Sweet Lies

Diana Hammond was born and brought up in Rio de Janeiro and later attended Northwestern University. She is a screenwriter and has published several short stories. Ms. Hammond now lives in Santa Monica, California.

Diana Hammond

Sweet Lies

Pavanne

published by Pan Books

First published in Great Britain 1983 by Pan Books Ltd,
Cavaye Place, London SW10 9PG
© Diana Hammond 1979
ISBN 0 330 26865 1
Printed in Great Britain by
Collins, Glasgow

Acknowledgments

I would like to thank Bernard Geis, Barbara Lowenstein, Joyce Thelen, and — from the beginning — Faith Motley for their help in encouraging things to turn out the way they did.

DIANA HAMMOND

Sweet lies are those we tell ourselves. They are the hopes we get by on, the private expressions of our own mysteries, the primary reality we have. Sweet lies are as seductive, as dangerous, and often as honourable as—what generally passes for—the truth.

Prologue

On a sharp, ice-blue day in the spring of 1977, an odd and tragic accident occurred at a ski resort in the French Maritime Alps.

The sky over the ice-cream slopes was clear. The pilot of the helicopter, a handsome—if disillusioned—Dutchman, was experienced. And the scene had been rehearsed.

Minutes after the disaster, it began to snow. By the next morning the only road leading up to the resort was pronounced impassable. Investigation was delayed. By the time the official findings were released, the shock and thrill of the story had slipped from the front pages. And the findings never clarified much anyway. The accident had been simply that: an accident. The helicopter, brought in to make aerial shots for a film company on location, had crashed into the scene it had been meant to photograph.

There were no victims among the regular guests of the ski resort. The nine people killed were all connected with the international cast and crew of *Lovers and Clowns*.

This is the story of those people and of that film.

Chapter One

We are—all of us—so paralyzed, so wasteful, so much of the time. This clouds our memory of the present. Distorts the lens through which we view our own scenarios. A clean, well-lighted moment cannot be measured in a dirty hour-glass. The sand spills through. Yet we go about each

7

day, each season, as if we were going to have it all forever. So did they.

They arrived on the Côte d'Azur in various stages of true and false, in the chilly February sunspill of the Riviera winter. No roses bloomed; they were all pruned to the ground. But pink-cheeked Ian Spencer met everyone— everyone, that is, whose contract called for more than a hundred thousand dollars—in a white Rolls-Royce that everyone assumed was his and of course was not.

At four o'clock on a particular Friday afternoon, a jet bearing its polyglot, trendy ragbag of champagne-damped, vinyl-bagged, wrinkled holidaymakers—and the three Americans from Hollywood—shrieked in over the wintry, sapphire sea to set down at Nice Airport just as Ian's Rolls pulled up to the terminal building and parked. Illegally.

Locked and strapped into her seat in the first-class cabin during the jet's last thrilling swoop over the pretty cutouts of the coast all done in fresh, primary colors, Djuna had pressed her face to the window and felt the tug of France, and wanted very much to cry because the moment welled up and demanded private, mysterious celebration.

Then they were down. Disembarking. The wind whipping at their hair, their clothes.

French faces. A wiser, more knowing sky. Snow on the Alps, bright water and expensive sunshine. All in the same frame.

As the three Americans emerged from Immigration, the photographers focused and flashed their cameras at Baker Martin, and it was difficult, in all the jostle and crush, for Djuna to stay at his side—particularly since he didn't seem to notice whether she did or not, and was, in fact, bestowing his cowboy smile and public charm on their traveling companion, his wily and famous agent, Lily Dunne.

It was Lily who had brought about the whole thing for Baker, having negotiated by phone from Hollywood what looked like the best picture deal she had ever made for him. No wonder she looked smug as she strode elegantly alongside him, her gold-bangled arm resting possessively

8

inside his. The part was originally to have gone to Jim Stark, a much bigger name, and Stark had actually come over for it but then had abruptly departed before the picture started. Now it was Baker's. It was to be his first starring role, at the highest money he had ever been paid.

Djuna was striking in the way some women with classic features can look their best after thirty. Familiar by now with airport scenes, she didn't worry about the photographers; she smiled pleasantly, that was all, and tried to keep for herself some sense of the private side of the experience—her first sight of the Riviera, her first trip to France since her university days. In the ever-flashing looking glass of the film industry she was Baker Martin's wife, and that was a far easier role than remembering, as the years went by, who she really was.

Inside the airport waiting area, Ian Spencer, who was to produce the picture, observed the arriving trio for a moment before moving up to welcome them.

The women would have too much luggage: hairdryers and face steamers, vitamins, mountains of shoes, framed photographs, and all the other rubbish they carted around the world with them. He would never get it all in the car. Why hadn't he left them to a taxi? To themselves? The pretty one would be Baker's wife. She was not an actress, so she would be either a tart, a would-be tycoon, or—worse—one of those philanthropic, environmental- or politically minded wives of actors who proliferated in American film circles today, determined in their humorless compulsion to bore you out of your skull if you gave them half a chance.

Lily Dunne, of course, was one of the biggest bitches in the business and not quite imaginative enough to know how to be charming at it. It must have been either extraordinary luck or blackmail—or both—that had got her on her way. As for Baker, he would be easy, grateful for the part, the prestigious French director, the big-name co-stars, and the splendid villa that had been leased for him in Cap d'Antibes. Ian was pleased to note the American actor's clean, suntanned look and wondered how much

Baker had heard about the troubles that had plagued the unfortunate film thus far.

Ian's head began to ache again. He was hideously hung over and still shaky despite the shot of B-12 that morning, a massage, and a quick, drugged nap. That ridiculous girl from Rome had almost destroyed the apartment he had rented for her and her sister (she *said* it was her sister) in Cannes. She was absolutely nobody, just an "actress" recommended to him, and yet she had smashed lamps, overturned furniture, torn from his wrist (now deeply scratched) his new digital watch and jumped up and down on it on the cement balcony floor in her high-heeled platform boots. It had all been perfectly awful, though possibly he had deserved every ghastly moment. When the film really got started and a more regular way of life began he would not be driven to look for such trying ways to while away the late afternoons.

He moved toward the arriving party now, smiling, a rangy, still-handsome man in his fifties, in casual silk elegance, his well-cut clothes hiding the red scratches and welts that now defaced his fashionable winter tan.

Chapter Two

On the beach, Djuna squinted, imagining she could see Africa. The sea was pale aquarium-green all the way to some little white boats, where abruptly it turned to cobalt blue. You could see the line where the color changed. Just like that.

She picked her way back across the rocks.

From the terrace of the villa, Baker watched her. He was already on the telephone, not really using it but just holding it to his ear, dialing random numbers. There was scarcely anyone to call yet.

When Djuna came onto the terrace he hung up guiltily

and said, "You haven't even unpacked yet. I turned around and you were gone."

"I was exploring."

"Listen," he went on restlessly, "what's the name of the hotel in Nice where we dropped Lily?"

"The Negresco. Aren't you glad they got us the house here? It's so much nicer. Did you hear Ian's secretary saying that Antibes was settled by the Greeks in the fourth century? Imagine!" She crossed the terrace and went to inspect a thick bank of red and blue anemones.

"Should I wear a tie tonight?" Baker asked. "Ian says he's having everyone."

Djuna felt the blackish earth underneath the anemones to see how recently they had been watered. To Baker, "everyone" meant only important people. "I wouldn't know."

"Listen," he continued, "there's only one real bathroom in this place, so you'll have to start getting ready soon. And see if you can use your fancy French to find out from the help whether there's a phone book around." He lit a cigar and leaned back in his chair to study, somewhat impatiently, the Mediterranean. Already there was nothing to do.

Djuna crossed the light-filled living room with its stone floors and hot-pink rugs. Baker was feeling insecure again. Actors! Like Alice, he had been getting smaller all afternoon, ever since they had arrived at the villa from the airport.

Of course, in the car with Ian, he had been "on" in the way she had once found charming and ingenuous but had eventually recognized as the line-perfect, characterless mask it was. Did she, herself, have a mask? Of course she must. But what did it look like? How different was it really from what she had become?

But no. She was too filled with the wonder and the newness of the place to want to deal with old problems. She would not be sucked in. Not yet. Not today.

"Here," she said a moment later, giving Baker the sky-blue telephone book. Now he could call Lily and he could chat until it was time for him to dress. It would put him in a good humor.

She went inside again. In their bedroom she crossed to the little balcony with its white iron railing. A few boats were still delicately impaled on the azure sea. The radiant afternoon had been particularly promising to winter sailors, but she thought they would have to come in soon. The sun was going down. She began to unpack. To decide what to wear to Ian Spencer's dinner party.

Theodora Spencer, ugly and splendid, with a cloud of ivory-colored hair, opened the door herself and announced that the butler was off sulking somewhere. Which indeed he was. Theodora, as Ian's wife, had lived in sophisticated company long enough to know that the smoothest lie was often simply a matter of producing, with an offhand smile, the offhand truth. She drew Djuna and Baker into a small white living room filled with people and the smell of Scotch whiskey, perfume, and eucalyptus glowing and smoking in the well-used, blackened fireplace.

The villa was in Juan-les-Pins and Baker immediately wondered whether that was more classy than Cap d'Antibes; whether his own villa, which he had liked perfectly well that afternoon, was second-best to this. After a moment he was reassured. The dirty fireplace, the thin worn rugs on the floor, and a generally fusty look erased any further unease.

Djuna, on the other hand, had immediately noted the Chinese horse in the entry, the fine old rugs in the living room, and the ikon on the mantelpiece. This difference in taste between Djuna and Baker had begun to erode the marriage more than anything else. How another individual assesses what is beauty and what is worthy shouldn't, perhaps, be all that important, except that the way things work out, it usually is. And while one can put up with contrary tastes in a friend, in a spouse it can spoil one's personal scenery.

Not that Djuna knew all that much about anything. It was just that she had always paid more attention than

Baker had. And in an interior sense, her goal was higher. In a touching, undefined way, she wanted the world. All Baker had ever wanted was to to be a movie star.

Theodora effortlessly drew Djuna into the tight little circle by the fireplace while Baker remained fixed in first position just by the entry, engaged in conversation with Ian. Baker had a routine. By the end of the evening he would have had a talk with every person in the room, elicited a great deal of information from each, and to one degree or another made them all like him.

Djuna had never ceased to be amazed when watching this practiced, oh-so-easy performance, though it occurred to her to wonder now whether it would work here. Baker had never made a film in Europe. Nor had they ever been in such "splendid" company on an equal footing. In a sense, this was Baker's debut in the Big Time. After years of routine actor's luck—bad, good, and none at all—he had finally landed a spectacular supporting part that, last year, had brought him an Oscar.

Theodora was now introducing Djuna to Baker's female co-star, Maria Marogodat, known to all the world as Maroga. The hawk-nosed Italian actress fixed her violet-smudged intelligent eyes on Djuna, and Djuna knew instantly that here was an actress who was also a woman of character. You didn't get a face like that just from being a star all your life.

Maroga, for her part, saw before her a creature of the kind she had come to fear more than any other of her own sex. Particularly when she was feeling anxious and dumpy as she was tonight. This wife of Baker Martin was a golden California girl of the highest type, beautiful, cared-for, probably expensively educated. She had that clear, sunny look. Like Robbie's wife. Oh, dear God, would the pain never go away? She glanced across the room at Baker. Would he be interesting? Would anyone ever be interesting again?

Baker met Maroga's glance and produced his automatic actor's smile. With a slight deference, to note the occasion, but—

Not interesting, Maroga decided with a dismay that was becoming all too familiar now that she was nearly fifty. The older she got, the more obsessively romantic she was becoming. It was crazy at this stage to be looking every day for the Prince. One reverted. At twenty, she had been more practical.

Baker, engaged again in conversation with Ian, positioned himself so he could continue to watch his wife being introduced to the inner group by the fireplace. These people would be the scenery of his life for the next eight weeks.

Bernard Trigère, the French director, was smaller than Baker had imagined from his photographs; a slight taut figure with graying hair and a deep forehead over heavy brows and very dark eyes. He had that elegant European presence no American man could ever attain. What was it? It couldn't be acted, learned, bought. It was as if it grew out of their goddamn elegant shoes.

And now, from his diffident position on the sofa, Joss McIvor, the young superstar, was rising politely to put down his glass of beer and to look down at Djuna. To shake her hand gravely. Baker watched with hungry, professional interest as the celebrated English rock star, whom he had never seen in person, greeted his wife with a brief, schoolboy jerk of his head and a hooded smile. McIvor was wearing a velvet suit of hunter green and a shirt with a ruffled collar, open at the neck. His patrician nose, very high in the bridge, had definitely been broken at least once.

Then Lily Dunne arrived in the room, giving Baker a possessive glance as she took his hand, pecked Ian on the cheek, and looked swiftly around, pausing to squint slightly at the circle by the fireplace.

"Sorry I'm late, Ian. Hope I have time for a drink. You English always have such a short cocktail hour. A gin, please. Just ice. What a super house! Is it nicer than yours, Baker? And what is that godawful thing Maroga has on her head? I hope it isn't her hair."

"Maroga's temper is uneven these days," Ian said as he

poured Lily's drink himself at the little bar set up on a refectory table by the entrance. "It's a cross we may all have to bear." He handed Lily her glass. "I can't stand to think what that will do to your insides, Lily. One should never drink straight gin after the age of twenty-one. We can get just as blind on vodka and only half as sick."

Baker swirled the ice around in his glass. He was feeling uncomfortable all of a sudden, a little out of sync, and he supposed it was jet lag. He waited for Ian or Lily to say something, but they were also silent for the moment, immersed in themselves.

Ian was appalled at how much the dinner was costing him. He had absolutely come to the end of his cash, and unless Vito brought forth the miracle he had been promising by tomorrow, not only would the film be delayed again but he and Theodora would be dangerously over their heads in personal debts. They'd been running up bills ever since they'd arrived two months ago. The big paper pyramids he could handle, but how to deal with the grocer, the wine shop, and the florist?

Lily was also tired. And suddenly very uneasy about a deal she had been uneasy about in the first place. Of all her clients, Baker was the one she felt most protective toward, and it was precisely because of that, to give him what looked like a terrific chance, that she had taken the risk of signing him for this picture. She saw Vito, Ian's associate producer, over by the fireplace and would talk to him right after dinner. He would know more than Ian when it came to details. Vito always did, the cheap crooked little bastard. She gulped down her gin as she saw Theodora herding people into the dining room.

Djuna was seated next to Joss McIvor. He gave his complete attention to the food until, toward the end of the first course, he said to her quietly, "This is very bad wine. It will give you a headache if you drink too much."

She stared at him.

"It's not that Ian is cheap," he went on. "But he has no palate. I promise you. I have dined with him before."

"Oh," she said at last.

He fiddled with the silverware. "Do you have children?" he asked.

"No."

He watched her hand go automatically to the thin gold chain she always wore to cover a scar in the hollow of her throat. "You're lovely," he remarked quietly. "A lady like you should have lots and lots of babies."

She said with a surprised laugh, "That's very old-fashioned of you. But also charming. I think."

"Oh, I expect I'm *very* old-fashioned about things like babies. Do you always wear that?" He nodded to indicate the chain.

"Always." She felt as if she had been identified. It was as clean and mysterious as that.

"Yes." Joss touched the chain. "It's very sweet."

She was astonished to hear herself saying, "You are completely different from what I expected." She glanced about to see if anyone was listening to them.

"So are you." He gave her an innocent look. "But it's lovelier for me. I didn't even know you existed." Then, after a moment, "How am I different?"

She considered. "Naturally, I've read about you. Seen you on television. In person, you don't compute."

"Oh," he said with a laugh. "You mean England's rowdy boy? Oh, well. It's all true. I can be very loud and very vulgar and I get into an incredible number of fights, it would seem. But I'm working-class, dear. When I see a lady I can respect, well then, I know how to behave, don't I?" He flashed his mischievous grin. "I promise you I won't let the shit fly till later. Not until we get to know each other."

She looked down at her plate with a slight smile. "I'm not all that easy to get along with, either."

"Oh, I know that," he said. Very offhand. "I could tell. And it's all right with me. I promise you."

Then they were both arrested by a sudden commotion at the table.

Vito's girlfriend, who was sitting next to Baker, had

fallen forward into her plate, her long black hair spreading its ebony silk into Baker's poached salmon.

Chapter Three

"I was *sure* she was only drunk," Djuna said. They were driving back to their villa.

Baker glanced at her impatiently. "You've said that three times."

"How could anyone possibly get drunk at the Spencers?" Lily groaned from the back seat. "They don't serve you enough booze to even get a buzz on."

It had been a long and grim evening, and Lily had accepted the Martins' offer to stay the night with them. She had left her rented car at the Spencers.

Baker chewed his cigar and watched the narrow turns in the unfamiliar road. "McIvor surprised me. He looked like Little Lord Fauntleroy in that goddamn velvet suit. But Jesus! He was trying to pump air into that girl while the rest of were still stuck to our chairs."

Lily yawned. "I thought Ian was going to throw up."

"Did you notice Bernard Trigère?" Djuna asked after a moment. "He stayed in a corner the whole time and just watched everybody."

Baker began to chuckle. "And how about Theodora? Can you believe that woman? 'But no one has had the trifle, darlings!' And trying to give some to the Inspector. What *is* trifle anyway?"

"Stale sponge cake soaked in sherry and a lot of fruit and cream. It's godawful and the English love it."

"I like it," Djuna said stoutly, suddenly loyal to she knew not what.

"Am I going right or not?" Baker stared through the windscreen at the winding road. It had begun to rain. "Jesus. Since I got out of bed yesterday morning, I've had no sleep, my dinner partner died in my poached salmon, the police inspector hadn't seen even one of my movies, and now, I apparently don't even know where the fuck I live."

"There." Djuna pointed suddenly. "I remember that house. We're round that little bend there, where the two big trees are by the gate."

When they had found the house and Lily had been given a room and one of Djuna's dressing gowns, they gathered by the fire, which had been thoughtfully laid out but which they were unable to keep going once they had lighted it.

They clinked their brandy goblets. Outside, thunder and lightning shook the skies and the wind rattled the windows. The noise of the downpour, which had begun as a light rain when they were on the road, was dense and steady, like the tropics. They were all very tired.

Lily held her glass high. She giggled and shivered. "To your first European film experience."

Baker took the cigar out of his mouth and raised his own glass. "To the tacky broad who made it all possible. You're fired, Lily." Lily smiled complacently as she raised her glass to Baker.

They drank. Djuna said, "Nobody seemed to know who the girl really was."

"People never know who a girl like that really is." Baker took the bottle from the mantelpiece and refilled his glass. "Don't look at me like that, Djuna. I'm just telling you how it is. Vito has had her around for a month and *he* didn't even know where her home was, who her people were. She was a high-class hooker someone introduced to someone, who introduced her to Vito."

"Who is Vito, exactly?" Djuna asked.

"He's Ian's co-producer." Lily sank into one of the flowered chairs. She crossed her ankles and stared at them critically. "He's hundreds of years old but he gets his blood rinsed and takes all those injections—anyway, he's been in pictures forever. He's strictly a money man. He arranges things. He's also a crook. He and Ian have been together for years, though I think Ian has managed to stay pretty clean."

Djuna finished her brandy and said good night. She knew they would talk for hours.

The bedroom was cold, and she hurried to get into bed, dropping her clothes on the floor, jumping under the celery-colored blankets. It was really a charming room, with its thick white rugs on tile floors, real lace on the pillowcases, the elegant turn of the carved bedposts, the window seat with its cushions and flower pots. She had planned to lie in the darkness and think about everything that had happened that day, but she fell asleep at once, in the same moment that the corpse of the girl whose last name nobody knew passed the villa in a police ambulance, followed by the inspector who had not seen any of Baker's movies.

Next to the inspector rode Vito, who had spent the last few hours in a state of gross spiritual discomfort. It was not the wretched girl; it was his blood pressure. It was the bad luck of it all. It was the waste of his valuable time.

At the Spencer villa, Ian and Theodora were getting ready, at last, for bed.

"I'd like to kill Vito," Theodora said viciously. She pulled the heavy Spanish earrings from her ears and threw them across the room at the dressing table, where they landed, clattering, amid the tangle of hairpins, necklaces, wads of cotton, and perfume jars.

"Oh, come off it, Theodora," Ian said indulgently. He was already in his tobacco-colored silk pajamas, sitting up in bed sipping his nightly cocoa. He had taken his sleeping pill and was beginning to feel warm and safe. "Come to bed and stop all that carrying on."

Now that he no longer really loved Theodora (or anyone else . . . after a certain point one simply ran down), he found her high-key moments very tiresome. There had been a time—oh, there had been a time when he was young!—when he had been always delighted and amused by her dazzling capacity for taking life in and filling her-

19

self to bursting with it. Theo's special style, her vitality and her wit, her intelligence—all had been captivating and fresh in the early days when everything was still new. They had been together for twenty-seven years. She was still more striking than ugly, but traces of a growing hysteria were evident not only in her face but also in her increasingly trying behavior. She was often consumed with fury at Ian, at what she conceived to be her failed life, and at the whole world for not taking any notice of the fact that practically nothing could make her happy any more.

"Between you and Vito," she was shouting now, "every slut on the Continent has dined at my table." She was going to wake the Navy. "And tonight I won the sweepstakes. I entertained a dead one."

"My dear, everyone who is born must die. Some do it at dinner."

"The humiliation!" She was going on. "How do you think this is going to look after your widely reported little escapade, that disgusting party in Rome last year?"

"Do pipe down, Theodora. No one gives a fig about a producer's private life. It's only actors who are required to behave."

"I hate it, do you hear?" She addressed his reflection in her dressing-table mirror. "I've hated it for so long I can't remember when I didn't. I hate you, you disgusting son-of-a-bitch, you filthy failure! You blockhead!" With one sweep of a still-elegant arm she sent everything on the table crashing to the floor.

She wasn't going to stop. After a last weary look at her, Ian closed his eyes and simply shut her out.

Theodora went down to the living room and put on a record, lighted the lamp over the piano, and poured herself a large glass of brandy.

She paced up and down in front of the cold fireplace for a time until the brandy and the music shifted the moment into softer focus. She sank into a chair. Ian had such rotten taste in music. It was nice to be hearing one of her records for a change.

Lovely Vivaldi, play on. She looked about the room at

all her dear things that she had brought with her from the London house to make her happy while she was here. She called the collection her traveling decor, curiosities she had collected through the years in her travels through Spain, China, Africa, and here in France as well, always the odd piece, something from the street. "Bring me something from the street," she would say to Ian whenever he went abroad. He had never understood that she meant something special, a kite, a basket, a length of cloth. Something you could only find once. Instead he brought back Gucci appointment books, electric toothbrushes, clever watches and clocks. Jet-set rubbish.

No wonder most of his films were so flashy and ordinary. Perhaps Trigère would correct that this time. Ian had never worked with the French director before. They had always moved along different tracks, across and through the same places, Trigère gaining increasing international recognition for his delicate, simple stories, his total control over every film he made; Ian building a reputation for "big" pictures, plots of adventure and espionage, swelling the profit coffers in box offices all over the world. The question was why Trigère agreed to direct *Lovers and Clowns*? The script was slick and ordinary, simply not his thing. The financing had been uncertain from the beginning. Joss McIvor probably couldn't act, Maroga was getting on, and as for the American, Baker—well, he had won an Oscar, but it was only for best supporting performance and who had really heard of him outside his own country?

Trigère probably had money troubles. It was always that. Was there anything to look forward to? Some more brandy to numb the pain? She poured another brandy, turned the record over, and floated back on the memory of a blue satin sash she had worn long ago. On that day the English sun had dappled the silver leaves of the beech tree shading her parents' seventy-five guests at an afternoon lawn party. And the announcement of Theodora's engagement to Ian Spencer, just down from Oxford, had been made. To hurrahs.

*

Trigère and Maroga walked down the hotel corridor to her room. They had driven back to Nice from Ian's dinner in weary, companionable silence, having tacitly agreed to speak no more about the black-haired girl's death at the dinner table.

They had known each other a long time, since their simultaneous but separate entries into the film business, since Maroga, plump and buxom, heavily lipsticked and very hungry, stumbled her way over camera cables and a horny assistant director through a small role she did not understand in a picture that would become a classic. Barefoot, in a torn dress, terrified by the director, secretly four months pregnant by her uncle, and with a raging gum infection that kept her teeth pink with blood so she had to keep licking them, she had given a performance that, as one critic wrote, "one could almost smell."

At the time, Trigère had been an apprentice to the fiery, gifted director of the film, Carlo Andretti. A few months before, he had abandoned his studies at the University of Paris to the dismay of his middle-class parents, taken the train to Rome, and wangled an introduction to Andretti. Trigère was crazy about film. He had seen everything, read everything. He talked well, showed taste and energy, and was willing to work for no salary. Andretti had finally told the boy he could stick around and make himself useful. When the picture in which Maroga made her debut finished shooting, Andretti let Trigère hang around the cutting room. Now and then Andretti would take him to a late supper, and they would talk.

Trigère was a handsome boy as well as a clever one. Early on in the picture he began an affair with the leading lady, an actress of some forty years who was beginning to require younger and younger men for her bed. They had a most agreeable relationship, and when she returned to her husband in another country she left her darling Bernard with a grateful check that enabled him to return to France with the wispy, delicate little script he had been writing between four and seven in the morning. Somehow he managed to make a modest, quite charming picture, using his niece and nephew and all of his friends. For the most part it was ignored, but it found an enthusiastic reception in limited circles, and thus Trigère was able to get basic financing for a second picture, then another, then another. He wrote them all himself, shot them all in the French countryside, using local people whenever possible. There was a rich, pastoral quality to everything he did, and he began to build a following. He also began to gather about him a group of players and crew with whom he formed a kind of artistic family. They lived together for long stretches of time and in a way it was sometimes hard to distinguish between illusion and reality, so naturally did all their lives spill into the idea of the film, just as what they were creating for the camera spilled into the rest of the day, into what and who they were as people.

In the fifties, the number of serious students of the cinema around the world began to increase geometrically. Trigère's films became known and highly regarded in those circles. And with the continued support he had always had from the critics, those were happy, successful years for Trigère. In the early nineteen-sixties, his film *Juniper Road* won an award at the Cannes film festival, and the first ripple of interest came across the Atlantic from America. Within the next few years he made his first color film, got married and divorced, sadly watched his group disband as everything to do with them, to do with him, got more complicated, and threw himself into a project that took him to Africa for a year. Now that he had money—which meant time—he was able to lavish the finest attention, the most exquisite detail on this parable of the desert, and when the film was done he knew it was his best. There had been four more after that, increasingly personal, decreasingly profitable.

He watched Maroga kick off her shoes and sink into a chair, holding her cigarette. She gave him her weary, luminous smile as he crossed the room with his gold lighter.

"Shall we go to bed?" he said. "It's late. And the word is that we really start to shoot tomorrow afternoon." He lit a cigarette for them both and began to loosen his tie.

"I don't believe we start shooting. Ever. There is something very stinking about this film. I tell you, I am crazy with this rain, with the hotel, with reading books—all this waiting. Bernard, do you know we have been here almost a month? You have been back and forth to Paris, to Rome, I sit here getting fatter. After a week I was already too fat to shop." She caught his amused look and made a face at him.

"You'll never be thin enough, beautiful enough, perfect enough, will you?" He took her hand. "How absurd you are, my dear. Well, shall we have a drink?" He went to the little bar. "What would you like?"

She sighed. "Oh, just a lovely water. In a wine glass, to make it pretty."

He poured the drinks, took off his jacket, and threw it on a chair. "Let's go to bed."

Rhetorically she asked, "You are staying?" Her centuries-old smile hid her resentment.

He kissed her forehead. "If I may."

Maroga went into the bedroom while he left a call with the operator and turned off the lights in the sitting room. When he came in she was already in front of her mirror, opening jars, going about her nightly ritual, wrapped in a large white towel.

Her resentment at the male assumption that making love with whoever was about was the desired ritual with which any sensible person ended a given day was mild; more archetypal than personal, more traditional and tolerant than critical. Women had had to deal with it for centuries—even women like herself, who liked sex very much.

Thus had the genders evolved and there wasn't much anyone could do at this point about biological differences. Men had cocks and women didn't. It was as simple as that. A woman didn't have, between her legs, something which absolutely had to be put somewhere—preferably, once a day—and dealt with as a willful ancillary brain almost all of the time.

A woman's reality was different. She had a single brain, lodged in her skull—and connected to her heart. And her real thoughts, her real life, were often dark and hidden.

But Maroga and Bernard were old friends. Like long-time spouses, there was a network of warm, dear lies between them. And to say "I don't feel like it tonight" to Bernard, to any dear old friend, dear spouse, would be a cold rejection. Men would never understand that "I don't feel like it" meant "I don't feel like it with anyone tonight. I don't want to be entered. I just want to lie here on my pillow and celebrate my right to rest, privately, from your cock. God bless it and I'm sorry you have this Problem, but I am also a person. Let me be."

The way it usually worked out was that you gave in. If you didn't, you hurt the feelings of someone you cared for, and left them with the Problem besides. The erected cock in a pair of pajamas. What to do? Over the ages it had become the woman's responsibility. It was quite comical, really. It also wasn't fair. Women had learned to accommodate the man's Problem. But the female problem was beyond solving; it had become part of the suppressed litany of the sex.

"Now that Baker has arrived, our cast is complete again," Trigère was saying, taking off his watch and putting it on the bedside table. "They've run out of reasons why we can't start shooting. Unless financial matters are worse than they've been telling us."

"But I don't understand." Maroga was scrubbing her face with lime tonic. "Isn't it American money? Isn't that what you said?"

"That is what I was told originally. The explanation has changed a dozen times since then. My dear, it has all become incomprehensible to me as well, but it is obvious that there is trouble and that there are lies, because there was no reason to wait for Baker to arrive to start principal photography. Unless the backers were holding up the money waiting to approve—or pick—someone to be signed for that third part." He eased his lean, elegant figure into Maroga's champagne-colored satin sheets. "I don't even know any more who the backers are. If there are backers at all. Ian does nothing but doubletalk."

She had been staring at him in her mirror. "I never get over it, Trigère. You're *that* gorgeous-looking. At your age. I could kill you."

Maroga got up and dropped the towel. She turned off the dressing-table lamp and walked toward the bed. He pulled back the covers so she could get in.

After a suitable interval, Maroga pretended to have a climax and hoped God would forgive her dishonesty. She was superstitious about that, lying with her body. But anyway, she was giving pleasure; Trigère was coming now, and how he came, that self-contained, dry director! She smiled in the dark. Dear Trigère.

He lay collapsed until, after a few moments, she heard his murmured laugh. He kissed her breasts once more and turned over on his back. He took her hand, as he always did, and fell asleep. She looked at his profile. He could have been posing for a picture. Incredible man.

Maroga adored Bernard Trigère. She worshipped his talent, respected his intelligence, and cared for him as a human being; but she would rather have gone to bed with his chauffeur, and in fact she had. It had happened on that horrible location in the American desert when Robbie's wife, the picture-book mate of America's top picture-book actor, had shown up, just like that, with children and nannies and her mother, and had rented a house just outside town, where she stayed until the end of the picture. Robbie had grimly moved there from the hotel where he and Maroga had been together every night.

Maroga, crazy with the kind of grief she was to suffer again when they parted for the final time, went to bed the very next afternoon with Trigère's chauffeur in her trailer dressing room. The boy had come to deliver some books Trigère had ordered for her from Los Angeles, found her weeping, and because he was very young and very literal, he did the only thing he could do well. Besides drive a car.

He had been very sweet, and somehow this unexpected exchange of feeling, while disaster was still open, still fresh, put some space on that day between herself and the pain.

That evening she had dined with Trigère in the hotel. He had taken her hand, saying, "You know, darling, don't you, that Robbie Brannigan will never leave his wife? They have nine children. He is a superstar. He is a Catholic. And he plays golf with the President. All of that matters in America."

"This is such a vile dinner," she had said, the tears starting to her eyes. "Such a vile place. What sadistic fancy led you to want to make a picture in the American desert?"

Trigère looked at her gravely. "You're much too good for him."

"I don't care. I love him. I'm wild about him. It's the answer to everything. And I wish I were dead."

She was to say that again many times before the affair finally came to an end, but that had been the worst, that day, that night, and the terrible five weeks in that dry, fierce desert, uglier and more desolate than any land she had ever seen. She had drunk herself into insensibility every night. The whole company had, except for Trigère and except for Robbie, who spent every evening with his wife and children in the rented house, watching television and going to bed early.

The night noises of Nice outside the hotel were barely audible now, muted by the steady falling rain. Maroga waited for sleep.

She thought about the film possibly beginning tomorrow and she looked forward to the adventure. The first day of a picture was like the first day of school. Scary and new, a chance to begin one's life over again. While you were gone they had washed the windows, put out fresh pencils, swept the floor. You entered to find new teachers, new lovers, new friends. She was anxious to start. She had not worked in eleven months. She needed the money, she needed the discipline and (she smiled in the darkness) she needed the attention.

Since Robbie there had been a few men, but she had

not loved any of them, nor they her. She had redecorated her house in Rome, spending money she could ill afford, gone to Greece, to Rio, taken up yoga, gone into seclusion to have her face scraped, hung around Paris for months in utter desolation, and then Ian had phoned and offered her the role. And she was happy for that, happy to be working with Trigère again, happy to be working at all.

When Joss arrived back at the hotel, he went straight into the bar. He was keyed up by the bizarre experience at Ian's and he realized it was more than the shock of that girl dropping dead at the table. Early in the evening, when he had been introduced to Djuna, he felt his blood change in the first moment, in a way that reminded him of something long ago ... something good ... what the hell was it? Better forget it for now. What he needed was someone in his bed tonight. But even that didn't seem likely. The bar was almost empty at this hour. Well, a lot of beer would help. When he was properly sodden he would go upstairs and fall across the bed with all his clothes on and go straight to sleep. Jimmy would put him right in the morning with Alka-Seltzers and hot tea.

Then he saw Ian's American bird at a table by herself in the corner, pulling on a cigarette, her long red hair looking black in the dim light. Kat, her name was. He'd spoken to her only once, in the lobby, the day she had arrived from Los Angeles. Ian had introduced them, and in the next moment Joss had forgotten all about her.

Joss stared at her moodily. He hated girls who smoked. They were a pain in the ass the way they always had to have a cigarette right afterward. They stank up the bedroom and their fingers always smelled of it, their mouth and their hair always smelled of it ... Anyway. It was someone to be with. It was two o'clock in the morning. She was far from ugly. And far from sober.

She was, in fact, quite tight. She had been sitting there since coming in from a movie, about eleven.

"Hello, Kat," he said. She knocked her drink over and they dealt with that, assisted by the lone waiter. And then

Joss sat down and ordered a beer for himself, another vodka for her.

"I suppose you went to Ian's dinner," she said. "Naturally, I wasn't invited."

"Naturally," he said cheerfully, but he didn't care about that or anything else except making up his mind whether or not he really wanted to sleep with her. He drank his beer in two gulps and looked around for the waiter. When the man came, Joss said, "Look, bring me two this time, why don't you? Save you running back and forth." Then he turned back to the girl. Well, why not? If he didn't, he'd end up going to his room and ringing up girls all over the world the way he often did when he was in a new place and couldn't sleep.

"Does shooting really start tomorrow?" she was saying. "Though I haven't minded the waiting. I've never been in the South of France before."

"Neither have I. I've been staying with a friend in St. Tropez the last few weeks. Came back today for Ian's dinner, and for tomorrow."

"That's why I haven't seen you around." She lifted her glass, stared into it doubtfully, and set it down again.

"Have you known Ian long?" he began conversationally.

"I don't sleep with him, if that's what you mean."

"Darling. Did I say a word?"

"Well, I'm telling you. Because I know everyone thinks I do." She looked gloomily into her drink again.

He led her into talk about the picture and the general gossip for a while. Her responses were sharper, more insightful than he had anticipated; still, uppermost in his mind was the question he really wanted to get to. He took a deep breath. "Look, would you like to come upstairs and spend the night with me?"

She looked at him uncertainly. "I don't know. I honestly don't know."

"Kat." He took one of her hands in his. "It's late. The whole world has gone to bed except you and me. Let's go and be sweet to each other. Come on." He stood up and pulled her gently to her feet. She was swaying a bit and so was he, and he realized he wasn't exactly sober either. "Come on. Here's your purse. Now where's your hand? There. That's a good girl."

They walked across the deserted lobby toward the elevator.

In his room he sat her on the bed. "Do you want a wash or something?"

She shook her head.

"Well, get into bed. Here." He pulled back the covers and plumped up the pillow for her. She leaned down and began taking off her shoes.

There was a knock on the door that led to an adjoining room. "I'm okay, Jimmy," Joss called out. "Go back to bed. And don't let me sleep past ten. I want to be at the studio by noon."

"Who's Jimmy?" She was staring at the door.

"Jimmy's my boy." He took off his velvet jacket and dropped it on the floor. He jumped up and down on it a few times.

"Your son?"

"No. Of course not." He looked at her with exasperation. "He's my man. You know. Like a valet."

"Your man," she repeated slowly. "Jesus. Like an English novel."

"I *am* an English novel," he said cheerfully. "From filthy Rags to filthy Riches."

"Not *that* kind of novel. I had something more elegant in mind. Lords and Ladies. Listen. Why did you jump up and down on your jacket?"

"I dunno." He went off to the bathroom. He undressed, peed, and then sat on the edge of the bathtub, holding his head in his hands. He had felt better for a few minutes when they got to the room, but now the emptiness was suddenly there again. Well. The main thing was he'd have someone warm to hold onto. He got up and began to brush his teeth. Then he wondered what she was up to, and looked around the corner into the room.

She was in bed. Her clothes were neatly folded on a

chair. She really looked rather sweet, with her long red hair falling over the covers she had pulled up just past her breasts. Which he hadn't seen yet. Would they have little freckles pasted on porcelain skin? Like her face?

"You all right?" he said, toothbrush in mouth.

She smiled at him. "Do you always brush your teeth before bed? No matter what?"

" 'Course I do." He grinned back. "I wasn't brought up like you, what with Water Piks and dentists all over the place. Mum and Dad didn't bother about seeing to toothbrushes till I was thirteen. When I cut my first album I paid a dentist a thousand quid to fix up the rot I had around my gums." He waved the toothbrush at her. "Now I'm in love with my teeth. Anyway, let's see yours." He crossed the room. "Come on, open your mouth. Let's have a look."

He sat on the bed beside her and she opened her mouth. He peered in.

"Aha! Very well-bred American teeth. Very good indeed." He touched one of her front teeth with his finger, looked at her, and then lightly traced the outline of her mouth. Her gray eyes looked back at him coolly. She put one knee up, under the sheets.

"Kat," he said. "It's bloody cold out here without my clothes on. Move over." He bent to kiss her and then he was pulling the sheets off and they were all over the bed, and he was having her as if he had made love to her a thousand times before, as if he had never had enough of her, as if he never would have enough of her. He couldn't stop, he didn't want to stop, and when she cried out several times and he thought it might be with pain he was all the more aroused.

He saw her eyes open wide with shock and he covered her mouth with his, tasting her tongue again. And when he felt her soft movement under him he was very still, learning her rhythm. He raised himself on his elbows, smoothed her hair, watched her face, kissed her eyes. "Kat," he whispered, "I'm going to come now," and he began to fuck her hard until it was over for him and he fell forward onto the pillow and all that tangled red hair.

After a few moments, he murmured, "I'm sorry if I hurt you." Usually this was a lie unless he really loved the girl. And he certainly wasn't in love with this puzzling bird. He turned sideways to look at her.

Her legs were still apart in the wide arc he had made for himself. They were very white, the legs, but well shaped. He raised himself on his elbow and looked at the rest of her with curiosity. She was quite thin, quite vulnerable-looking, less than beautiful and more than pretty. He supposed it was all that white translucent skin on a young frame. She didn't have that trace of puppy look most girls her age retain; she was already sculptured.

She hadn't answered him, so he said again, "I'm sorry. I expect I was a bit rough. Are you all right? Kat, open your eyes. I know bloody well you're not asleep."

Her eyes opened. "Well, nothing is broken." She stared down at herself, found the covers, and pulled them up to her chin. Then she announced coolly, "You are my first famous fuck."

"I'm your *what*?" He sat upright, staring at her in outrage and disbelief. "How *dare* you refer to me in that manner? Famous fuck indeed! You silly bitch, you're going to fuck straight out of here, that's what." He jumped out of bed, stood up, and glared at her.

"Oh, Joss. Really." She looked up at him, took his hand. "I'm sorry. Sit down, please. I'll explain."

He stared at her suspiciously. "Now what are you up to?" And he sat down, ostentatiously covering his cock with a bit of sheet.

She sighed. "Look. Look at the way you picked me up. When you walked in that bar tonight you didn't see me at all. You saw a lay. I could have been a chicken. And you'd have brought the goddamn chicken up here and fucked feathers all night, the horny condition you were in."

He looked at her gravely. "Okay. That's fair enough."

"So." With her finger she traced a circle around his kneecap. "I wanted all of a sudden to hurt you back for that. I wanted to make *you* feel like nothing. I don't *like* being treated like a chicken. Like nothing. That's all." She looked up at him.

He got up abruptly and stomped to the bathroom. "I have to pee," he said.

She called after him. "Well, do you understand or don't you?"

"Of course I understand," he shouted over his shoulder. "And you're a very odd girl, I can tell you." His words were drowned out by a sudden roar in the toilet, and then she heard water in the sink and a lot of splashing.

His head came around the corner of the open door. "Do you want a drink of water?"

"Thank you." She propped herself up on the pillows and he brought her a glass of water. He lay across the foot of the bed. "Anyway. Have you always wanted to be an actress?"

She took a swallow. "I've never wanted to be an actress. What are you talking about?"

"Well, I thought—I mean, darling, you *appear* to be one of Ian's birds and they usually get a small part in whatever picture he's making at the moment."

She looked at him. "I want to be a director."

"A *what?*" He was shouting and had sat upright once more. "A director, for Christ's sake? But you're a *girl!* A bird!"

"God almighty," she muttered and threw the covers back, swinging her feet to the floor. "I don't have to lie here and listen to news bulletins from the nineteenth century!"

"Christ, now what?" he muttered. "Get back into bed, you silly ass. Go on." He pushed her back, drew the covers around her neck and pinned her down by getting on top of her. "You! With your American lady-lib shit. Go and direct *War and Peace* for all I care."

She glared at him. "I will not be humored by a stupid, conceited pain in the ass."

He started to laugh. "You're a lot of trouble, you are.

Perhaps I would have been better off with a chicken." He saw her try to hide her smile and decided to press his advantage. He gave her a long kiss which, after a moment, she accepted. Her mouth was very sweet.

Chapter Four

A good film is the result of a miracle, nothing less. Getting one made at all is a thousand strokes of luck. The audience never realizes this, and why should it? On the face of it, money, talent, and drive would seem to be the requirements. These three elements are usually present at the beginning of any movie project, in the form of one person or another person or even a lot of persons, but there is a more important factor that characterizes the production from the very beginning and ultimately determines its quality, though not its fate—*that* comes under the Miracle and Luck Department. This factor is the answer to the question: Why is this film being made? Like children, a lot of films get born for the wrong reasons.

Traditionally, the idea for a film is supposed to begin in the head of a producer, who hires a writer. Or it begins in the head of a writer, who finds a producer. These are beginnings which generally have the most promise, but the fact is that often the first candle is lighted in another corner: by an unfulfilled contract, somebody's wife, a hungry agent, a secretary, an unemployed movie star who needs his roof fixed, a businessman with tax problems.

In the case of *Lovers and Clowns* the first candle was lit because Ian needed a picture. Desperately. At the time that the principals arrived in the South of France, Ian had been nursing the project for over a year, the screenwriter had had an alcoholic collapse and was dying in Hong Kong (which didn't bother Ian one bit; he had very little use for writers anyway), and Vito had lied his way back and forth across the world several times, exchanging hope/lies. Hope/lies are very common in the motion picture business and are generally condoned, forgiven, forgotten, repeated, and even improved on. Hope/lies are made in good faith as often as in bad faith, and they go on forever because, every once in a while, they come through as firm deals.

The script of *Lovers and Clowns* had been knocking around for years. It was a banal anecdote, stretched to one hundred and ten pages, but the fact that it was thin and ordinary hardly mattered. What mattered was that Ian was broke and needed a picture, the screenwriter was broke and had to make a sale, and Vito (who might have exercised better judgment about it all) had been on his yearly holiday at a special sanatorium in Switzerland at the time Ian had optioned the script and started the ball rolling. It was like that.

And it was not really all that surprising that such Names as Bernard Trigère, Joss McIvor, and Maroga became associated with this project. Each of the three was told, on the same day, that the other two had already signed. In this particular case, the hope/lies worked. But that had been the last of Ian's luck. So far.

By eleven the next morning, the ancient salty sea along the soft coastline of Antibes had gone from slate gray to cobalt blue. The water made frills around the pretty rocks. At the villa the sun had already started across the terrace where the three Americans sat at a little table with a heavy white cloth, hot croissants and coffee, a plate of pale green pears, and fresh cream in a china jug.

Lily puffed on one of her little cigars. "I should get my ass back to the hotel. I have a dinner date in London."

Djuna wondered what it would be like to have a dinner date in London, to have a job, to not be married. But these familiar questions were merely rhetorical this morning. She sipped the strong black coffee, felt the sun on her face, smelled all of history in the air, and was happy.

Baker got to his feet. "There's been no call, but I think

35

I'll go to the studio anyway and have lunch. Ian said everyone would be there. Do you want to drive in with me, Lily?"

"Remember? My car is still at Ian's. Why don't you go on? Djuna can take me over there in a while. I'll go back to the hotel, pack, and maybe catch lunch with you before I go to the airport."

"That's all very well," Baker said, "but how do I find Nice? I need a chauffeur, Lily. How much is a chauffeur?"

Lily got up, pulling her borrowed dressing gown tighter around her waist. "Come on, Baker. Let's go and look at those maps in your car and I'll point you in the right direction."

They moved off the terrace into the house and Djuna gratefully heard Lily saying, "You're unreal, Baker. You've got a goddamn villa when everyone else is at the hotel except Ian—and he comes here every winter anyway. Now you want a driver, too? You think you're an international star already? You want to give Harold another heart attack?"

Harold was Baker's business manager. Before they had left Los Angeles he had taken Djuna aside. "Look, honey, I'm counting on you to keep an eye on The Big Spender. He's bad enough here where he *knows* I'm around to chew his ass out every Monday morning. But Jesus, when I think of him for eight weeks on the Riviera! Promise me you'll remember the whole time you're away that your expense-clock will be ticking here, too, while you're on location. It's not like everything stops. And don't let Baker forget it either."

Harold was a necessary fixture in their lives. Baker spent money obsessively and Djuna was only a sporadic and ineffectual check on his rashness. Almost every time they had a fight about his extravagance, and particularly when it was over his frequent gambling losses, he would promptly go out the next day and charge something of equivalent value that was just for her. She would find on her pillow, or at her place at the table, a first edition, a fur-lined trench coat, a turquoise necklace. It was bribery.

It had made her a troubled partner in his addiction to more and more of life's comforts, of society's valuables.

Djuna stared at the sea until Lily came back to the terrace.

"One more cup of coffee," Lily said, settling into her chair again, reaching for her sunglasses. "And then I'd better go. Tell me what you thought of everyone last night. You're going to be playmates with them for the next eight weeks."

Djuna felt the pot and poured. "Oh, I don't think so. You know Baker always goes to bed early when he's working. Except for poker, he's antisocial on location."

"I don't think they start shooting till noon here. So his schedule is going to be different. And I suspect Baker will want to stay close to the other principals. And they to him. I may just have the A.M. blues, but apparently a lot of people have been here almost a month and no one has been paid."

"But don't they have contracts? And isn't EFX putting up the money? I don't understand. Does Baker know this? Do *you* know what's going on?"

"Only a little. Baker and I talked about it last night after you went to bed." Lily omitted, of course, what had happened later. She had taken Baker to her room and blown him for what must have been half an hour, until her jaws were nearly paralyzed, and practically nothing happened. And then they had gone into the old white kitchen with its cold floors and marble sinks, put milk and bread and cheese on a tray, and returned to the living room to play gin rummy and gossip until dawn.

"Anyhow," Lily went on, frowning, "the main problem is Vito. I think. I know he's up to his ass in trouble—he's mixed up with a lot of things that have very little to do with movies. Ian has always managed to stay clean; he's not a crook like Vito, but he's greedy. It looks like EFX pulled the plug on them, and Ian and Vito are keeping it quiet while they're trying to get new financing. Meanwhile nothing happens."

"But I don't understand. Why did you—"

"Because I'm a schmuck." Lily lit another cigar. "I was conned. Like everyone else. Everything *looked* fine. Ian's promises, the EFX money, Maroga, Trigère, Joss McIvor. And the part was *made* for Baker. I wanted it for him. I wanted him to get a shot at it. Maybe I made a mistake. We'll see. There's a lot invested here, and I don't want to be hasty or pull him out of the scene until I have to. I'll be around. I'll be in London for a few weeks but I'll stay close." She stubbed her cigar out in a small white ashtray and stood up. "I think I'll go put on last night's rags, and you can take me to my car, if you will."

Djuna drove Lily to the Spencer villa in the little black Fiat that had been rented for her. She waved goodbye with relief when Lily got into her own car and started the motor.

Djuna returned home, enjoying the adventure of driving the tiny car along new roads in a new land. She passed several men on bicycles, a few women in kerchiefs and woolen suits, gossiping in a cluster by the bus stop, clutching their string shopping bags. At the corner, where she turned toward the water once more, a small boy and his fat, starched nurse gravely watched a very young puppy tear around in ecstatic circles.

The color of everything was heightened by the clear day. Even in the shadows you could see purples, magentas, mustards, and a dozen shades of earth. Under its coloring-book sky, Cap d'Antibes had a washed-down look, its high gloss polished with sea spray.

She ran up the steps of the villa. Thank God Lily had gone. For a moment last night there had been a three-way camaraderie born of the bizarre events at Ian's, but this morning the sense of distance Djuna always felt from Baker when Lily was around had come back.

Whether or not they were having an affair was only part of her unease. It was their chummy, professional solidarity. It was The Business. They were Hollywood provincials. Inbred. Insulated. Their talk was all trade gossip—names and money, money and names.

As for herself, she had been merely marking time for

years now, gradually letting go of the arrogant illusion that she deserved—or would know what to do with—an interesting life of her own. During the winter she read novels, masturbated, tried on clothes, and went to movies by herself in the afternoon. In the summer she spent the afternoons lying on a float in their swimming pool. By mid-June she always had a mahogany tan. In the mornings she made phone calls and lists: lists for the housekeeper, lists for herself organizing the marketing and other shopping, the cleaning and laundry, the care of the garden, the pool, the menus for the dinner parties and barbecues that occupied most of their evenings and weekends.

Baker liked to have a lot of people around. So there were frequent houseguests who were mostly people who knew you when, who ran up large phone bills and burned cigarette holes in the electric blankets and peed in the pool. They asked to borrow sunglasses, hats, tennis rackets, your car, and very often money.

What else did she do? She redecorated rooms, watered the fifty-seven potted plants throughout the house, answered the telephone, kept up Baker's scrapbook, drank too much at lunch with other women who drank too much at lunch.

It was an absurd life, and most of the time she saw this clearly. Her difficulty with the notion of separating herself from it a little—or altogether—had to do with defining her commitment to Baker, to the lost ideal of herself. For a long time she had been paralyzed with fear that when she finally found the courage to deal with it she would discover that she herself was not worth the bother.

As she walked into her pretty new Cap d'Antibes living room, the gauzy white curtains at the French windows fluttered and framed a Dufy tableau on the water. Little boats with flags on a crayon sea. Was there anything anywhere more enchanting than France? Had there ever been a more beautiful day than this?

Djuna held her breath. She was—and this might even save her—a child of Hope.

Chapter Five

A little way down the coast, Joss had just arrived at the studio. He found Ian's offices empty and walked over to the restaurant. He had been advised that nothing would be happening today but had come anyway, as was everybody else's custom, on the chance there might be some hard news.

On his way to the private dining room, he saw Kat sitting at a table by herself in the main part of the restaurant. She had wrapped a lime-green scarf around her head and wore funny-looking sunglasses, jeans, and a short fur jacket. She was smoking, of course.

He walked into the room, up to her table. "Why aren't you lunching with Ian?" he asked, and removed her sunglasses to look at her.

She blew smoke at him. "It's Theodora's day to lunch at the studio. Do you see those two dykey blondes in the corner? They forgot it was Theodora's day, too. We were all dumped in here. And now we have to pay for our own lunch."

"That so?" He put her sunglasses back on, suddenly not liking her as much as he had. "I expect I'd better run along in there. See what's happening."

"Don't let me keep you." She began a pretense of eating her lunch.

He considered. "What gives *you* the right to be so prickly?"

She stuffed her mouth full of bread and butter. "I have the right to be anything I please."

"When I woke up this morning you were gone. Why?"

"I went back to my room because when I woke up I felt marginal."

"What do you mean, marginal?" he asked in exasperation. "Hung over, I suppose."

She sipped her wine. "That's obtuse of you. Actually, my frame of reality was slipping. I had to be alone."

He chose not to deal with it. "I'm going in to lunch. They'll have started." He turned and walked away. She was interesting. And the hell with her.

Ian's table was smoky, noisy. Wine had been poured and the first course was being served. Joss took the only empty seat and found himself between Bernard Trigère and Lily Dunne.

"Where's Vito?" somebody asked, and the table fell suddenly silent, attentive to the answer.

"Damned if I know," Ian replied, looking around with his bland smile.

"Has the cause of death been determined?" Lily asked next, in her brassy New York accent. "It's a bit much to believe it was natural, like they said last night."

"Darlings!" Theodora fluttered her bread and butter in the air. "We are a *family*. And we must keep this awful thing to ourselves as much as ever we can!"

"So that's what we are." Maroga squeezed a wedge of lemon into a glass of water. "A family. I knew we weren't a movie company. A movie company makes movies. We just come here every day to have lunch."

Ian picked up the wine bottle near him, frowned at the label, and set it down again. "Actually, my dears, we are *indeed* going to start shooting this week." He smiled at everyone again. "If not tomorrow, Wednesday for certain." He looked up to see Chin-Chan, his petite Chinese secretary, entering the dining room. She came over and whispered to him and then went out again.

Baker turned to Trigère, saying in a low voice, "Can you tell me what the fuck is going on here?"

"You have never done a picture for Ian and Vito?" the French director asked with a smile. With his fork he rearranged the parsley on his fish.

"Why is it Ian *and* Vito? I thought Ian was the producer."

41

"My dear Baker, usually wherever there is Ian there is also Vito. In the last few years whenever they make a picture there is . . . somehow . . . trouble. Always to do with money." He shrugged. "I suppose they are a bad lot and I should have listened to my agent, but my function on this film was to be purely artistic, or at least that is how I excuse myself for this somewhat questionable association."

On the other side of Trigère, Joss was paying slavish attention to his lunch. Seeing his glass was empty again, he started to look around for some more wine.

"Here," Lily said, noticing. She passed him a bottle.

They had scarcely spoken throughout the meal, but now she said, "Do you think you're going to like being in a movie?"

He spread some yellow sauce on his remaining piece of fish. "I can't very well say, can I? I signed with Ian because it was terrific money." He considered, and lied again. "Also, I was curious to know if I could act. So far I haven't had a whack at either. Do you know nobody's been paid yet? Good luck to Baker is all I can say. Do you know why everyone turns up here every day? To make sure they don't miss out on anything. Like news or money. And Ian always pays for lunch."

"Did you know Ian—I mean, personally, before this?"

Christ. Did he know Ian personally? *My dear Miss Dunne,* I didn't know Ian at all. It was his darling niece I knew. Fifteen years of age and her father with a title, only she said she was nineteen when she showed up in my dressing room that night after the concert. Friends had brought her.

She had close-cropped black hair on an exquisite small head. Great sooty eyelashes and a long graceful neck plunging toward incredibly plump breasts that kept spilling out of a tight silver dress. And a floor-length fur over her shoulders.

He loved fur. He loved sooty eyelashes. It was the last night of that tour, and when she looked at him from her perch on the dressing table where she was sniffing at the champagne he could see the high flush of excitement on her cheeks. He hadn't known she was on school holiday, that she had borrowed the dress and the fur, or that she was Ian's niece and godchild.

They had gone to supper in a crowd, and then he had taken her back to his hotel. He had been terribly drunk by then and out of his head, and her sudden astonished fright, standing there in her little minislip, seen through his stepped-up perspective, had led him to actually rape her there on his bed at the Savoy with all the lights blazing. So he had seen the blood. All over the bed. And also the vomit when, afterward, she threw up.

He had ripped her. He had also—the lawyers informed him—made her pregnant. *I am making this movie, Miss Dunne, partly by way of penance.*

Joss looked across the table at Ian. The stories he had heard about the suave producer weren't so pretty either. It was said that Ian's girls did more performing than anything else. It was said that these days he didn't take anyone to bed but merely watched women make love to each other.

He suddenly pushed his plate away and drank some more wine. What about Kat? Was that what she was up to? But she didn't fit the part! He felt the familiar resentment. It was all fucked. Everything was fucked. Shit and pain flowed through everyone's veins, including his own. He tried to think about his music. About Djuna Martin. Especially about Djuna Martin.

Next to him, Lily was weighing choices. She should probably not leave tonight, after all. She should stick around until she was sure the picture really was going to start.

Of course, there had been no real reason for her to come to Nice in the first place. Baker could have found his own way across the Atlantic. But she had been coming to Europe anyway.

When she'd had a word with Ian earlier, he had been as bland, as enigmatic as ever. He hadn't answered a single question. He had airily met all of her queries with "Not to worry, dear girl. Not to be paranoid! Of course we are going to start this film. Do you think for a moment I would be dallying here if we weren't? I have to earn a living, too, you know."

Lily twisted the set of heavy gold rings she always wore on her right hand. There was nothing she could do except wait like the rest of them and she might as well wait in London as her schedule called for. Tonight she was going to go straight to her hotel in London and get stoned right out of her little mind.

The years that led to her success as an agent had eaten away at her energy and her nerve. She had had to give more and more of herself and instead of it getting easier it had, on the contrary, drained her of her vitality and her drive. So she got stoned a lot.

One day about a year ago she had simply run out of juice. She had lain in her bed, staring out the window at the leaves in the pool, knowing she had a ten-o'clock appointment and a lunch date, and not wanting to go. For the first time in her career she didn't want to go where there was money or a deal to be made. She found she couldn't even remember why she had chosen this kind of life—or indeed if she had chosen it at all. All the things that had once seemed so important to her seemed to have lost their original meaning. Nothing was new any more. Everything was old. Old and hard.

Eventually, of course, she got herself out of bed and went to the meeting. She knew what to do and she did it well, no one ever knew after that that she was only playing a part.

No one had loved her for a long time. She had hoped at one time that she would mean something to Baker. When he married Djuna, she had gone to Mexico for ten days, stayed completely stoned, and then returned to hope again. Their friendship was one of the few good things she had. She knew that he depended on her—and maybe it was only that—but surely he came closer, in his way, to a kind of affection that was more authentic than anything she got from any of the men she made love to. Men rarely made love to Lily; she did it to them. It was her act, it had always been her act, and she would do it over and over because she really didn't know any other way.

Joss was looking for the wine bottle again. Lily passed it to him.

In the main dining room, Kat had finished her lunch. She collected her long, rust-colored muffler from the coatrack and walked out through the empty bar. She could hear the chatter coming from Ian's table behind closed doors at the far end.

Screw them. She felt out of it. Out of everything.

She hadn't traveled much and didn't know the art of coloring in the empty squares of time that make up a foreign afternoon, and so she often fell victim to traveler's vertigo, that edginess of the heart and throat which comes from being non-affixed, floating just off the ground above the newsreel faces of a foreign crowd that never notices but just goes about its daily business, crossing streets and buying bread.

When she got outside she didn't know what to do, so she strolled aimlessly for a little while along the road that led to some of the exterior sets. The afternoon had turned sulky and gray.

Nothing was happening. Through a window in one of the studio buildings she saw a man asleep at his drawing board in a deserted office. A plane roared over the buildings and a striped cat scuttled away from a bush with hard, spiky flowers. Kat picked one and threw it away.

She thought of California, of the apartment in Westwood she shared with two other girls who were also students in the film department at UCLA, of their Mexican rugs and posters, of the one bathroom always dripping with everyone's pantyhose, and the late-afternoon sun coming through the pepper tree, through the window panes, hitting the living-room wall to make bright, moving images.

Home. She had quit it so triumphantly. Like the innocent queen of a crummy beauty contest. Even her sophisticated stepmother had been impressed with Ian. An English gentleman. Gracious and amusing. A graduate of Oxford. Or maybe it was Cambridge. An international movie producer.

Since Kat's arrival in Nice, Ian's fatherly interest in her consuming passion to be a director of films had undergone an unpleasant change. He was still paternal, all right, but his manner with her had become maddeningly off-hand and extremely tyrannical. She found out very quickly that she was to occupy a fixed place in his life here. She was the junior, untried member of an entourage she hadn't known existed, and she had a specific primary function, which was to be available to him at all times. Whether he was summoning her to meet him for cocktails at the Carlton or sending her out on errands, to buy him cigars or pick up a package at the airport, it was always with the same easy air of a privileged person who is used to instant obedience from everyone.

He had paid her fare, for her rented Peugot, and he was taking care of her bill at the hotel, and she had thought it all simply wonderful until it had dawned on her, after a few days, that she was not the recipient of his philanthropy. She belonged to him. She was not his protégée; she was his lackey.

Not that he wasn't charming to her. A lot of the time he was benevolent, interesting and even funny. He introduced her to a fascinating variety of people, took her with him to dinner, to the casinos, on shopping trips. And once he took her to Paris. But whereas before she had always been Kat, with her own sense of separateness and identity, here she was domestic help with privileges. She was "one of Ian's birds." She was stuck fast in the cogs of his glamorous, crooked machinery.

She looked down at the short fur jacket he had bought her in Cannes. She stroked the plump pelts, running her hand up and down slowly. They felt nice. He had also bought her some very smart high-heeled boots, a shoulder bag, and a pair of huge sunglasses. "Bigger than California," he had said, smiling at her in her new Riviera-hippie finery.

She was realizing, feeling strangely grown up and strangely sad, that their relationship was to be mostly—and merely—a transaction. So she must at all times keep her objective in mind.

A few months before she had met Ian, one of her teachers at UCLA had invited her to what was called a Special Evening at the Directors' Guild in Hollywood. For the first time in Guild history they were honoring a woman director, and naturally every female who had ever directed a film (not that there were many of them) turned up to join an overflow crowd of film professionals paying tribute to the only woman director in America ever to make "big" pictures. It had been a long, emotion-drenched, and in many ways bitter evening. Certainly it must have been bitter for all the aspiring directresses to contemplate that only one of them had so far succeeded to such visibility.

Possibly it was also bitter for the honoree. It had been thirty years since she had directed a film in Hollywood. Although she appeared to be in excellent health and was extremely sound of wit and younger than some of the big-name directors on the podium who were still making pictures, the reason for her early retirement was not dealt with by any of the men who spoke. They seemed to think it absolutely extraordinary that she had directed those pictures at all. And indeed it was.

At intermission, having had most of them pointed out to her, Kat found her directorial sisters to be a sallow, tight-haired lot. With the exception of a glamorous, ballsy actress who had directed a number of television shows and was considered one of the pioneers of women in film, the directresses were a tacky, tubercular-looking group, Kat thought in dismay. They looked poor and proud; even the few little rich girls among them who produced their own films in a blue world of vanity and ridicule lacked style. They appeared totally devoid of female grace. It was as if, in the terrible struggle to be admitted to the holy ground of directing, they had all lost their complexions.

Kat was struck with one woman in particular. She had a genuinely bizarre appearance—oily looking hair, ragged red cloak, sunken eyes, and a dirty baseball cap. She was quite well known because what she had done was serious and good. She had sacrificed everything to make her few early pictures. She was still young. But she hadn't had any work for years.

Kat was going to do it another way. And Ian was going to help her. None of this had been planned; it had sprung from happenstance—the good fortune of meeting Ian, and being invited here as an "apprentice."

Her determined, if vague, resolve had to do with her ambition, her sense of self, her good looks, and what she had been able to understand so far about her own process. She was too young and too inexperienced to perceive things as they really were. So she saw them as she supposed them to be. Which often—of course—can be the same thing. She was dealing within the limitations of what she knew. And to that extent she was clear.

The only way for a woman to become a director was not to ever forget she was a woman. To be simply talented was not enough. Not yet.

She came upon a large exterior set, a romantically pretty, peeling mockery in the silvery light of the winter afternoon, surrounded by wasteland grasses and pockets of fresh mud. Many years before, Trigère had made *Juniper Road* on that set. It still stood. Others had used it, dressed it, changed its face, but she recognized it instantly. There had been that long opening shot, the swelling music, the first titles . . . she knew every scene. She had seen the picture a dozen times.

She picked up a little pebble from the edge of the set and put it in the pocket of her fur jacket. Souvenir. Then she turned and started back to her car.

A little way off, a black Jaguar passed on the road that led out of the studio. She saw Joss at the wheel, and a girl. They were too far away for her to see who the girl was.

Joss would always have a girl. She could be sure of that. She felt diminished even while she accepted it. And she was glad she had been shitty to him in the dining room.

Joss, for his part, would rather have been with Kat (spiritually) than the thirtyish Swedish production secretary he was taking back to his hotel with him, but on the other hand, production secretaries presumably knew their place. And Kat didn't. There were times one wanted a bird of paradise, to be sure; there were also times one wanted a nurse or a Mummie, and this was one of those times. He had had a lot of wine at lunch and he didn't want to talk, argue, or work hard at anything; he wanted, rather, to be worked upon, and glancing over at the peach-colored Scandinavian bird beside him, he congratulated himself on his sensible choice. Sex was the only way to anesthetize himself for the rest of an afternoon with nothing to do. He was used to the sharp, busy edge of life in London, used to all-night sessions in recording studios, to airplanes, to New York, Houston, Chicago and Los Angeles, Australia, Japan. In short, he had become used to his life. France was different altogether, rather like a soft, endless holiday. It was dreamlike, remote, like the colored pictures in books when he was a little boy, temporary and indistinct, like naps, memories, dreams. The Scandinavian Peach was like that. Done in rounded, untroubled pastels.

By the time Kat got back to the hotel and went into the bar, Joss was upstairs, swimming in peach juice, it might be said, while his valet in the next room read a comic book and listened to the enthusiastic Swedish groans of pursuit and plunder. Why did women always make so much noise?

Downstairs, Kat ordered a Kir and reread Eisenstein's notes for *Potemkin*.

Chapter Six

After lunch Lily left to pack and catch her flight to London. Baker had planned to spend the rest of the day at the studio, but Ian had disappeared right after dessert. No one else displayed any interest in Baker's continuing presence, so he got in his car and drove back toward the Cap.

He followed what road signs he could decipher and looked for the landmarks he had memorized on his way to Nice that morning. The scenery was a California mock-up. Gas stations, apartments, roadside places. On his left the water was choppy green. Then he saw the ramparts of Antibes and its tiny port, and knew that he still had to thread his way through the Old Town, come out on the water again, follow the slick modern beachfront, and then head south on the pretty coast to the villa, which was hidden from the road by immense pine trees and a high stone wall.

He was feeling diminished. Those people at lunch, all chattering in French and Italian to one another, lingering over each course, each cigarette, each opinion. They were languid heirs to a way of life to which Baker would always be an impatient stranger, never really understanding their style or their patience with history, and especially with time. He was an outsider.

He wished now that he was staying in a hotel. He was feeling foolish about the villa, just as he was feeling foolish about everything—the picture, the quiet, almost-deserted studio, and the rest of the empty afternoon.

Did the struggle ever end? Was there no such thing as a moment when you knew you had made it? There had always been something to keep each hard-won victory from becoming a clean contract with the future. When you got what you wanted there was always only about twenty seconds before new shit started; the compromise to do with the billing, or the part, or the money, and often with the picture itself. The best performance he had ever given, and the one which could have won him an Oscar years before he actually did, was in a movie otherwise so mindless and shoddy that it had disappeared from the theaters within a week. The reviewers had ignored it altogether. Even when he had finally won the shiny statuette, that hadn't been clean either. He had garnered the votes, but the Academy audience had clapped with politeness and little enthusiasm; he was clearly not the emotional favorite, and the next day a lot of sons-of-bitches were saying his agent had bought him the award with the high-priced campaign they had run in the trade papers. Even Djuna had helped to spoil it, with her strange restraint over his triumph.

And now *Lovers and Clowns.*

He had thought that for once everything was going to come right; his biggest part, biggest salary, biggest billing —and the French Riviera thrown in. He had finally made it. He was going over the title. He was going to be a star.

Shit.

It was evident they didn't have the money pinned down. If he had been conned like that at home he would have walked out in a minute. Here, everything was different, hazy, confusing. He tried to reassure himself. Ian and Vito weren't amateurs and they knew the consequences. They had been in the movie business a long time. They had been, in fact, a successful combination—Ian with his reassuring, upper-class bullshit connections, backed by the busy, secretive Italian. Certainly they had managed until now to keep their international high-wire act going. They had produced some very big pictures over the years.

At lunch, Trigère had told him that despite Ian's successes, the houses, the cars, the mob of people he kept on his personal payroll—or perhaps because of all that—the word was out that he was down to his last penny.

"Perhaps," Trigère had said, "he has lost his touch.

51

Perhaps he never had the touch, perhaps he was only lucky and now he has become unlucky. They say he had a lot of his own money riding on that last film he and Vito made. In America. It was an extravagantly expensive production. And a disaster."

Baker held his nose. "I saw it."

"Precisely. They all had—how do you say—their heads up their ass. The director, Carmelino, got carried away and tangled up in some kind of tedious, didactic message he wished to give the world, and they were too stupid to understand what he was doing. All three were accused of being unfriendly to your country's ideals. What do Vito and Ian know about America? What do any of us know? I tell you, I made a film there and afterwards I felt like a fool. Anyway . . ." Trigère twirled his glass of wine reflectively. "Anyway, Ian's picture was so bad that not only did the Americans stay away but all over the world people somehow knew it was false and boring. They say that is what broke Ian's—how do you say—piggy bank. They say that is why the money was pulled from this one."

Baker drove through the villa gates and parked the car. He went inside and found Djuna on one of the flowered sofas in the living room, reading the script.

"What happened?" she asked, looking up. "Anything?"

"Nothing." He glanced around the room restlessly and picked up a little Greek figurine from the coffee table. He stared at it and put it down again. "Ian says we start Wednesday."

"I've been reading it." She pushed her glasses up on her forehead. "I know this isn't being the supportive wife and all that—but really, Baker, it's nothing. You mean all these people have been brought here for *this*?"

"Djuna," Baker said dangerously, "be a supportive wife. Go on. Try. Just for once." He sank into a chair opposite her. "And get me a beer. Or tell Fatso to get me a beer."

She put the script down and walked to the door on the other side of the dining room that led to the kitchen. Then she paused.

"His name is Gerard," she said sharply. "And he understands English. If you persist in calling him Fatso we'll lose him. We'll be the only American couple to have imported the servant problem to France. I've lost three housekeepers in two years because you can't treat people decently."

She was so quick to find angry fault in the moment that she knew—and he knew—that the wound in the side of the marriage had opened again. It seemed to have stayed closed only long enough for them to have applied for passports. To have crossed the Atlantic.

Baker wondered if he should keep his mouth shut and let it pass. Djuna's irritation with him had very little to do with how he treated the help. It had everything to do with what a pain in the ass she was getting to be about everything.

On the other side of the room, Djuna felt a familiar, dark rage fill the inside of her head. The way Baker treated the servants was the way he would have liked to treat everyone, including her. His system was watertight. He lacked empathy. He shared a sense of reality with no one. His mother had seen to that.

As usual, Djuna and Baker were having separate experiences of the experience. They would have been further dismayed had they realized the degree to which, and how often, their connections to a given situation differed. The evidence of this had always been there but had rarely been noted; they subscribed to the myth that spouses should be able to understand each other. Several years of this well-meaning muddle had made them angry and confused. Both of them felt betrayed by they knew not what. They dared not blame it completely on the other; when a house of cards caves in, absolutely nothing is left standing. So over and over again, they rattled their marriage chains at each other.

Baker was still trying to persuade himself to keep silent but lost this argument with himself. He stared at Djuna angrily. "What's the matter now? Are you going to tell me you've had a bad day? That the flowers didn't come up? That one of your forty-dollar fingernails broke? Jesus!

Doesn't anything ever change? Did we have to travel ten thousand miles to reproduce the same scene, the same set, the same dialogue?"

She said in a dreary tone, "Flowers. And fingernails. Is that what my life is about?"

He replied in the same dreary tone. "Why didn't we tape this conversation the first time we had it? Then we could schedule it into our activities, say once a week. Just listen to the dialogue. God knows, it never changes."

She said nothing and went into the kitchen. He picked up the script from the sofa and turned the pages idly, trying to find comfort in the healthy number of his lines. Maybe the storm would blow over. It hadn't reached such an advanced stage that it couldn't be deflected. Maybe he could say something funny to make her laugh. Maybe she would suddenly turn into the sunny girl he had courted. He didn't need this shit today. Once the picture started he would have that magic insulation that working gave him, like an extra layer of skin, against hostile afternoons like this. He felt raw and exposed. And more alone than ever.

Djuna came back with an angry mask on her face and his glass of beer. She handed it to him and said bitterly, "We can be sorry, but we shouldn't be surprised. A marriage on the rocks is a marriage on the rocks. You can buy it a first-class flight over the Atlantic and install it in a fancy French villa, but it's still the same—a marriage on the rocks."

Baker hurled the script across the room. It hit an alabaster chess set and all the pieces went flying. After a moment he said dully, "Don't start that divorce crap unless you mean it."

"I think I do mean it," she said slowly. "It's being here, on new ground. I had an insight today—"

"I don't need your goddamn insights!" he shouted. "I don't need your goddamn dramas or depressions or pissy philosophies of life. I'm an actor, trying to make a living in a tough business. I need someone who will support me and believe in me and not drive me nuts. My head should be examined for marrying an overprivileged neurotic like you!"

The phone in the entryway had been ringing and now Gerard entered to say, "Telephone for you, Monsieur. Monsieur Trigère is calling."

Baker went to answer it. When he came back he said, "Trigère and Maroga are going to have dinner at some place halfway between here and Nice. Joss McIvor will be there, too, and they've asked us to join them."

"Naturally you accepted," she said sarcastically and sat down. She lit a cigarette.

"Yes." He stared at her. "Naturally I accepted." He chewed on his cigar and watched her warily.

"I'm not going," she said.

He came and stood over her. "Don't give me any of that spoiled-little-girl shit. I'm not going to put up with a temper tantrum or any other kind of asinine behavior from you. You're going."

"I'm not." Tears spilled down her face. Scenes like this with Baker made her feel violent, lonely, crazy. There were no words in the language with which to protect or explain herself. Only the act of weeping, a flimsy, wildly flapping woman-cloth braced against the dark, whistling wind, gave her some sense of immunity. The tears would make her invisible until it was possible, bearable, to move into the next moment.

The familiar hopelessness overwhelmed them. The afternoon became one of those desolate domestic life-stops that exist outside time and never contribute to the record, only erase from it. Baker had left the room with the onset of the tears, and Djuna had continued to sit there, smoking cigarette after cigarette.

It began to grow dark and she got up at last to turn on the lamps. Baker came into the room again. But he could tell by the way she was sitting that she had not changed her mind. She always punished him with herself. Her rules of conduct were complicated, couched in the primitive language of surprise.

"Are you going to come with me or are you going to sulk here like a spoiled child?"

When she didn't answer he merely said "Fuck you," and went off to take a shower and change.

When Djuna heard his car start and drive away, she went into their bedroom and threw herself face-down on the bed. She lay there a long time in the angry prison of herself.

A little time passed, and this homely magic made it possible for her to entertain the idea of coming to the surface again. She lifted her head and propped herself up on her elbows.

In how many rooms and on how many beds had she thrown herself down to die a little? The first occasion had been on the huge four-poster bed with the woolly white spread in San Francisco, in the house where she was born. She had been five years old. The fuss had been about a certain red pinafore she refused to wear to her cousin's birthday party. And so she had not gone to the party but had remained face-down and weeping wildly on the four-poster.

She smiled a little now at that little girl. Not wanting to wear that ghastly red pinafore had been something to fight for. Of course, in those days all the issues had been clear. Seeing another's point of view was, obviously, a disease one only caught when one got older. She stood up, turned on the lights, looked at herself in the mirror, made a few funny faces, and went back to the living room, where she poured herself a very large drink and addressed herself to the possibility of resuming her life.

Perhaps she should change clothes and have Gerard drive her in the other car to the restaurant. Baker had been gone less than an hour; they would still be having drinks.

It wasn't so much to make up with him that she would hurry there, but to quickly heal herself, close the circle once more by getting dressed up in her role again. And it would be enough for Baker. They never really made up any more; too much hurt had piled up and the weight of it was too heavy to move. So without being able to resolve (or in most cases even define) the issues between them, they merely turned on the marriage machinery again, bought gifts for each other, watched television together, entertained friends, went shopping and to restaurants, and planned yet another trip to New York, the Springs, Mexico.

She poured some more vodka into her glass and went to run a bath. She would wear the white silk pants. And all her pearls. Why not? And her hair very long and straight. Thank God she was pretty. It was disguise, it was solace, it was power. She raised her glass and toasted herself in the mirror. And hoped that her frequent attacks of anger and craziness were caused by her marriage. And not by the fact that there might be something really wrong with her.

Chapter Seven

The restaurant was lighted by candles and an open fire-place. The room was crowded and smelled smoky and boozy and of hot butter and garlic and of perfume and fresh linen. There was a small dance floor and very loud music coming from an exuberant combo of three.

Djuna saw Trigère and Joss at a table near the dance floor. When they saw her coming toward them they both got to their feet. The three of them shook hands, Trigère signaled for another chair—which came immediately via a flustered hostess-proprietor—and Joss held it for Djuna.

"I thought this was to be a quiet dinner," she said over the noise. "Where's Baker?"

"Over there." Joss pointed out Maroga and Baker on the dance floor. "We thought you weren't coming." And he smiled and looked her over with unmistakable gratitude at her sudden appearance. "We're all half drunk already," he said cheerfully. "At least I am. And Maroga is pissed

57

off because there's a table of Americans over there who came and asked me for my autograph and didn't even notice her."

"Or your husband," Trigère added dryly. He glanced across at the table of young people. "Now they're staring at you, Djuna, and wondering who you are."

"I can't help them," she said with a grin. "I don't know either." But she was feeling fine now.

"Anyway," Joss said, putting his glass down with a decisive thump, as if he had been thinking over the matter and it was of great importance, "it's fucking marvelous to see you. I can tell you that straight off, darling. Now, what will you drink? Madame!" He shouted and waved his arm in the air at the harried hostess.

"A vodka. Thank you." She took off her fur and let it fall back on the chair. He helped her with it and they quickly exchanged frank glances of curiosity and appraisal. Djuna decided she'd better stop this, so she looked down and reached in her purse for a cigarette.

Joss picked up some matches from the table and lit it for her. "Why do all beautiful American women smoke? I hate it."

Trigère examined the end of his own cigarette and said mildly, "I suppose you don't smoke because of your voice."

"What—my voice?" Joss replied carelessly. "Bugger my voice. I don't smoke because I've always done sports." He smiled at Djuna. "Really I have." He started to say something else but instead knocked over his wine glass. "Shit," he said pleasantly. "Look what I've gone and done. Madame!" he shouted again and began to blot up the wine with his napkin. "Anyway, I'm going to quit the music business soon. I'm going to buy a desert island somewhere and eat coconuts and run around all day in my knickers."

The hostess came by with two large napkins and deftly rearranged the tableware over them to hide the stain. Joss gave her a sunny look. "Been naughty, haven't I, Mum?"

She smiled patiently and went away.

"Do you really mean that?" Djuna inquired with amusement. "About the desert island?"

"Of course I do," he replied, scowling now. He touched the watch on her wrist and fiddled with it absently "Made up my mind. Going to retire when I'm thirty."

"From what I've heard of the music business," Trigère commented, "I think that course would be wise."

Joss answered in the slow way he had when he was thinking things out, and was with people he knew to be more articulate than he. "I can't say the film business looks all that much more innocent. Though I'll admit the meals are more regular." Then with a smile at Djuna, "And the women are more beautiful. But your people at the top seem as gross and as crooked as ours."

Trigère hesitated a moment, then said dryly, "I think I was talking about life expectancy. In your business there is rarely a success that isn't savagely paid for, and paid for young."

Joss was scowling again. "I never got into the heavy drug scene, if that's what you mean. It wasn't my thing. That is, not after I'd tried everything once." He looked at the other two for a moment. "Actually, being who I am is bloody tiring. I can't say it any plainer than that. Of course, I'm grateful. And I'm rich." He looked up with the sudden shyness that sometimes affected him. "I'm afraid the problem tonight is I've had too much drink. My brain is all muddled. Not to mention my mouth. Anyway," he continued, suddenly cheerful, as if to placate the audience, "everyone's a crook except us. And we're lovely." He blew a kiss at Djuna. "Aren't we, darling?" He grinned at Trigère. "I won't blow a kiss at you, dear, or it'll get in the papers."

And then Baker and Maroga were suddenly upon them, Maroga in a red silk caftan with fringe that fell from her wrists to the floor. She threw a theatrically surprised look at Djuna.

"But you came after all! I thought I had Baker all to myself for the evening. I was in heaven. Now I shall be stuck with Bernard, who is utterly bored with me, and Joss, who is far too young."

"Too young for what, darling?" Joss leered evilly at the Italian actress and, without getting up, held out her chair for her.

Baker sat down, lit a cigar, and looked across the table at Djuna. "Feeling better?"

She reached across and took his hand. "Much." And she smiled. It was an act. It was partially for the others, mostly for themselves; a familiar device by which they could make up in public so that when they were alone again they wouldn't have to deal with it.

"Well." Baker looked around for the hostess. "Let's get some menus and eat."

"Madame!" Joss yelled in all directions. "*S'il vous plaît!*"

Maroga arranged the onyx rings on her fingers. "We shall have to leave a very large tip, the way Joss is carrying on."

Joss leaned back in his chair and regarded her affably. "I'd like you to know, dear, I've had to leave some very large tips in my rowdy career." Whereupon the chair tipped over and he landed on the floor.

"Christ," he was heard to mutter as he sat up and rubbed his elbow. From the floor, he looked up at Djuna. "That's not in my performance, I promise you. Anyway, come and dance with me, my love. I'm covered in shame and need to hide in your arms."

He got to his feet, bowed, and took her hand. The other three watched in silence as he led Djuna to the floor. Once there, he threw his head back, his knees forward, and went to it, to the delight of the other dancers and the people in the front ring of tables.

After a moment Maroga remarked, "I suppose he is going to be our resident *enfant terrible*."

"He was so different at Ian's," Baker said, still watching the couple. He'd forgotten that his wife was a very good dancer. "I suppose he's had a lot to drink. Isn't he here with anyone? I thought rock stars went around with huge entourages."

"Actually," Trigère said, "I'm beginning to see that Joss does not fit anyone's conception of what a rock star should be. Though to answer your question, yes, he did come here from London with a group of people. His manager, a secretary, a valet, part of his band, and a few girls. Except for the valet, they all disappeared after a week or so. Ian told me that Joss sent them away because it was his first opportunity in years to have an excuse to be by himself."

"But most of the time," Maroga added, "he has been in St. Tropez with Maria Andretti. That's hardly alone. And, of course, here he picks up girls like flies. He had my maid in the broom closet. She said—can you imagine—that he was like an angel!"

"In a broom closet?" Baker's eyes went to the dance floor again.

Trigère had been frowning at Maroga and now she gave a little laugh. "Bernard gets furious with me when I gossip. He thinks it is—how do you say—tacky?"

"It is usually unreliable information," Trigère said with a gentle smile at her. "You adorn your story with the premise that Joss is some sort of musical rapist who picks off maids in hallways. Perhaps he went to the broom closet at her invitation. Perhaps she seduced *him*. Why should a healthy young stud like Joss pass up an opportunity to get off for a few minutes against a belly and tits like that?" His eyes twinkled. "Suppose he was walking down the hallway on his way to the elevator. The maid comes out of your rooms and they say a word to each other. She gazes up at him, takes his hand, puts it inside her blouse and with the other hand . . ."

"Oh, do stop it, Bernard," Maroga interrupted crossly. "What fantasies you men have! You think you are all irresistible. The trouble is that the history of the world has been written by men and every last one of you has bought the serving-wench myth. The truth is that the reason a great many women make love at all is because they don't know how to refuse."

"If that is so," Trigère said drily, "my life has not been half so meaningful as I had imagined."

Baker was looking at the dance floor again. "I suppose Joss *is* very attractive to women. My wife seems to think so." He turned to Maroga. "What about you?"

"Oh . . ." She shrugged. "He's very sexy. There is no doubt about that."

Baker lit another cigar. "Sorry. I can't see it."

Trigère was also looking at the couple on the dance floor. "I think that it is the dichotomy in Joss' personality that makes him so appealing to women. It would be quite the same if he were a merchant seaman or a minor jockey and not famous at all. I believe him to be very innocent and, as it always follows, very cruel. To women that is a traditionally fascinating and romantic combination."

"Yes?" Baker puffed at his cigar and then added coolly, "I think he's an asshole."

With a final clatter and wail the music stopped.

They ended the evening, for no particular reason, at a plain, flat-lighted waterfront bar in Old Antibes. It was Joss' idea and they had all gone along because none of them wanted to go home, not really, not ever. At least not until they had to.

Joss and Djuna in particular did not want the night to end. The little flame that had first spurted up at Ian's dinner party was between them again, hot and bright.

Baker decide to put up with it. The pair were at the bar, drinking brandy and talking to the young bartender only a few feet away from where he himself sat with Maroga and Trigère. The three of them were at a small, wet table, playing a gambling game he had never heard of with two dice and a green felt field. A few young Riviera bums who painted yachts out of season, or were itinerant nannies or chauffeurs to the local rich, hung about, made side bets, bought drinks for the trio, and the trio bought drinks for the bums. Trigère had more or less given up on the game,

Maroga felt she was not in it at all, and Baker was slowly and determinedly beginning to win.

At the bar, Joss said, "I came here last week and met a girl, an American girl. She had been here for ten years and I asked her what she did and if she didn't miss home, and she said yes she did miss home, and that she hadn't really done anything for the ten years that came specially to mind, now that she thought about it."

A brandy-and-love-induced tear welled out of Djuna's left eye and rolled down her face.

"Now I've gone and made you cry," he said with a shame-faced but nevertheless triumphant look.

"Djuna!" Baker called from the table where he was collecting his winnings. "Let's go."

Chapter Eight

The next day they were actually shooting. It was as if the long wait had never been. By two o'clock in the afternoon Ian was looking around the set with satisfaction. *Lovers and Clowns* was under the lights at last.

There was Trigère, his glasses pushed way up on his forehead, with his arm around Joss, saying something quietly while he squinted at the set. Nearby, also in make-up, sat Maroga, doing needlepoint. Next to her, Baker was sprawled out and relaxed, his eyes closed, the base-ball cap he always wore when he worked pulled down to cover his face.

The actual shooting area, dressed as a pub, was beginning to clear out. For the last few hours it had been cluttered with crew members pulling cables, moving lighting equipment, carrying props in and carrying them out again. Now a silence was settling. All the people who had been measuring positions, polishing the glasses behind the bar, consulting their clipboards, standing in for the three principals, positioning the boom, moving the reflectors, arguing and taking orders, laughing, complaining, watching Trigère and Hans, the Hungarian cameraman, waiting for approval of each small, physical detail—now all these people were moving to the darkened areas on the sidelines, out of the brilliant pool of lights.

The sound man sat quietly before his equipment. The script girl whispered a question to the assistant cameraman. The assistant director stared anxiously at Trigère, who was still in conversation with Hans.

In the darkened area, behind the camera, Ian settled himself in a chair next to Kat. She looked up from the composition book she had been writing in.

"Why are they starting with this?" she whispered. "Don't you need an establishing shot? And they haven't rehearsed. Doesn't Trigère rehearse?"

"Kat, darling," Ian replied benevolently, "shut up. Don't bombard me with your American efficiency."

"But isn't it unusual to do close-ups before setting up the master shot? I don't understand."

Ian patted her on the knee, smiled absently, got up, and wandered off again.

The young camera operator who had been standing just in front of them, smoking a last cigarette, turned around and whispered to her, "Hey, dummy!"

She stared at him and he came up to her chair and crouched by it. "My name is Jack. And I heard your question. They need sixty-five extras for the establishing shot. And a completed set of the pub interior. They weren't ready. Or they didn't have the money. Take your pick. I have a feeling this production is going to be ass-backward all the way. But it's not the director's fault. Hans told me Trigère wasn't let in on the plans either. Crazy Ian just woke up this morning and decided to start today. As for rehearsals, I've never worked with Trigère, so I don't know about that. Maybe he just wants to scare the shit out of McIvor. If possible." He grinned. "You from the States?"

She nodded. "You?"

He put his cigarette out. "I've been over here for a couple of years. Came over for a location in Spain and decided I'd stick around to see a little of Europe. I ran into a commercial producer in London, so I did stuff for him all over the place—Hong Kong, Ceylon, Malta. I got on this thing by a fluke. I was just staying here on vacation—that means I was unemployed—and I was up skiing and I met Ian Spencer's wife. She's old as the hills but she skis like crazy. Anyway, the operator they'd hired got tired of waiting for the picture to start and went back to wherever he came from and they needed somebody fresh for Hans to bully. So a few weeks after I met her the first time, I ran into her again at a restaurant, and this time she was with Ian and she told him about how I'd shot all over the world and what a cute kid I was and so on. We had a few drinks and he asked whether I'd stay around and work on this and I said why not and here I am. Do you work for him?"

She hesitated. "I guess you could call me an apprentice." Then she changed the subject. "But don't they have unions here, and how do you get around that?"

"I don't. Ian and his partner take care of that. Can you have dinner with me tonight?"

"Thanks. But I'm busy tonight."

"Are you busy every night?"

"No."

"Then I'll ask you again." He nodded and turned away.

On the other side of the set, Maroga had just sat upright and was looking under her arms. "*Merde!* I am cursed. My body, as usual, betrays me."

Baker pushed back his cap, turned to look at her, and she pointed to her soaking armpits. The circles of wetness were spreading.

"Don't you use deodorant?" he asked with the cruelty of the fastidious.

"Deodorant is for people who don't perspire!" she said with contempt. "They think they don't perspire because of the deodorant, but I am telling you it is because they don't perspire."

"Maybe you don't use the right one."

"Nothing works on Italians."

He smiled. "Well, you are a passionate people. Have wardrobe sew shields in your blouse."

She replied tersely, "You do not understand. There are already two layers in there. I am like a faucet. I get a little nervous and pssss . . ." She looked around for the wardrobe girl, but Conchita was already coming across the set, carrying a tangerine-colored shawl with long yellow fringe.

"It needs this," the woman said blandly, arranging and tying the shawl around Maroga's shoulders.

"It doesn't go," Maroga grumbled. "What are you thinking of, Conchita? I am not playing a Spanish dancer."

"Yes, that's good, Conchita. Thank you," Trigère called from where he was still standing with Hans. "Only tie it a bit lower, and to the side. Thank you."

"He has eyes in the back of his head," Conchita muttered, and retied the shawl.

Maroga stood like a sulky child, her eyes on Conchita's deft hands. Then she sighed. "So be it. Everyone has at least one humiliating affliction. Tell me that is true, Baker. Tell me that you also suffer from some physical embarrassment."

Baker supposed chivalry was indicated. "I get hemorrhoids," he offered gallantly.

"What is this—hemorrhoids?" She looked at him curiously.

"Well . . ." He paused for a moment, not knowing how to proceed. "Henry Miller described it in one of his books as feeling like you have grapes up your ass."

She looked interested. "But that is more exotic than humiliating, no?"

Baker put his head in his hands. "I don't believe I'm having this conversation."

She saw he was shaking with suppressed laughter, and she pulled his hands away from his eyes, shrieking in mock fury, "You are making fun with me. Stop it at once and tell me!"

His eyes had begun to water and he dabbed at them with his cap. "Look. You must have them in Italy."

They looked at each other and started to laugh. He tried again. Delicately. "You know. It makes it hard to go to the bathroom—"

"I know, I know!" she announced jubilantly, and then put her hands to her mouth. "But you poor darling, and all those pictures you made on horseback."

"Where do you think I got them?" He lit a cigar.

She sat back in her chair again. "I am thinking," she began reflectively, "that I prefer to perspire always, rather than to have hair all over my bottom like Adriana Conti. The humiliation!" She looked sideways at Baker and giggled a little. "When someone—how do you say—turns her over!"

She continued musing. "It is true that everyone has something like that. Marthe Striemer snores like you cannot imagine. She cannot fall asleep on airplanes because she is afraid to be heard, to destroy her sexy image, to be laughed at, and when she went to do that picture in Australia it was thirty hours, that awful trip, so she took pills to stay awake the whole time, poor thing! Ah, Baker, the world makes us crazy with shame about our bodies."

From under his cap, Baker smiled, comforted by her silly actress prattle, by the cozy, familiar sounds of the set.

"Isn't it a shame about this bloody weather?" Theodora said, pouring a second sherry for Djuna and for herself. Outside the Spencers' villa the February rain was coming down again in glassy gray sheets. The wind was up and on the beaches the water was foaming.

"Unless we have a miracle they won't be able to do exteriors for days," she continued, handing Djuna her glass. "How lovely you look—all that white wool. So California."

Theodora settled herself again on a couch covered in aquamarine linen. "How I *adored* California. When Ian went over to do his first picture in America I went along and we took an absolutely charming place in Santa Monica."

In reality, Theodora had hated Santa Monica, Los Angeles, and America in general. The Southern California sky had been locked in perpetual haze, the Pacific Coast Highway, which ran along their back door, had been noisy and dangerous with traffic and humanity, mostly teenagers with rubbish, motorcycles, soft-drink cans, wetsuits. Ian had practically never been home to dinner.

She had taken long walks along the rough, nut-colored sand, watched all that incredible daytime television, and written a great many letters to her friends in England and elsewhere. Sometimes on weekends Ian had people to the house, but the men were usually dull-eyed and preoccupied, the girls very young, very bare, very shrill. They were all heavy drinkers and absolutely no one had anything to say.

She had not made one real friend, even though she was lunched once or twice a week, usually at the Polo Lounge or Ma Maison. She was always glad when the lunch was over and she could leave the bright, fickle, overheated air of Beverly Hills and go back to the private gray slice of beach.

It had been a terrible period. She had read more than fifty paperback mysteries, changed her hair color three times, grown fat on snack foods, smoked endlessly, and when it was all over and she was back in London she wondered why she hadn't used the time more importantly, gone more places, done more things. The answer lay somewhere in the confusion and paralysis she had experienced in that alien landscape.

She wondered whether Djuna was going through a similar disorientation on what was for her, after all, foreign ground, so she said, "Now the picture has started and everyone is at work except us, we can gad about together. You must see everything whilst you are here. I consider Ian absolutely lost when he's filming. He's simply never home."

"Baker is," Djuna said pleasantly. "He needs his sleep. And when he's working he likes his home life to be very ordered and serene." She didn't want to gad about with Theodora. What she wanted was to settle in, start a life of her own, explore Antibes and all of this part of Provence, learn to grocery-shop in French, and maybe be a bit in love with Joss McIvor. All things seemed possible here. "Baker isn't much of a swinger," she continued. "When he comes home he wants his phone calls, his dinner, and television, in that order."

"But, my dear, how dull for you," Theodora murmured.

"Well, I didn't know any of that before we got married," Djuna replied with a laugh, and then wished she hadn't said it. It was the sherry. She put the glass down.

"We never do, do we?" Theodora said with her merry laugh. "The hell of it is they *never* get to know *us*. Twenty years later they are still thunderstruck every time we try to tell them who we are."

"Oh, I don't know. I try to avoid that position—the idea that men are all alike, and lumping them together like a bunch of bulls. It's not fair. And certainly not true."

"My dear! You must be in love with someone." Theodora got up to poke her head into the kitchen and ask for lunch. Then she poured herself another drink and brought it back to the low table that was piled high with expensive color picture books on flowers and pornography, a Greek chess set, a large silver bowl filled with black walnuts, a catalog from Neiman-Marcus, a gaily painted Bavarian music box, a pack of cards, and an Oscar.

Theodora lit another cigarette. "What I mean, darling, is that generally those periods when we convince ourselves that men aren't alike, that they don't only care about money and football matches and their mothers . . . well, that means we've found someone new." Her eyes twinkled.

They went in to lunch.

The Spencers' man was standing by the table, which had been set at one end with a rose-colored embroidered cloth. The lunch was fish soup, cold meat, and salad, very good, much better than the dinner a few nights before.

Djuna ate hungrily and drank two glasses of the excellent cold beer.

"I do think beer is so much better at lunch than wine," Theodora said when they were finished, lighting another cigarette and smiling at her guest.

Djuna put a last salty, black Greek olive in her mouth and chewed with satisfaction. Theodora was really not all that bad. Behind the scattered, silly-sophisticated veneer, she was obviously intelligent. And despite the cynicism, she was kind. She would have something to offer. They would get along.

The lunch had been marvelous. The villa was beautiful. The rain was beautiful. France was beautiful. Bright new scenery hung all over Djuna's private world. She had never had such an astonishingly clear sense of her own history. The moment was filled with drama and hazard. There was a distinct color of time as well as place to the antique white coastline with its pretty treasures, its slanted silver greenhouses, its wooded villas, its distant, spectral glaze of snowy alps. Her connection with it, and all that would take place here, was a natural act. She was a story within a story. It was like those nested wooden boxes people give children that fit inside one another and that have to be opened and opened until the very last one is reached.

With happy wonder, Djuna sensed she had been found.

Toward midafternoon, Vito arrived at the studio in a taxi. He instructed the driver to wait and hurried to the set. He entered the stage and spotted Ian sitting next to that red-headed American girl they had met in America.

Quickly he reached his partner's side and hissed into his ear. "Have you gone mad? I told you there was nothing doing when I phoned you from Amsterdam yesterday. We can't pay for any of this, you English turd!"

Calmly, Ian looked up at Vito. "My dear man. We are making a film here. Kindly keep your voice down."

Vito's eyes were round with agony. "Tell me there has been a miracle, Ian. Tell me that since I talked to you EFX has changed its mind. Tell me the Aga Khan loaned you five million dollars. Tell me this isn't happening." He looked around the set. "Jesus Mary Joseph." He rolled his eyes toward heaven. Then he leaned down again. "Come outside with me at once. I have to talk to you."

Ian flicked his cigar ashes and they scattered down over Vito's black patent loafers. He looked unperturbed. "There is nothing to talk about. The picture had to start. So I started it."

"But, Ian," Vito said more patiently now, convinced he was dealing with a lunatic, "you cannot make this picture if there is no money. How are you going to meet the pay-roll on Friday? What about the studio? How did you manage it? How can you do this to me? We are already in so much trouble we should both be on a plane to Brazil this very afternoon. Now listen to me. I'm going to Geneva to see the Alvarez brothers. I will telephone you tomor-row. You must promise me that when you wrap today you will close down until we have something to go with."

"I promise nothing."

Vito stared at his partner. "This is the most unbeliev-able thing that ever happened to me. You *are* mad."

Ian did not even glance at the Italian as he turned and left the set. He smiled at Kat and lighted another cigar. He looked at the brightly lighted action taking place, ring-ed by a hushed circle of darkness filled with attentive faces. Everyone was happy now. They were working. It had been so easy. He had ordered the production manager to put out a call and to refer all queries and problems to himself. Bugger Vito. Bugger EFX.

For a moment, Ian blinked and felt very, *very* peculiar . . . It occurred to him that he might really be crazy. What if the decision to start shooting was not the forceful, ima-ginative act he had been congratulating himself on since morning? What if it was indeed utterly irrational? Or worse, early senility? If Vito failed in Geneva—what then?

Never mind. He focused on what lay before him phy-sically. It was real, distinct, sharp enough to chase away the vaporous fears. The queer feeling was probably only his blood sugar. A way would be found. Someone would come through. This was a big film with big names and a top director. It would be one of his most luminous successes. It would sweep triumphantly, in all its stylish glitter, through every merrily tinkling box office on the globe. In America it would reap huge grosses and he would be vindicated.

They would say again, as they had in other times, that Ian Spencer had the Midas touch for assembling all the right ingredients that made for huge international successes in the cinema today. He hadn't shown anyone, not even Theodora, the wounds that had been inflicted on him by the American reception of that last picture. Or, by the outraged director, after Ian had personally, at the last moment, supervised a complete re-editing of the film the night before the opening. He would not soon forget the young Yugoslavian crying out wildly in the lobby of the theater, "It's butchery! You have committed butchery on my picture! What does a man like you know about the art—the *art!*—of editing film!"

A man like you. Even now, Ian wanted to put his head in his hands and cry with bitter rage and shame.

"Cut," Trigère said quietly. "And once more. Quickly, please. Joss, the same thing. Exactly the same thing."

Joss looked puzzled but nodded his head. The camera moved in on him again.

Ian glanced at Kat. She was leaning forward, a pencil clutched between her front teeth, a cigarette smoldering between long, translucent fingernails.

All that precocious intensity, all those freckles in the heart-shaped face, all that silky red hair. Charming. Even if sometimes she simply would not shut up. Even if she didn't always understand her place.

Lately he had grown weary of the jaded professionalism of certified international parasites, kept "actresses," hangers-on and other paid drifters who moved in and out of his traveling circus from year to year. They were a ferocious lot, all of them, young and old, hard-eyed and adept at surviving—at his expense. Ski bums, failed writers, soldiers of fortune, relatives, retired military officers, pugilists, and whores. Over the years they had eaten at his table, lived in his houses, traveled with him, hung around the fringes of his films, "worked" for him. The more clever they were the more they got from him, and the most successful of them all, of course, had been the women, the sleek suntanned string of platinum-haired, stiff-lashed beauties of every variety and nationality with whom he had traditionally adorned his public life. He smiled in painful recollection. Some of them had been tarantulas.

They had always seemed to arrive on his scene quite unconnected to their pasts, amiable, agreeable to everything: the dinner, the necklace, the small part in the picture. And then, as soon as they had what they deemed to be some sort of tenure, came the onslaught. The fur left in Rome at a pawnshop that had to be redeemed, brothers with rheumatic fever, mothers who needed operations and private nurses, sisters studying to be engineers, police records to be fixed, abortions and hysterectomies, dental work—it was incredible. After a time they developed highly expensive tastes. They wanted large apartments, servants, antique furniture, electric appliances, hypnotists, masseuses, good luggage, golf lessons, lovers. Expensive, expensive.

Despite her youth, Kat was already a person in her own right. That was clear, and it was one of the reasons he liked her. She was a nice American girl with her own camera, her own typewriter, her own hair dryer, and her own traveler's checks. She was good-humored, intelligent, and so far did not appear at all shocked by what she had heard, seen, suspected. She was merely curious, and occasionally asked some very funny, very ingenuous questions.

Perhaps it was her generation. They didn't seem to think anything was nasty or odd, only new.

And he wasn't *that* nasty or odd. It might even be a phase; possibly in a few years he would return to taking pleasure in ordinary sex as he had all his life until his forties, when suddenly he couldn't seem to get the dear old thing up. Absolutely nothing happened for ages. Then on a trip to New York he had stayed in someone's apartment in Gramercy Park, and on a hot summer evening, standing at a window, he saw another window opposite. In the room, there were two people on a bed. They had just started. The man rubbed the girl's nipples with both hands and then sucked her breasts. He began to move on her. Ian had remained for the entire performance, and when the couple came to climax so did he.

He was very pleased and surprised, and after that he found ways to arrange tableaux of every variety for himself. It was now absolutely his favorite thing, and the only way he could get off.

Of course, it had all got more elaborate over the years, and in fact, in a London apartment, he had a closetful of quite fantastic costumes. But really, what harm was there in enjoying oneself? The only problem was that he suspected Theodora knew everything and this sometimes troubled him.

Kat was watching Trigère, who had been under the lights with his three principals. He nodded to the assistant director and walked back toward the darkness. She felt so excited she wanted to cry, wanted to fix the moment forever, to impale it on memory in some indelible way. All of her past fell away. She was here, she was real, and her canvas chair was planted squarely at the crosshairs of the mechanical illusion. She felt a rush of happy connection to everyone on the set, to all the people who were here to frame the magic.

Absorbed in the scene before her, she held the collar of her fur jacket closer around her neck and stroked the pelts. She wriggled her feet inside the exquisite lining of her new boots. Was there anything more exciting than this? She opened the composition book on her lap and wrote at the top of the first page: *"Lovers and Clowns*. First Day. Studio. Int—Pub."

Chapter Nine

Extract from Kat's Journal
Lovers and Clowns
Ext. Flower Field
Third Day

The rain is gone to Africa and we are outside today for the first time. Also, for the first time we started shooting very early. The crew was here at six.

Obviously Trigère wants a lot of pretty atmosphere for this scene—mist over the greenhouses, masses of dewy flowers, sea spray, the works. He's got Maroga in white and ivory lace and a hat with real violets. She actually looks wispy and frail. Though I'm beginning to realize she can look anything she wants to. Yesterday in the studio she made her eyes go red. She didn't cry, she just got red all around the rims for that particular scene. She's incredible. Right now she's sitting under a lone olive tree. The art director said he chose this spot just for that tree, and I can see why. Its branches are crazy and beautiful. Joss is sitting at Maroga's feet, looking very romantic and sexy in a white linen suit.

I have not had one word with him since that day in the studio dining room and I haven't seen him around the hotel, even though I've been in the bar every night after dinner. And not by myself either, I should add. Now that the picture has started I've gotten to know a lot of the crew and the staff. Jack, the assistant cameraman, the one who asked me to dinner the first day of shooting, seems to have found a steady girl. If I hadn't turned him down, maybe I'd be that girl. I don't want *that*, but I wouldn't mind having dinner with him now and then. It's too bad that men are always in such a hurry to sign up someone who will be *theirs*, someone they can count on, like a home base. Like a loyal pet. From which they give themselves permission to roam whenever they please. I think the reason that women don't always need that home base is because we don't know what it's like to have someone always around, waiting for us. We only know how to be around, waiting for someone.

I am telling everyone I am here on a scholarship sponsored by Ian to learn all aspects of film making. I just took it into my head to say that one night. I wanted a legitimate reason for being here so they wouldn't all keep assuming — like Joss did — that I was just another bird in the traveling circus.

Ian's wife came to the set yesterday and he introduced me. He more or less had to, since she turned up to surprise him, and there I was sitting next to him. He told her I was a student, and the daughter of a "dear friend" in America. Theodora asked me right away what I was actually doing here, so I told her I was studying film production. "You're not an actress, then," she said, and she seemed relieved, but she took her time looking at my boots and my silver-and-turquoise belt.

She's quite fearsome and ferocious but also rather attractive. The only way I can put it is to say there is an awful lot of Theodora. She has big green eyes that notice everything. And she has this wicked, sophisticated air. She can also be really funny. I mean, being outrageous is definitely her thing. Naturally I had wondered about her a lot and how she and Ian acted with each other. The surprising thing is that they are really affectionate, and it didn't look at all phony to me.

Baker's wife was with her and the thing I noticed most about *that* was the way Joss' head snapped around the minute they walked in, and though he stayed very busy over in a corner with his script, he kept sneaking quick looks at her and then looking down at the pages again, smiling.

Of course, Djuna is terrific looking. I would like to have that kind of style when I get older. There's no way for me to do it now. Not only do I not have the money or the time (or the looks!), but I think it probably has to sort of happen to you. There's no way to look or be like Djuna when you're only twenty-two. I've still got puppy fat in my brain and I know it.

I only saw her look at Joss once, but she had her sunglasses on and that's all I can report.

I sound as if I spend a lot of time watching Joss, but actually I watch everything—that's mainly what I do. I sometimes think my eyes are going to fall out of my head, there is so much to notice. I didn't think about it before I came—I was so thrilled with the idea of observing a production from start to finish and learning as much as I could. I see now that there's even more to observe than I thought, that layered inside every movie is another movie. Already it's hard to separate us from what is going to get on film. We flow into it and it flows into us.

Chapter Ten

They were in the field of flowers.

Trigère looked around once more and felt his own uneasiness. He had somehow to contain this space. The field, the row of greenhouses, the little wooded road gently sloping toward the sea. And he had to make the scene work—make all the words and actions in that terrible script work. All morning he had been playing, introducing extra elements, trying out new ways for sounding, coloring, filling the frame with his own sense of beauty, of flow. All morning he had been moody and withdrawn.

Maroga wandered up, the only one in the company privileged to break his solitude. She looked at him quizzically from under the violets of her lacy hat. "What a face! What is it you are looking for, Bernard?"

"I only know that I am looking," he replied simply. "I am staring into space, into the veins of the leaves, into the faces of the flowers. Choking down my stage fright. There is lead in my throat, in my heart."

"But, Bernard, it's been going well. You said so yourself. Yesterday."

He shook his head impatiently. "That was in the studio. The scene was preliminary. Problem-solving. Mechanical. Today I have finally come to grips with the meaninglessness of what we are doing. What is down on paper, Maroga, isn't going to do. Why didn't I see that before?"

"You *do* have stage fright," she murmured.

"I am such a fool," he continued quietly. "I have wasted a day and a half in this pretty field already, dallying like a dreamy schoolboy, staring at my fly."

"Stop it!" she protested loyally. "We have accomplished a great deal."

"I hate this film, Maroga. I see that now. It explains—but does not excuse—everything—everything I've done so far, everything I've let everyone else do wrong." He removed the violets from her hat. "Even these are wrong." He handed them to her with a bitter smile.

She turned the little bunch of flowers in her gloved hands. "It would be more reasonable of you to blame that idiotic script instead of yourself." She looked up at him affectionately. "And the working conditions. You are accustomed, after all, to controlling everything about your own pictures."

"It's more than that," he said after a moment. "Less honest than that. I did not start with the necessary kind of connection to it. My connection was based on the fact that there was absolutely nothing in the bank. And I did not prepare. I avoided. Then, there are all the uncontrollable things. Where did Vito disappear to and do we really have the money to go all the way through?" He ran his hands through his short gray hair. "I like a film to have walls around it. Walls I can see."

"Look." Maroga was pointing toward the water. "What is all that?"

Where the wavy grass sloped down to the little beach they were coming with pink and white striped awning and tablecloths, painted wooden furniture, champagne coolers, and large picnic hampers. Five musicians set up their instruments, the breeze off the sea fluttering at their shiny black coats.

"A scene out of Fellini," Trigère murmured. "The very naturalness of the unnaturalness. We need a midget, a nun and a clown."

The tablecloths were now flapping in the breeze. Waiters laid the silver, crystal, and bowls of flowers, and a flock of pale yellow birds flew in stately formation across the scene, in obedient rehearsal for an unknown impresario. Behind Maroga and Trigère the members of the company moved up to stare.

"Where is Ian?" Trigère looked around. "It must be his party. It is certainly not mine."

The burly production manager approached, out of breath. "What the hell is this? Lunch is already ordered —it's over there in the truck. Or is this some sort of joke? A scene not in my schedule? Another movie altogether, perhaps?" He glared sarcastically at Trigère.

"My dear Armand—" Trigère began.

"Look," Maroga was saying. "Here's Ian."

The Rolls drew up and out of it stepped Ian with a short, fat rumpled-looking man in very black sunglasses and a statuesque blonde wearing white plastic boots and a white ermine Davy Crockett hat.

Ian and his party approached. "My dear Trigère, and darling Maroga! Do you like my little surprise?" He beamed down at the festive scene. "May I present Mr. Henry Reed and Miss . . . ah . . . Miss . . . anyway, come along, all of us." He waved at the staring company. "Everybody down to the sea! *Lovers and Clowns* is having a party!" He took the fat man's arm and led him toward the festive scene. The blonde traipsed after them.

"More craziness," Trigère muttered as people surged forward toward the table and the champagne glasses were filled. The musicians began to play a wispy waltz. Trigère turned to Maroga and the production manager. "Is all this for Henry Reed? Do we know who he is?"

"I've heard his name," Maroga replied. "He's an American financier or promoter of some sort. On the shady side, I believe."

"And the blonde?"

Maroga lifted her eyebrows. "Darling, I don't think the blonde is anyone."

"The blonde is never anyone," the production manager said acidly. "But she'll be charged to the production along with the fancy lunch. Lots of luck shooting this afternoon, Trigère. The crew is going to be something with all that champagne in their pants." He walked away toward the catering truck, saying over his shoulder, "As for Ian, I think he's off his rocker."

Whether or not he was off his rocker was precisely the question Ian had been asking himself for the last few days.

He tried not to think of it now, as he sat at the head of the gaily decked table by the blue-and-white Mediterranean, the champagne fresh and sharp in his mouth and the whole party scene colored in the delicate, pale yellows of the winter Riviera. He had not heard one word from Vito.

What was a man to do? For thirty years he had been making pictures, one after the other. It was all he knew. It was his life, it was everything he was about. He had known for months that he and Vito were at the end of the line. After the disaster in America and all the ensuing problems, they had to get *Lovers and Clowns* off the ground. If it went under there was nowhere to go, not a shilling to be had anywhere in the world for their watery promises.

That damn-fool script was the only thing in the world he owned free and clear, except for his socks and his ties, and if there had been any further delays he would have lost his stars. Really, there had been only two choices: start production or go to the villa, shut the door of his bedroom, and shoot himself.

He sipped from his glass, felt the sea on his face, and watched Joss chatting up Henry Reed's blonde, Henry Reed chatting up Chin-Chan, Maroga and Baker gaily toasting each other, and Trigère quiet, smoking, watching the hired musicians play their tinny little waltz against the plaintive breeze, the popping of corks, the clatter of silverware and talk. They had begun to eat. Movie people were always hungry.

Ian gazed at Henry Reed. If only the man could be induced to put up something to get them really started. Maybe the others Vito had been talking to would then come in.

Ian had known Henry on and off over the years and didn't care for him much. Henry was cheap-spirited, ugly, and no gentleman. He had been involved in some very strange deals. But he had money—or at least the ability to produce it at all times, as if it simply came out of his hat. So far his only involvement with films had been a sideline: a lucky string of pornos. But he was clearly fascinated with the movie world of big features, big money, big people. He also favored heavy sex in his personal life. Ian had learned never to discount such a factor when there was a transaction to be made.

He had run into Henry in Cannes the evening before, and they had had a drink together. Henry had come to the South of France to engage a yacht on which he planned to entertain during the film festival in May. He had decided to branch out, change his image in order to have more friends, more money, and more fun. He said so frankly to Ian.

"What's with *Lovers and Clowns*?" he had said next. "They were making book in Hollywood that it will never get made. Yet I heard yesterday that you were already in production. Is it true?"

So naturally Ian had had to put on this litle show. Which actually was turning out very nicely.

If only Vito were here! He would know exactly how to handle Henry. Ian had always depended on Vito to close. He himself was only skilled in opening.

Henry was looking absolutely popeyed over Chin-Chan, who was, after all, spectacular-looking. People who worked for Ian rarely noticed that because she was so purely functional. She wore her glasses low on her nose, and with her mincing little steps and precise Cambridge English, she took care of everything in his life with a great deal of efficiency and a minimum of show. Perhaps Henry had never had an Oriental girl, though it was doubtful. Henry had probably had everything.

In any case, Ian was not prepared to offer Chin-Chan. The very idea of her could not be spared. She did everything he told her to do, never asked questions, never was cheeky or lazy, had absolutely no private life, and was afraid of no one but him. He paid her very poorly and considered her indispensable.

He had hoped that Kat would turn out to be equally agreeable, and he sighed. One day he would learn to stop being so impulsive. It was not only that his financial resources had changed drastically since he had met her in America and invited her here, but it was obvious that she was not a docile creature who knew her place like Chin-Chan. Kat was good company and something of a novelty but she was in no way profitable to him, and her hotel bill was an expense he could do without now that his situation no longer allowed him to indulge himself in his traditional penchant for largesse.

Well, she was a darling girl. But Ian liked everything to come out even. He didn't see why she shouldn't be made to pay for her supper. She was overdue for a personal contribution.

Dessert was served, a milk-white glacier pudding looking like a fairy castle, with black walnuts and red fruit for doors and windows. No one ate it. The wind was up now, and the striped awnings flapped wildly from their poles. The sea changed color, people continued to drink champagne and coffee, and a few couples danced on a huge and ancient flat rock.

The hired musicians were pleased. They smiled and played with more zeal. The production manager looked at his watch.

Chapter Eleven

Yesterday we had a special lunch on the beach, orchestrated by Ian. Trigère and the production manager were furious because it lost so much time and naturally half the crew got drunk. The script girl's sister, who was visiting from Marseilles, threw up. Into her purse, I might add. Resourceful girl!

The lunch was given for Henry Reed, an American, a sort of promoter, I guess, with a lot of money, who Baker says is an asshole and a crook. He's also creepy and disgusting and I'll get to that later. His girl friend was cheapo blonde and about six feet tall. Her clothes were tacky and she wasn't even pretty, but the way Joss acted with her one would have thought he was really attracted. The other men reacted in the same way, staring, trying to be near her, talk to her. Even though they were laughing about it, they were still doing it. Maybe it's the fact that there is so much of her—all that hair, pounds of make-up and lipstick, giant breasts, giant legs—maybe that turns men on. Who knows! (Who cares!)

I seem to be avoiding the main event. Ian told me we would be having dinner that evening with Henry and Eva (the blonde) in Cannes, where Henry has rented a huge villa.

Ian picked me up (that is, his chauffeur appeared in the lobby for me) at eight-thirty. I wore my one long dress and my contacts. The whole way to Cannes, Ian talked to the chauffeur about football while I wondered who would be at the dinner besides us and whether it would be any fun. With Ian you never know. He mixes with an incredible variety of people. Some of it is very high class and interesting and some of it is pretty low and not so interesting.

Of course, I didn't realize until I got to France that sexually he's a bit weirdo. He'd never tried anything like that with me but I'd heard stories, and before the picture started he took me to a couple of parties in Villefranche that were very heavy. I was scared out of my wits the first time and wanted to run, but it turned out we weren't going to do anything, just watch. He stroked my arm a bit hard and that was it.

Back to last night. We arrive. Henry opens the door, all done up in a quilted satin jacket. And sandals. His toenails are horrible, yellow and thick. I hate men with ugly feet.

Eva didn't have a stitch on. Except jewelry and some really crappy bedroom slippers. Ian kissed her hand, murmured, "Absolutely lovely, darling," and floated into the sunken living room. We followed.

For the first hour we watched a porno. It was French and very strange—more creepy than porno—and it was a terrible print. Everyone drank martinis, even me, and I never drink martinis.

Eva sat next to Henry on the white sofa, and toward the end of the picture I saw she had her hand in his trousers. He just sat there with his legs open, looking at the movie, puffing at his cigar. When he came, it was just a grunt. That was it. Like a burp. Ian appeared not to notice anything. He was very absorbed in the movie—he was laughing a lot in a dreamy way—and as for me, I sat in my chair and drank the martini and planned my escape.

After the film was over we had more martinis and Henry said Eva was going to make blintzes. Sour cream and blintzes. On top of the gin. They called that dinner? I thought I would be sick.

There we were in that opulent house (and it really was —it had Grecian terraces and sunken bathtubs and rooms filled with so many plants you thought you were in the jungle) with Henry and all his money, and there must have been a dozen servants for a place like that so we could have expected a terrific dinner. But no. We all traipsed out to the kitchen where the light was harsh, like an operating theater, and the huge old appliances, all white, made it look like we were backstage in a restaurant.

The Hungarian bombshell tied an apron around her curvy waist and, bare-assed and bangled, starts darting and humming from the refrigerator to the pastry board, while we stood around like clowns, drinking our gin and asking if we could help. We might as well have been in Burbank, and at this point I was really depressed.

Another gin, and I crossed over. My sense of options got lost. I was reacting, not acting. I forgot that life was supposed to offer choices. It was the gin, it was my inexperience, it was the distortion produced by both, it was the way things turned out.

The table, very long, dark, and carved at the corners with griffins (so were the chairs), was already set, so all we had to do was carry the stuff in from the kitchen, for which I was grateful. Out of the fridge came a glass bowl of caviar. I decided things were looking up. Of course, I didn't realize how loaded I was. All of a sudden—it seemed—we had finished dinner. Eva got up, went to the kitchen and came back with a tray. Coffee and a bottle of brandy. She poured for everyone. Henry was telling a long story about some exotic baths he had been to in Santiago. I didn't listen because I was trying to remember whether Santiago was in Chile or Goa. It was driving me nuts.

Then, after a while, Eva came around behind me. She lifted my hair and hung it over the back of my chair. She put her hands on my breasts and began to kiss the side of my neck and the tops of my shoulders.

My reaction to this startling move will be understood by other idiots and well-brought-up people of the world.

I didn't do anything.

I saw Ian was regarding us pleasantly. Henry, too. They smoked their cheroots in cherubic silence. Dimly I perceived that I was a player in a set piece. And that nobody but me thought what Eva was doing was odd or embarrassing at all.

The men took their coffee and brandy down into the sunken living room. Eva got me by the hand and led me through a sky-blue hallway to a bedroom, where she handed me a baby-doll nightgown and started putting one on herself.

I now knew pretty well what it was I was going to be asked to do and yet I delayed my refusal while I pondered the idea of actually going through with it. My reasoning was as follows: I have always wondered how people like prostitutes could do it with people they didn't like or didn't know. I know so little about sex anyway. I was also wondering if perhaps I wasn't overly naïve—whether I had limited myself by always having to "feel" something, even if it was only simple, healthy attraction. And/or loneliness, like the night with Joss.

There is so much talk about how sex should be free and unashamed and how anything you do is okay, and how come I'd never really felt that way, and maybe I should conduct an experiment to see what it was really like. It couldn't do any harm. I wasn't going to get hurt, I didn't care about any of the people, and no one would ever know back home. If I was going to be a director and writer of movies, I would have to know about every kind of human experience.

All I had to do was jump at the paper scenery, go through the hole I'd made, and be instantly on the other side, older and wiser.

This is what I was thinking when Eva sort of lifted my hair and looked at me curiously. "You okay?" she asked.

"Not really," I answered. She lit cigarettes for us and we sat on the edge of the bed and I tried to tell her the story of my life, which I felt at that moment to be of paramount relevance. I don't know whether she listened or not because her eyes got kind of drifty, and right away she was asking whether I was ready to go back to the living room and start. So I asked what it was exactly we were going to do, and that's when we really got talking.

She said she was very surprised that I'd never made it with a girl or in front of anyone and, if not, why had Ian brought me, and why hadn't he told me I was to be part of the after-dinner entertainment?

She asked how we knew each other, and when I explained about being a protégée and so on she just said, oh well, as if the reason I was there was now the easiest thing in the world to understand. To Eva, all relationships between men and women are a simple transaction. You give and you get.

That point established (for her), we got on to the next thing. She looked at it as a theatrical situation and she said that since I was so new at the game the best thing would be to play a seduction scene. She would seduce me, and generally all I would have to do was to react, but I'd better be sure to produce all sorts of maidenlike, quivering, pelvic stuff and sound effects. I must have looked doubtful—God knows I was—because she patted my hand and said it would be easy. The two old codgers were already tired and yawning after their dinner and all they wanted was a mild *divertissement*.

"We'll give them twenty minutes," she said firmly. "After all, I had to cook those blintzes, too."

I thought about my room back at the hotel and the half-read novel on the bedside table and the familiar sounds of Nice traffic outside the window. It was true I was paralyzed with fright, but at that point it was the very fright that was egging me on. More than anything, I hate to be afraid of things. When possible, I do the thing I fear. (I don't really, but that's what I was telling myself.)

Also, I knew a lot more about Ian than I had that morning. He had simplified everything by bringing me to this place. I now knew my position with him. If you were a woman, you were nothing. You started with that.

I decided I could kill two birds with one stone: I could go through with it and have a brand-new experience, and also avoid being sent back to film school, where I'm beginning to see I didn't learn all that much about the way things are.

And so, I did it. In a way I'm rather proud of myself. It was crazy of me—and of course I never would have done it sober. The gin, as I said before, greatly exaggerated my curiosity about life. Yet, drunk as I was, my reasoning still

87

makes some kind of sense this morning, if you look at it practically and intellectually.

But when the scene plays back in my mind I find myself shutting my eyes and wincing and even moaning to myself to make it go away. It's not because I'm ashamed—how could I be ashamed of something I did of my own free will? It's just that I, Kat, didn't like it, and some of it I hated beyond any description I could put here because you can't say feelings like that.

The only thing that got me through it, frankly, was my pride. When we started, I was pretty gung-ho, of course. And I did try to feel sensuously. I tried to separate my mind from my body. I wanted to be pure, erotic sensation —like I'd heard about—but that only lasted as long as the preliminaries. Eva had said I would only have to react, but obviously we weren't on the same wavelength because she made me go down on her. I can hardly write this. She forced my face up between her legs and right away started moaning and heaving, and Ian and Henry were sitting there with their cheroots, and their cocks up, diddling away, and I really got desperate. I wanted to weep. I wanted to scream. I wanted to die. But I knew there was no other choice but to go through with it. I was giving a goddamn performance and to stop at that point would have been more ludicrous than what I was doing. So I kept sending myself messages, saying never mind, Kat, never mind, it's nothing, it's only physical, it's like the dentist. It's going to be over soon.

Anyway I'm definitely not bisexual—I know that now!

I'm sorry I didn't get more of a chance to talk to Eva because the mentality of her scene still fascinates (and horrifies) me. She can't care about herself *as* herself or she couldn't live like that. And also, that whole mythology men have cherished about The Whore with the Heart of Gold is a crock of shit. It's how they (men) avoid the issue —which is simply that the woman fakes passion in exchange for money. Deep down, men probably can't accept that. I think it's why they romanticize whores in novels and movies, and rosy them all up with heroic virtues and

88

pathos and all the rest. What bullshit! Eva doesn't have a heart of gold. I don't think she has a heart at all. I think one has to be subhuman to do what she does, what all women like her do.

It's as if their spirits were retarded. It's like, in terms of evolution, they are way back *there*, dealing with survival on the most primitive level. Which makes them cunning, dishonest and immoral, and capable of playing the clever, historical (and not too funny) trick they have performed on men through the ages.

Of course, it works both ways. I mean, look at men like Henry. Ian has a *few* good things going for him, but doesn't Henry really *deserve* Eva? She thinks he's a piece of shit, and laughs at him behind his back and will take him for everything she can. He treats her like a machine that makes sex and blintzes, and both of them think *that* is *life*.

It's all very depressing and complicated to think about. Anyway, I'm sure that by tomorrow I'll feel more like myself. Even though I *am* changed.

And not really sorry.

Chapter Twelve

The winter sun was bright and the sky all along the coast was clear. The production schedule had called for an exterior, yet they were shooting at the studio. Everything about this picture was inexplicable.

The lunch was lamb chops again, and a soggy salad, three shades of wet green. But there was plenty of wine, lots of fresh bread and butter, and in the dining room where the crew was eating spirits were high. It was payday.

At the table with Ian were, as usual, Trigére, Maroga, Baker, Kat, Joss, Chin-Chan, Hans, the art director, the assistant director, and today there was also a pair of girls, flaxen-haired twins from Holland, about seventeen, with very plump braids, striped knee sox, miniskirts, and low-cut blouses. Everyone ignored them—even Ian, who had invited them.

Joss was watching Kat. On the set earlier that morning, Baker had said to him, indicating Kat in her usual place, scribbling in her notebook, "I understand Miss Film School has an exotic life none of us suspected."

Joss had scowled. "What kind of rubbish is that?"

Immediately, Baker wished he hadn't said it. You never knew how McIvor was going to react to anything. Arrogant son-of-a-bitch. The look in Joss' eye egged him on. "Let's put it this way," Baker said, defiant and foolish. "She'll suck anything. Even women."

In a rage, Joss grabbed him by his collar. "Who told you a thing like that and what kind of shit are you to go round spreading nasty stories about people?"

There were stares and murmurs around them, and Joss yanked his hand away angrily. The assistant director moved toward them. Baker held up his hands in peace. "I'm sorry. It's just something I heard this morning. And," he paused, "I didn't know you cared."

"Go to hell," Joss muttered and walked away. He hurled himself into his chair and scowled down at his script.

Baker tried to look unconcerned. But he had misjudged Joss again. What had made Joss so angry? Was it because he had some connection with the girl, or was it just repugnance at Baker's admittedly shitty piece of gossip? The kid never let you be chummy with *him*. *He* chose the moments. *He* let you in. Who could have predicted he would be shocked at a little gossip, however gratuitous, about a groupie broad? Joss, who looked up every skirt like some kind of adolescent Casanova and was, at times—and in front of anyone—foul-mouthed beyond description!

Fuck him. No way would they ever get along.

Now, at lunch, in a state of agitation and gloom, Joss stared down the table at Kat. What had she been up to? He realized that he hadn't really talked to her since the morning after the night they had spent together. They said hello every day and that was that. He hadn't felt the slightest need for her; his days and nights were filled with the film, and he had taken most of his evening meals with Maroga and Trigére. He had a new appreciation of them now that he had watched them work, and he found it pleasant to be in their company after hours. Also, he had been going to bed early. There *was* someone he had thought about a lot in the past week, and of course that had been Djuna Martin. He had very much wanted to telephone her but hadn't been able to think of an innocent excuse. He would have to wait for the next opportunity when they would be thrown together again.

Lunch was over. Everyone was standing up and moving toward the doors. Joss hurried outside and waited at the foot of the steps for Kat, who soon came plunking down in her sandal clogs, the ubiquitous blue jeans, and goggle sunglasses.

He caught her arm. "What've you been up to, anyway?"

She squinted at him in the bright light. "Not much."

He tried to say it lightly. "You haven't been naughty, have you?"

"What?" she said absently, and turned her head to where the others were disappearing through the doors of the stage. "Let go of my arm. I want to get back."

"Look, do you want to go somewhere on Sunday? Cannes? For lunch?"

She took off her glasses and stared at him. "You mean with you?"

"Of course I mean with me. For Christ's sake. Do you or don't you?"

"Well, actually, yes." She put her glasses back on. "I'm just surprised. That's all."

"I've been very busy."

"I didn't mean I've been crying myself to sleep every night."

A noisy plane flew low over their heads, making for the airport.

"Yes. Well, look." He took a breath. "I thought you said you weren't one of Ian's birds."

"I'm not," she replied coolly.

"And I thought you came here to study production. Period."

"Get to the point."

"Well I *thought* you were a nice girl!" he shouted, feeling like a complete ass.

"Nice! Nice!" she shouted back. "You're weird, McIvor! I don't know what you're talking about."

"Then why have you gone all white in the face?"

"Because," she said, and suddenly there were tears in her eyes, "you are making me very angry and upset."

They stood, toeing the gravel, glaring at each other. The assistant director appeared from around the corner.

"Joss! Trigére is looking for you!"

"Coming!" Joss yelled over his shoulder and turned back to Kat. "Look. I may not have a chance to speak to you again today, so shall we say half past eleven? I'll meet you in the lobby." He was already starting away, running backward, waiting for her answer.

She called, "I don't know whether I'll be there or not. I don't know whether I want to go."

He waved cheerfully. "Half past eleven. Or I'll come up and kick your fucking door in."

She watched him run off and she noticed he was slightly bowlegged. She began walking slowly toward the set.

Had someone told him about the night at Henry Reed's? She couldn't believe it had been Ian. Not his style. Yet someone had been talking. Could it have been Henry Reed? The chauffeur? It was obvious that on location practically everything got to be known about practically everyone. Hadn't she herself been the recipient of innumerable stories? Theodora's rages, Maroga's torch for Robbie Brannigan, Vito's connection with drug traffic, the production manager's obsession for the young Danish grip—it went on and on. And now was her own story to be added to the collective history of the company?

All at once she felt sick and thought she might lose her lunch. She hurried her steps. Shit. For everyone to know! Who would ever understand—or care—what her convoluted, on-the-spot motives had been? They would only hear the story and never know who she was at all.

And then the very idea of expecting anyone to believe her weird, precocious reasoning suddenly made her smile. In a minute she was wondering whether she hadn't been assuming an awful lot. Maybe Joss had just heard the standard rumors about her relationship to Ian. Maybe his questions had nothing to do with Henry Reed at all.

She entered the stage, and when she passed Jack he gave her a friendly wave. "How's it going kid?" he said, and she felt warmed. Trigére came over to talk to Ian and patted her absently on the head. It was okay. McIvor was being gratuitously paranoid. He was part Jesuit, part rapist. And he had a nerve.

She looked across the set at Joss. There was a fluid, natural arrogance to the way he stood, waiting for the shot. It was the performer in him. He was already on.

He had surprised everyone by taking his work very seriously. They had expected him to be difficult, but instead, from the very beginning, he had been quiet, attentive to everything going on, always knew his lines, and was plainly anxious to please Trigére. The director, in turn, was gratified by this unexpected cooperation. Kat had heard him say to Ian, "I'm not going to ask an amateur to express complexity. But I am encouraged. If we do a little of this, a little of that to the part, he might come off very strong. If I try to work with his style instead of against it, we may have something."

The assistant director held up a hand. "Quiet!" he called. The camera moved in.

Chapter Thirteen

On Saturday night at seven o'clock, Baker arrived home and went straight to the telephone in the living room, shrugging out of his coat and letting it fall to the floor as he crossed the room, and saying over his shoulder to Djuna, "I've got to call Lily. No one is getting paid." He dialed, spoke carefully to the operator in English, and paced up and down holding the telephone.

"But I thought that had all been solved," Djuna said. "How could they have started shooting? I don't understand."

"No one knows what's going on. Vito hasn't been seen since the first day of photography, which nobody worried about until today. Suddenly there's no one around to answer questions. The production manager has gone to Naples to his sister's funeral, or that's the story, anyway. Ian disappeared, and either he didn't go home or he's not answering his phone."

"I see," Djuna said, her private world starting to crumble. "But what can Lily do?"

Baker stared at her impatiently. "She can't *do* anything. But she might be able to find out a few things we don't know here. If they're serious about making this goddamn movie, I'll be happy to stay. But Jesus, they already owe me for two weeks, and then there's the villa and the cars— Hello, Lily! Hello! Yes. No, I am *not* okay!"

Djuna sat down on one of the flowered sofas, lit a cigarette, and thought *But it can't be over. It can't.*

Her week had been perfect. Now that Baker was working he had come home every evening in a good mood. They had not quarreled once. She had spent the short, pretty days in a new mode altogether, experiencing her freshly aired-out self. And thinking about Joss McIvor.

Gerard and Marie took care of everything that had to do with running the villa, so Djuna was free to read or daydream on the terrace, drive into Antibes, or take long walks in the wooded lanes and along the water, breathing the air of other centuries, examining with happiness and respect a puff of cloud, a shiny leaf, a man with pink cheeks on a bicycle. She saw everything, and she saw it fiercely and with joy. The new geography had become the new spiritual definition of her existence, and she would find herself trying to stop time, to stamp each bright moment into the record, so that when she eventually had to give up this place and this time, she would still get to keep all of it forever.

It was all very sentimental and very good for her and somehow she knew this. She cried a lot, and she knew they were very old tears, released at last to drain violently from her eyes, and evaporate into the magic air.

She heard Baker saying to Lily, "Well, see what you can find out, and let me know. Okay, babe."

Even when he was upset, he was always nice to Lily.

"So this is where you're hiding!"

Maroga stood on the threshold of the living room at the Spencer villa where Ian and Theodora were seated cozily by the fire, playing scrabble and drinking whisky. They looked up at her in astonishment.

She had come straight from the studio, eluding Trigére (who would have tried to stop her), and had burst in unannounced.

"Where is the money for this picture?" she cried now. "Where is Vito? How dare you do this to us? It's no wonder you left the studio early. You coward! You villain!"

"Maroga, darling," Ian replied calmly, "sit down. Let me give you a drink. And do stop all that shouting."

"I will shout as much as I like! Do you realize I have no money to pay my people? My secretary, my maid—they are threatening to leave!"

"Those people are your affair," Theodora said crossly. "The production hired you, not them. They have nothing to do with Ian. Don't be so hysterical."

"Theo, darling," Ian said mildly, "please shut up."

Maroga turned on him. "You should be ashamed of yourself! Sitting there playing a game by the fire like a stupid clerk home from a stupid day. With everyone in the terrible shits because of you."

She began to pace the room, her long fur scarf trailing on the floor.

"What's to become of us?" she wailed. "I demand to know what is going on, Ian. I demand satisfaction" She sank into a chair. "I demand a vermouth. Tell the man not too much ice." She looked mournfully at her host. "I am too old for aggravation like this. How could you do this to me? An old friend! You have fuckered me up, Ian. Now I will have to sell my jewelry to pay the hotel bill."

"But, Maroga, darling." Theodora drawled benignly, "what else is jewelry for but to sell in hard times? And anyway, it's insured, isn't it? Why not arrange to have it stolen? You'll come out better that way."

"Stop it, Theodora." Ian frowned at her impatiently. "Your criminal fantasies aren't in the least helpful."

Theodora made a face at him and turned to Maroga. "Darling, you've had your little say. Now that it's over, will you stay to dinner?"

"I hate English food. And I'm dining with Trigère. But," Maroga looked at Ian, "before I go I must have some answers from you . . . my dear friend."

Ian's eyes glazed over. "I can't give you any answers. Yet."

"But, Ian, are we to assume that everything is over, or is it just . . . temporary trouble? That will get put right?"

The butler entered to tell Ian he was wanted on the telephone.

"I am waiting," Ian said to Maroga. "Like the rest of you." And he went into the hallway to take his call.

Maroga turned to Theodora, who was smiling again. She had been smiling a great deal. "What is going on with you, Theo? You are insufferably smug tonight."

"My dear, I couldn't be happier," Theodora replied airily. "I hope with all my heart that the whole bleeding picture goes down the drain hole."

"That's wicked," Maroga gasped, and crossed herself.

"Is it?" Theodora looked at her calmly. "Perhaps. But I'm tired and I'm geting old and I want an end to all of this—an end to Vito and the traveling circus and this silly, dangerous, extravagant life." She got up and began pacing the room. "Do you think it has been pleasant for me all these years? Don't you see this is my chance? If *Lovers and Clowns* doesn't get made, Ian is finished."

"You are mad!" Maroga cried. "Pictures are Ian's life!"

"I'll buy him a set of tin soldiers. Or some paper dolls. We'll go to the cottage in Cornwall. Live simply." Tears suddenly ran down Theodora's face.

"But, Theo, you are talking about smashing a career, smashing a man's life!"

"Do you realize what Ian could have been? Do you know he had honors at Oxford? He could have been an ambassador. He could have been anything. You know who his family is, you've met his brother . . ."

"And to make movies is so bad?" Maroga inquired gently.

"I've had no control over anything," Theodora went on as if she hadn't heard. "Life happens like that. In the beginning, I thought it would be such great fun. It was so interesting. So glamorous. I invented a fantasy role for myself and played to an empty stage. Ian was always off fucking, and rubbing his body with money."

"Nonsense! You are upset."

"I didn't understand, you see. Odd, isn't it, how much we assume, we invent, about people we love? I was so certain that I understood what Ian wanted. In the beginning it seemed so simple to me. To make beautiful pictures. But all he really wanted was to climb that filthy ladder. It was money and power all the time, Maroga, starlets and yachts and the best table everywhere—*that's* all he wanted!"

And why not? Ian thought wildly, overhearing this last from the hallway where he had just put the telephone down. What was wrong with money and power? It was excitement. It was knowing you were on top. Theodora had never understood that. What Theodora wanted was something she had made up, something that didn't even have a name, something he could never provide. And how dare she imply his pictures weren't good? They were very good, most of them. They had cost a lot of money and made a lot of money. No one could take *that* away from him.

He fiddled with the Chinese horse that stood on a table in the entry. The little figure was dense and translucent all at once. Was it jade? Nephrite? On what trip and in what year, in what place had Theodora found it? Had it cost a fortune? Or nothing?

It was a beautiful piece. He stroked it so he could feel its coolness in his fingers. He heard Maroga say in low tones, "We've all been under a strain. You won't feel like this tomorrow."

"You don't have to humor me," came Theodora's strident theatrical accents. "Nor be sorry for me, either. I'm quite sound of mind. It's just that *he* isn't any longer. You don't know what it's like. You've never been married. A wife suffers the consequences of all her husband's actions. That's what a wife does. That's what a wife is. I know I look like a cat chasing my own tail. But tragedy doesn't have to get on the evening news in order to exist."

She was off, Ian thought in dismay. The failure of his life, the failure of hers—it would go on all night. Quietly he let himself out the front door, got into the Rolls, and drove toward Villefranche.

Sometime later, Maroga left Theodora pouring herself a fourth whisky. She drove back to Nice, where she found Trigère in the hotel bar at a table with half a dozen other people from the company. When he saw her he excused himself and led her to a table in the corner.

"Where the devil have you been?" he asked irritably.

Maroga settled herself, along with her fur scarf and her large alligator bag. She shook out her long black hair, waving at the waiter with her cigarette holder. "I went to Ian's. Don't be angry. I had to drive a bit. I had to take off steam. It was a ridiculous trip. I forgot about the traffic at this hour. I found Theodora and Ian playing scrabble by the fire—*playing scrabble!*—and got nothing out of either of them."

"But you must have learned something," Trigère insisted.

"Well, didn't you?" she asked crossly. "He said he rang you when he got home."

"All he said was that we had to wait for Monday. There would be no news until then."

"Well, what are we to do? Wait for his miracles, or walk away before it gets worse?"

Trigère sighed. "First, I think we should talk to Baker and Joss. The four of us should consolidate our position. After all, our contracts add up to a great deal of money, if it comes to a lawsuit." He smiled thinly. "I can't tell you what a fool I feel."

"Or I. I called my agent in Rome."

"And? What does he say?"

She shrugged. "Please notice that I smile bravely as I say this. He says that if I walk away from *Lovers and Clowns*, I will walk away to nothing. He reports that there has not been one call for my services lately. He also told me that Vito was seen in Hong Kong."

"Perhaps there's movie money in Hong Kong."

"Bernard, there doesn't seem to be money for this movie anywhere in the world. *Merde*. It wasn't a bad part. And it was work. *Merde!*"

He took her hand. "Maybe there will be a miracle after all."

"Look, there's Joss. Let's catch him."

Joss saw Trigère wave and came to the table. "I can't join you. I'm meeting a bird. What's up? Piece of shit, isn't it? Does this happen often in films?"

"Maroga and I think we should have a meeting of the principals," Trigère said. "Shall I ring Baker? Perhaps we could all get together tomorrow."

"Right," Joss replied at once. "I'm going to Cannes for lunch but I'll be back whenever you say."

"If you can wait a moment, Joss, I'll go and ring Baker now." Trigère got to his feet.

Joss nodded, pulled a chair over from the next table, and sat down. Trigère left to telephone.

"You know," Joss said after a moment, "I was getting to

enjoy all of this. Staying more or less in one place. Sunshine in the winter. Going to bed early. Rather like a holiday from my usual frantic life."

"Please don't talk like it is over." Maroga shuddered.

"Isn't it? Well, I hope you're right."

"You don't find us boring?" She smiled slightly.

"On the contrary. And you're good sports, too. That's why I've been so well-behaved." He flashed his boyish grin. "Hadn't you noticed?"

"And imagine," she teased him. "We all thought you would be very difficult. Very bizarre."

"Oh, I *can* be bizarre," he said quietly. He took some nuts out of the little glass dish and chewed them thoughtfully. "Films are more relaxing than the music business. And more serious. In the best sense. Also, there's a wider separation between your act and your life."

"But we don't have an 'act.' Not like you. On stage you are always in the same role. Yourself. We play a different part each time."

"Bullshit you don't have an act," he said scornfully. "I'll grant that you don't have a fixed *performance* like me. But you've all got your 'act' and you take it from part to part. Only one I ever saw who didn't was Olivier. Now *don't* get all upset, for Christ's sake. I think you're a perfectly marvelous actress and you've taught me so much already. There's a good girl." He offered her a nut.

She lit another cigarette. "You know nothing yet. Believe me. It's not like that at all."

Trigère returned. "Baker has asked us all to dinner tomorrow night. Here's the address." He handed a slip of paper to Joss. "I accepted."

"Perfect." Joss nodded and put the paper in his pocket. "See you there." And he was happy. Djuna Martin. The long suntanned legs, the quick, tilted flash of smile, those lovely odd eyes. She used some sort of white make-up under them, probably to hide the dark circles. How old was she anyway? He wondered how she would look with a bare face. In the morning. In bed. *If* he ever got her there.

"Well," he said, moving off. "There's my young lady

for the evening. See you tomorrow." He nodded and went to meet the buxom Italian starlet who had been imported by Ian to play a small part in the picture. She was perfect for tonight, and Joss congratulated himself. He was tired, he wanted a good dinner and two bottles of wine, maybe two and a half. And something gorgeous to look at across the tablecloth. And a nice bit of in and out before he went to sleep.

Maroga watched the young couple go off, and turned back to Trigère with a dry look. "You know, you *don't* have to dine with me every night. If there is someone you fancy ..."

He laughed and said, "I thought you knew that my light comes from only one lamp. It is only between films that I indulge myself, star in my own absurd little dramas and comedies. I have a terrible time making a film if I am in love."

"It doesn't inspire you?"

He shook his head. When he saw her smile, he added, "Truly. I have an obsessive nature. One passion at a time. Two passions and I cannot make clear daily choices about either, or even identify the priorities. My work becomes infected by what is going on in my life."

"But can't that work to the good?"

"No. Scenes become lopsided, angry. Or worse, dull, and even sentimental. The worst film I ever made was when I was being crazy over Lithe. I go red with shame whenever I see that it is playing again."

"But the critics love that film!"

"They don't understand it. So ... where would you like to go to dinner?"

"Actually, I wouldn't. Would you mind? I am overwhelmed with the day. A hot bath and a massage are all I want. Paola is off tomorrow and my eyebrows need to be done and my legs—you know, that sort of thing."

"And you want to be alone."

"Will you find something to do? And forgive me?"

"Of course. I think there's a soccer match on television tonight. I shall order up two dozen prawns and wine and I'll be relatively happy."

They walked into the lobby toward the elevators, and kissed each other affectionately before parting to go to their rooms.

Their departure was followed with much interest by another occupant of the bar, a small, flashy blonde of indeterminate age, with a face-lift, a nose job, capped teeth, silicone breasts, a deep tan, and a great deal of Indian silver and turquoise. She was the "Hollywood" reporter for a television station in Los Angeles, which meant she had a five-minute segment on the news each night, during which she reported gossip, both real and invented. She was well known in Southern California, but no one in Europe had ever heard of Altrusa Galway, and this cramped her style a great deal, since she was honeymooning with her fourth—and adoring—husband, a used-car-lot owner from Culver City. They were "doing" the Riviera and had only arrived in Nice that same afternoon.

Altrusa would always be a star-gazer. "Doesn't Maroga look like Gang Busters? And she's fifty. At least."

"It was seeing Joss McIvor come in that gave *me* the thrill," her husband said. "Not for myself, of course. What do I know from rock? But for my kids. They've got all his records. If you interview him could you get his autograph?" He had two daughters and a son who lived with their mother in San Diego.

"Honey, I'm on vacation," Altrusa protested grandly. "In fact, come to think of it, I'm on my honeymoon." But she had heard a drift of a conversation from some of the crew at another table. This was a big picture. Yet it sounded as if there was deep trouble. She tried to remember what she knew about Ian Spencer. Perhaps she would phone her friend at *Variety* in the morning.

After a few more bourbons, she was saying, "Maybe I could tape a show over here, or at least get some film on these people. Maybe I'll contact one of the television stations."

Her husband nodded happily, not understanding yet that the budget for her "show" allowed only for office space, telephones, and a few slides. The film she used was all handouts or borrowed. He looked at her mistily. She was attractive and she was tough and he loved her.

They had a few more drinks and lost track of the time. About eleven o'clock they made their way upstairs to their room, attempted somewhat unsuccessfully to screw each other (that was how they always referred to it) and fell asleep, after a not-too-serious search for one of Altrusa's eyelashes that had come off in the fray.

On an upper floor, Maroga had been asleep since ten. She had enjoyed the evening by herself, whereas Trigère, who couldn't get any kind of consistent reception on the television set, finally got restless and went out to walk along the waterfront for a bit.

When he returned there was a message for him from Joss, saying that he was at a hospital just outside Nice and for Trigère to come at once. On the way back from dinner he had smashed up his car on the autoroute. The Italian starlet had suffered lacerations of the face and shoulder. She was hysterical, but Joss had been unharmed.

Joss and Trigère did not get back to the hotel until very late. By that time, the remaining crew members, who had been drinking in the bar earlier, had set fire to the piano and been thrown out. The bill for the damage was considerable.

It was a restless night elsewhere.

After waiting vainly for Ian to come home, Theodora wandered upstairs with her drink, put on a trailing, gauzy gown from another era in her life, and came down to the living room to dance by herself to the music of Delius. She danced beautifully, gaily, until she tripped against a table and broke her toe. She was too foggy to call a doctor; instead she swallowed an exotic combination of pain killers and passed out.

Theodora came awake about an hour later and vomited into the hand-painted toilet of the bathroom downstairs —the whisky, the pills, everything. This probably saved her life.

*

At the Martin villa, Djuna had said all the wrong things to Baker at dinner. And he had replied in kind. By the time Trigère's phone call came they were not speaking to each other but were sitting, "reading" in the pretty living room, each of them chaotically locked in that painful state of wild despair that results from having been married long enough to have misplaced one's sense of options.

After talking to Trigère, Baker came back from the telephone and informed Djuna that the director, accompanied by Maroga and Joss, would be coming for dinner the following evening. When she didn't answer he could not restrain himself from adding, "And see if you can keep your eyes off McIvor long enough to act like a gracious hostess."

"I'm missing your point," she replied coldly. But her heart was pounding.

"That night at the restaurant. And at the bar, later."

"I didn't do anything," she answered with honest heat, "except dance with him. Talk to him."

"Djuna, he was all over you. And you let him. And I'm warning you it's not happening again. Not in my house. Not anywhere, ever. I'm not going to play the fool because McIvor is after every piece of ass he can get."

"I'm not a piece of ass." She sent him a dangerous look. "I'm Djuna. Someone you used to know. Someone I used to be."

"You say that like it's my fault. Why do you always twist everything?"

"I asked you to see a doctor, Baker. I asked you that a year ago. I was willing to go into therapy with you, counseling, anything—"

"Bullshit!" Baker shouted. "I don't need a doctor! I need a woman who loves me! A woman who doesn't think, deep down, that sex is a dirty act!"

She died a little. Sometimes she even believed it herself. He had accused her of it so often. She was quiet, her mind racked and muddled as it always was during these painful exchanges of their shared agony, their private shame.

"It's the other way round," she said after a moment,

trying to think clearly, trying to think what she had been like before she married him. "It's you. It's you who doesn't know how to love. What all this is about, what it has always been about, is your impotence with me."

He stared at her. "And your hysterical reluctance to deal with it."

Scenes from the marriage played all around the room.

"Baker, I have never said this to you before—"

"Then don't." He averted his eyes, lit a cigar.

But it had been too long in her, like a shame, and she was weary of carrying that shame. "Do you have any idea what it is like for a wife, time after time, to have to look at the physical evidence that she is not desired? That only *it* is desired? To have to begin sex always confronted with limp flesh, softness, refusal? It's like being on trial. The responsibility is always mine. The failure is always somehow mine." She took a breath. "I've taken a terrible whipping in our marriage bed, Baker."

"So have I." He was expressionless.

Each was thinking back, to the beginnings of their relationship. Going over the old ground. Circles and more circles. Baker had married Djuna because he was tired of coming home to his apartment every night and figuring out what to do with his life. Djuna had married Baker because he represented a brand-new fantasy. And each had called it love. Believed it to be love.

Their chance meeting at a party, their first dinner alone, their first weekend—all this had rushed them along the special track of other pleasant and exciting "firsts." After Djuna visited Baker on location in Utah, they flew to San Francisco to meet her parents, and within a month they were married.

A quick romance like that can throw a lot of sand in a couple's eyes, particularly when the husband lives the life of a successful actor. They were always doing something, going somewhere, and after a few weeks were "simply exhausted" every night when they went to bed, so it was only "Good night, darling." And then in the morning there never seemed time, or there was some plausible excuse, and suddenly they were avoiding each other. But why? Had Djuna only appeared passionate and inventive in bed before the marriage because she wanted to land him? Or had she been sincerely hooked by the fantasy?

Had Baker been easily erected because of her newness, because there was no pattern, no record, only excitement? Or were they both merely victims of a culture gone high on instant gratification?

People used to get married because they expected—and frequently wanted—to spend the rest of their lives together. No matter how you approached it, Djuna and Baker had wed because it seemed like the fun thing to do. The sexual spark between them had been only a tiny, mutually manipulated flame. The truth is that making love to the same person for a lifetime can, even in a good marriage, turn out to be boring, merely okay, hardly ever —or all three. In a bad marriage it can turn into nightmare. Which it now had.

In a jail cell, you must sleep in the same room with a stranger. In a bad marriage you are expected to make love to that stranger, and he or she to you. Marriage counselors, sex experts, psychiatrists are only too happy to give you instruction on how to turn your partner on, how not to be bored or disgusted by what bores and disgusts you. What is extraordinary is that it never seems to occur to people in this situation, least of all the experts, that it is really quite normal not to want to fuck someone you don't like. Djuna and Baker were, at best, tolerant of each other in a sad, disassociated way, but they no longer liked each other very much.

It would have been far more logical to have accepted the fact that they were simply not suited to each other, by personality, by history, by values, or anything else. And be done with it.

But listen to them:

Baker: What do you think it's like? For me. To know you hate it?

Djuna (*turning her face away*): You can't get it up for me, Baker. Yet you've continued to insist that *I* was

cold. That *I* wasn't passionate enough. For a long time
I believed you. Now I know. Our sex life has nothing to
do with "making love." Can't you see that? We are
confronted with a mechanical problem.

Baker (shouting): That's what I said! You hate it.

Djuna (shivering): I was never much good as a performer.
Sex between lovers should be a natural act, Baker.

Baker: Then how come you do everything you can to
avoid it? How come *you* aren't natural about it? You're
a goddamn neurotic! You're the one who slams the
door in my face whenever I want you.

Djuna: It's not because I'm neurotic—it's because I'm
always so frightened! I'm terrified, I'm wooden every
time because I know it's not going to be normal. I'm
going to have to work and work—

Baker: Shut up! That's enough! Maybe no one ever
told you you were a lousy lay! Well, you are! You're a
goddamn boring, prissy, terrible lay!

Djuna (bowing her head): I see.

Baker (suddenly kneeling before her, weeping): Honey,
I'm sorry. You know I love you, Djuna, goddammit, you
know I love you.

Dear God. How to separate the hurt one got from the hurt
one gave?

Djuna put her hand on his head, which was now resting against her knees. But it was not love that had made
her hand go out; it was autonomic response to his suffering. One human being to another. They were in this
together.

They remained for a time in that same final position,
Djuna's hand on his head, his tears on her lap, both of
them silent. There seemed to be no option except to be
sorry, to let the moment pass into another moment. And
another.

They had dinner and talked gently about problems with
the film. Afterward, Djuna read some French fashion
magazines and Baker watched television. At ten o'clock

he said he was tired and went into the bedroom. They said goodnight, wearing their careful masks. It was marital truce. The combatants retire to their corners to assess the extent of their wounds.

When he had gone from the room, Djuna went into the kitchen and looked around. Gerard and Marie always left everything shining. There was nothing for her to do. She got a glass of water and looked out the window into the kitchen garden.

She had spent a lot of her marriage looking out windows. Bedroom windows, car windows, hotel windows. When I hurt inside, she thought, I always go to a window. In a way, I think tonight is the worst it's ever been. Baker has destroyed a lot of me that I care about, not that I really understand *what*. There's a whole piece of me missing that was there before I married him. I *know* it was there.

In the bathroom, Baker was brushing his teeth and trying not to swallow the water. He walked into the cold bedroom, thinking of the house back in Los Angeles, the king-size bed with the electric blankets, the big color television by it and, outside, the jacaranda tree by the pool, and the bright moving slices of brilliant headlights far below in the valley.

He got into bed and opened his book. Outside the balcony, everything was black. The night, the sky, the silence; it was all very poised, very silky, very French. Djuna loved it here. He sensed she was gaining some new kind of strength, in that strange way she had of absorbing the most minute experience and taking it away to a private space he knew nothing about. He was afraid of that, and of the look in her eyes lately. She, like the film, like everything else, was getting out of control.

The trouble with marriage was that once it got going, it was impossible to start over. And it got so crowded with shit. For a moment, he longed for Lily's frank, rapacious sexiness. And the clean simplicity of the relationship. But to give up Djuna! Life stretched out like a wasteland, devoid of style, of comfort, of surprise. She was lovely and clever and ran his home life beautifully. The last thing he wanted was to be alone again. After all, he had his career. His home. Lily. He liked having Djuna for his wife. Period.

Chapter Fourteen

In the morning Djuna slept late. When she awoke and threw back the covers she was still warm with dreams.

She sat for a moment on the edge of the bed, staring at her bare toes and smiling. A new day was a new life. And she was going to see Joss tonight.

She crossed the room and opened the high glass doors to the balcony. It had been gray all morning. The sun was only now beginning to color the sea. The air was still chilly but she stood there a little longer, hugging her arms to her shoulders, her long Mexican nightgown with its rough lace border flapping at her ankles in the chilly breeze.

It was just noon.

Along the green-walled Boulevard du Cap, a few hundred yards behind the villa, the dented Jaguar roared on its way down the coast to Cannes.

Kat was leaning back, watching France whip by. Joss had been silent since their departure from gray, windy Nice, but she didn't mind. He had explained the accident and all that had befallen him the night before, and, of course, she had seen the terrible dents and gashes on the side of the car.

"I'm very hung over and very pissed off," he had announced at once with a tight smile when they met in the lobby. "I'll be all right once we get going."

So they drove along like an old couple on a Sunday,

content with the scenery, with being anywhere at all. Once or twice she peeked at his profile. It was remote, leonine, self-absorbed.

It was nice to be with someone normal. Normal! She rolled her eyes comically at herself. She certainly had come a long way since arriving in France. Joss McIvor was glitter and fame, he was an international figure, he was anything *but* normal. Yet the connection was clean; their relationship had begun on a private note, where it had stayed. All communication between them had been personal, ordinary. His public image was somehow excluded. Even his arrogance she accepted as entirely his own, still fresh, straight from the playing fields and the pubs. He wasn't difficult because he was a star. He was difficult because he was Joss.

He broke the silence now to ask, "Tell me how you got hooked up with Ian. I haven't got that together. You met him in America. How?"

"Oh. Well, he shot a part of his last picture in Palm Springs. My stepmother has a house there. Ian came to dinner. He and Vito and some girls."

"Who is your stepmother?"

"Nobody. But her boyfriend is in distribution. He's the one who knew Ian."

"Your stepmother's boyfriend." Joss frowned and looked at her. "You're losing me. What about your father?"

"They're divorced."

"Then what about your mother? Your real mother."

"She died when I was little."

"Sorry. Go on."

"About my family or Ian?"

"Either. Look here, do you mind if we stop in Juan-les-Pins? I've got to have a beer. I'll die if I don't."

"That's okay." She looked out the window. "Is this it?"

"Shortly. Haven't you been anywhere? Forget I said that. It'll be nice. I promise you. You were saying?"

"Well, naturally, I told Ian I was in the film school at

UCLA and that I wanted to direct movies. He was very interested."

"In what?"

"Don't be tacky."

"I can be a lot tackier than that," he retorted. He reached over and pulled at one of her nipples.

"Stop it. Anyway, I didn't know anything about Ian except he was very nice, and distinguished-looking, and a movie producer, and he wanted to help me. You know what he's like. 'Darling, you must come over for my next film; it will be a splendid opportunity for you—don't even think about expenses, we'll find something for you to do and you'll adore the South of France.'"

This time he leaned over and kissed her on the nose. "You're a mimic, too. There's no end to your talents. You sound just like him."

"Of course," she continued, thoughtfully, "now I know that he's always done that. Just picked up people all over the world, like some people buy postcards. And after that, he thinks he owns you. No one in the traveling circus is really free. I mean, look at Chin-Chan. You aren't even allowed to argue back. Actually, I think Ian could have been more successful in the underworld. You know . . . the secret, vicious head of a cabal smuggling heroin and white slaves. His mind is criminal, I've decided."

Joss glanced at her. "What a kinky imagination you've got!"

"Well, if he isn't criminal he's absolutely amoral, then. That upper-class manner is how he gets away with it."

Joss glanced at her again. "You're not slow, are you, darling?"

They drove in silence for a time, and then he said, "I expect having been to university helps one to—to think with confidence. And to know all the right words. I never had that. No one in our family has ever been to college. When I have to write letters I tell my secretary what I want to say and then she puts it right for me."

She smiled across at him. "Intelligence and education are two different things."

He looked at her crossly. "I don't need you to tell me I've got a lot of good machinery in here." He tapped his forehead. "I know that, darling. It's just that it's a pain in the ass not to always have the words. It's why I have to use my fists now and then. It's certainly why I hate interviews. Ah, we're here. Now look for a place right along the front."

He had slowed down the car and was in the right lane, peering at the cafés. "Christ, everything is so crowded."

"Well, of course. It's a super day. How about *there?*" She pointed to the first place she saw, a small green-and-white restaurant with a rolled-up awning and a boxy veranda with potted palms. The sunlight, when they got out of the car, was brilliant and hot, and they could smell the water. They stood for a moment, looking at the curve of the bay and the people and the traffic, and then they went inside the café.

After they had ordered a drink, Joss said with a frown, "You shouldn't be mucking about with Ian. You're too young, you're not his sort. And you might get hurt."

"What do you mean?" She was choosing an olive from a small glass dish.

"You're a clever girl when it comes to most things, but you're not all that brilliant about the most important thing—yourself. Look how you came whizzing up to bed with me that night. Pissed out of your mind."

She stared at him. "You're unbelievable. You were only interested in me as an object and now *you're* giving *me* a lecture on *my* morals."

"Well, I thought you *were* an object, didn't I? Until I found out you were the subject." He grinned ingenuously. "We've already had that conversation. You're just lucky it was me. That's what."

"You're conceited and self-satisfied beyond words," she said as she sipped her beer.

"Look." He played with the olive dish and then looked at her squarely. "What I'm getting at is, have you got yourself mixed up in any of Ian's little frolics? Because if you have, you'd better stop it."

"Coming from you, that's pretty rich."

"Granted," he replied easily. "But I can take an interest, can't I?"

"Am I to assume that you care about me?"

He looked ruffled. "Now don't start boxing me in like that. I won't put up with it."

She looked at him in surprise. He added oddly, "Naturally I like you. Or I wouldn't have asked you to lunch, but I'm not exactly proposing or anything like that."

"Well, for heaven's sake," she said, laughing, "I didn't think you were." But she was moved by this chance display of his vulnerability. She felt she had been touched in a new place, and in exchange, offered him her lie.

"Ian hasn't bothered me one bit," she said casually. "Not that way. He has me on a chain as far as running errands and shit, but that's all."

"Good," Joss said quietly. "Let's have something to eat." He gave her a menu and began to study his. "I fancy the *crevettes*. Anyway, I expect Ian's so preoccupied with the troubles over the film that he hasn't had the time to be up to his usual tricks. We're going to dinner at Baker's tonight, that is, Trigère and Maroga and me. To have a powwow."

They had a long, heavy lunch with lots of beer, during which they exchanged random bits and pieces of their short histories, and then they got into the dented Jaguar and went back to Nice where they stayed the rest of the afternoon in Joss' bed.

Joss experienced the same quick pull of Kat's sexuality that he had on the first occasion, and she, who now liked and trusted him, was no longer afraid to show her tenderness or to ask for his.

On the same floor, a few suites away, Maroga was lying on her bed, a thick blue paste all over her face. She peered at the cloisonné clock with one eye.

Five more minutes and she could pull the mask off. She practised deep breathing and longed for Rome. The South of France in winter was pretty and all very nice in a metaphorical way—that is, if you were freezing in Scotland and dreaming of a warmer clime—but truly, the place palled. At least in the summer one could play with the obsessive ritual of getting a suntan, be invited to go on someone's yacht. In winter there seemed only the rain.

There had been nothing to do since morning but wait all day for dinner.

How did life get wiped so clean, so empty, so quickly? She had turned her back on everyone for Robbie, and when that had been over she had expected to throw herself into the arms of her former friends, only to find they had all meanwhile drifted into other orbits.

She had thought that when she came to start this film a new life would begin, as usual. And a new love. But nothing at all had happened. And without Trigère she would have died. Their long history of shared experiences and their practiced easiness with each other had shored up her faltering sense of self. Every day she wanted to flee. But the question was where.

She got off the bed, and before she peeled the mask off she took a tranquilizer. She would have preferred a drink, but these bouts of anxiety were occurring with greater frequency and, in the daytime at least, Librium was safer. Besides, no amount of it would affect your face.

It was frightening to have lived almost half a century and to have nothing to do on Sunday but take care of your waning looks and eat tranquilizers to stave off the desperation. The knowledge was bitter that there was no one in the world who needed her or who required her presence for his happiness. Who waited for her, who longed for her to come home.

She walked up and down the room for a while, looked in the mirror several times, did chin exercises, and waited for the pill to work. The phone startled her. An American voice introduced itself as a "Hollywood" reporter. "Could they possibly meet for a drink in the bar?"

Maroga considered. And agreed to appear downstairs in an hour. She always gave interviews to Americans because there was the chance Robbie would read them.

Besides, it was something to do. It was hours before dinner.

Trigère stood looking out the cutting-room window. Behind him, leaning against a table, was the assistant editor, with nothing to do. The print was gone. A phone call had determined that the negative was safe—and, of course, why shouldn't it be? A phone call to Ian had elicited the information that the producer had left early that morning for the airport, to Paris, Theodora thought, but she wasn't certain. Obviously, Ian had taken the print with him.

Trigère dismissed the editor, advising him not to say anything to anyone about what had occurred. Should he tell the others tonight? Perhaps it would be better to wait until Ian's return. He left the cutting room and walked down the steps to his car. He drove back to the hotel, wondering what to do with himself, and he was filled with remorse at the laziness, the compromise, the vanity that had brought him to the Côte d'Azur, to the film, to this absurd situation, to this empty afternoon.

Ian's offer to him in Paris last year had coincided with a period when his personal life had been in transition and teeming with an unwanted population. The walls of his world seemed to be papered with claimants: ex-wives, ex-lovers, ex-business partners, his three sets of children, and all the nannies and schools and pets. Everyone needed money, attention, understanding. He had no picture in the works and money for new ventures suddenly seemed sparse everywhere in the world.

The offer of *Lovers and Clowns* had been seductive. All that American money. Anything he wanted, or so Ian had promised. All he had to do was direct—not write, not procure, borrow, or pray for money. What actually had come to pass could not have been foreseen and yet somehow he felt it was deserved. He had no business playing with the likes of Ian and Vito. It was more than a question of integrity; it was simply against all common sense.

Passing through the lobby, he saw Maroga in the bar and started toward her, but then he saw she was sitting with a woman, a stranger in a studded jeans suit. So he went upstairs.

And found himself looking out the window again. Years ago he had come here to the South of France, made a picture at the same studio, been happy. It had been at the end of summer, a wistful, dreamy, memory-laden summer.

They had all taken a house together. That was when he had his "troupe," the laughing, serious, beautiful-plain girls, the strong, brilliant young men. The intensity, the wit, the talent! He wanted suddenly to weep. They had all eventually scattered and most of them, like himself, had been successful. So successful, in fact, that three were now dead—of suicide, of murder, of alcoholism. Lita, his favorite, had married a South American dictator, disappeared from the European scene entirely, and now went to mass every morning in a bulletproof Lincoln. He had recently seen a picture of her, stepping out of the limousine, clutching her missal and her rosary, disguised behind huge black sunglasses. Those magnificent legs, descending to a hot, foreign pavement he had never seen.

At least for now, he had Maroga. Her sturdy spirit, her womanliness, and her laughter all comforted him. Yet she seemed so distracted, and lately she had not looked well. Her passion for Robbie had been one of the most painful scenes of innocence betrayed he had ever witnessed. For Maroga *was* innocent. There were women like that. They knew no other way of being. She had never had a chance with Robbie. Loving him the way she had, and trustfully expecting him to love her in the same way, she had not really understood anything about him. What on earth had attracted her? Perhaps she had mistaken his physical strength and all those boring, heroic roles he played for a kind of courage and simplicity that women like Maroga always looked for in men. Little girls and mothers. All of them.

It was five o'clock. He would read for a while and then have a bath.

*

At eight o'clock that evening, as Djuna was bringing a white pitcher of anemonies to the glass table in front of the flowered sofa, the doorbell rang.

She heard Gerard answer. In a moment Joss was in the room.

His presence, life-size was a clean shock, replacing her softer, dreamier composition in which he had been only still-frame and memory. The reality standing before her was big, uneven. She caught her breath and was happy.

They shook hands gravely, like children do over important matters. He smelled of soap, of limes. He might have noticed her noticing, because he said, "I washed behind my ears and everything."

They were so brilliantly exposed, alone like that for the first time, that Baker's step in the hallway was a relief to both of them. It cut through the bright, nervous, first light.

"What would you like to drink?" Djuna was asking by the time Baker came into the room and the two men shook hands.

"May I have wine?"

"Red or white?" Baker asked, moving to the drink tray.

"Red, thank you. I'm glad you aren't going to require me to drink cocktails. I hated that in America."

"I don't know what you mean," Baker said evenly. He handed Joss his glass. "We drink wine in America."

"Yes ,of course you do. That isn't what I said. On tour the locals always wanted to entertain us. And sometimes one absolutely had to accept. Being fed bourbon and orange juice in Dallas was not my favorite experience, I can tell you. Thinking back, Texas was a nightmare altogether. I don't know which was worse, the acoustics or the population. I found the Texans a difficult people to care for."

Baker said affably, "I'm from Texas."

Joss looked at him for a moment. "How lovely for Texas," he said just as affably. "Put my foot in it, didn't I?"

Djuna sat on the sofa. "Tell us what you've been doing all day."

"Not much." He paused, while residual flashes of Kat played in his head. "Had lunch in Juan-les-Pins. Took a nap."

They smiled at each other and Joss sat down next to her on the sofa.

Baker tapped his foot restlessly. Djuna reached for her drink. Joss looked around the room curiously. She lived here. He tried to place her. What would she be like in bed? he wondered for the hundredth time. What would she be like in general?

So he said to her, as if he were only inquiring politely, "What do you do with yourself all day long?"

She sensed that he was really asking: Who are you?

How wildly unreliable the facts of one's life were—and how unfair. Her history was suddenly inexplicable. As a child she had been authentic; she had believed in her own power. Since coming to France she had become connected again to what she remembered about how that had felt. But what about everything that had come between? The record of events was insufficient claim to an original sense of purpose. She wanted to say to him: Trust me. I exist.

"I have a car," she replied instead. "I run about looking at everything. I love it here."

"So do I," Joss agreed at once. "It beats England." And it was true. But it was not only the country that pleased him. He liked being in the borrowed time-capsule of a film. Whereas on concert tours he was constantly moving from city to city and there were always endless appearances, the press, problems with the hall, with the equipment, and all the exhaustion of transiency, here there were softer days and nights, life was contained and there was time to explore his adventures instead of only having them.

The doorbell sounded and Maroga swept in. She was wearing a scent that smelled of delicate orange and spice. Everyone smiled at her, including Trigère, who had followed her in, and Joss wondered again how a woman with slightly bucked teeth, and pushing fifty if she was a day, could generate so much sheer physical flash every time she entered a room. She was kissing Baker, she was kissing Djuna, she was putting her arm around him, praising the flowers, smiling at the hovering, respectful Gerard, and waving graciously across the room at Marie, who was peeping from the dining room.

"Darlings! How charming! And such a lovely warm fire. Yes! A vermouth. Thank you! But, my dear, how did you find roses with everything pruned to the ground at this time of year? Let me tell you," she settled herself in a chair, "that I spent the afternoon with an aberration! I have bored Bernard all the way here but, really, she was so impossible—one of your American television reporters with a cheap mentality, but also some very accurate information about the troubles we have with our little film."

Baker looked interested. "What's her name?"

Maroga made a comical face. "Altrusa Galway. She says that in your trade papers in America they are saying that *Lovers and Clowns* will never be made. That Ian and Vito are finished and that all of us are preparing to sue them."

"Not an entirely inappropriate suggestion," Trigère added with a tight smile.

"Well," said Baker, "unless we can find out what's really going on, I'm for it. Let's light a fire under Ian's ass."

"Ian is not our man," Joss said abruptly. "Can't you see that? Ian's just a ninny."

"What do you mean he's not our man?" Baker gave Joss a challenging look. "He's the producer, isn't he?"

Joss looked around the room at everyone. "My view is that Ian started shooting without any authorization. Without a shilling of backing. He simply told everyone to show up."

"That's impossible." Baker stood up. "That's the most asinine suggestion I've ever heard. I know you think that being in the movies is fun and games, McIvor, but the fact is, this is a *business*. Producers are in it for the *money*. They don't start pictures because they love to hang around a set."

"I'm telling you, old man. That's what he did."

"He'd have to be crazy," Baker argued. "It would be a criminal act. He'd be found out."

"He *has* been found out!" Joss shouted. "And he's bonkers as well! That's what we're here to talk about. Christ, Baker, would you bloody sit down so we can get something done?"

Baker turned to Trigère. "Man to man. Do I have to put up with this shit in my own house?"

Trigère held up his hands. "Please," he said quietly. "Joss' theory is not all that impossible. A criminal act is usually a desperate act, and perhaps Ian is more desperate than we know. It is possible he has lost all contact with reality. No one wants to be the victim of extreme circumstances, but perhaps we are. If that is the case, we have to find Vito immediately, assess what the real situation is, and proceed accordingly."

"But where are we to find him?" Maroga asked. "And did he disappear from the face of the earth because of the film, or because of trouble with the police over that girl?"

Trigère shook his head. "As far as we know he was cleared of any connection with that."

"But Altrusa told me that it had been in the gossip columns that the death was hushed up."

"What was there to hush up?" Baker inquired, impatient with everything now. "The autopsy said it in one line. She had a brain tumor and she died."

"That girl still haunts me," Djuna said, looking down at her lap. "She died there in front of us all. Yet it's as if she never existed. Nobody cared then and nobody cares now."

"Djuna, it is only because we didn't care about her in life either," Trigère said gently. "That's all. We're not heartless. An anonymous person's death—well, it is like an item in the newspaper. We are not touched."

"But that's what's so sad," Djuna went on with a frown.

"She must have belonged somewhere. But to die at a table of strangers like that, and no one even knew her name except Vito. And even *he* had trouble with her last name. What kind of life had she had? And then to die like that. It's horrible."

"My dear, what pathos!" Maroga drawled, with a nevertheless interested look at Djuna.

Joss had also turned on the sofa to face Djuna. "Look here, darling," he said quietly. "Maybe you've got it all turned around. Maybe she loved her life as much as we all presumably love ours. It's very likely that she thought it was glamorous to be carted around Europe by Vito. Maybe he was even kind to her." He smiled. "Maybe others were kind to her. She might have gone out in glory. Her kind of glory. Come on, there's a good girl. Drink up. We don't want you to be sad." And he handed Djuna her glass.

Baker chewed on his cigar. That asshole McIvor was putting the make on his wife again. He had spoken to her with the same grave attention one might use in comforting a child. The kid had an endless bag of tricks.

"Djuna," Baker said now, "you'd better see about dinner."

"It *is* being seen to," she said with a clear look at him, but she was chagrined that the others had seen how Baker positioned her and angry at him for always treating her, in the last resort, as a creature of function. "We have time for one more drink."

Trigère decided to share his discovery in the cutting room with the others. "I went to the studio this afternoon. I wanted to review some things and I discovered that the film is gone. It looks as if Ian took what we've shot so far to show to someone. He left town this morning, presumably for Paris. It probably means he's found someone who's interested."

"It's nice to know," Maroga said sarcastically, "that our names might count for something. You know, I am more and more believing, like Joss, that Vito washed his hands of everything and flew away, leaving Ian to tell everyone the bad news, and that's when Ian started his craziness."

Baker said in disgust, "Jesus. I didn't need this holiday. I could have used the work. Frankly, I'm inclined to cut my losses, pack my bags, and go home."

"Shouldn't that be decided by all of us?" Joss inquired with a studied look at Baker. His dislike was plain to everyone. "Isn't that why we're here?"

Djuna went to the kitchen to see if Gerard was ready to serve, because it was time and because she needed to put some space between herself and what was going on in the living room. She looked at the roast beef, and at how the salad had been arranged, tasted a bit of the dressed lettuce, and then went into the little bathroom off the back hallway and looked in the mirror and said hello to herself. For luck.

She had lately come to believe that beyond the villa, beyond France, the world fell away sharply into the alibis of the past, that all that had ever mattered was being accounted for now. How much did it have to do with Joss? she wondered. Did it make it less real or more real? Why were we taught to suspect our strongest sensings of our own mysteries?

She returned to the living room via the front hall, pausing in the entry to straighten out the dusky-pink rug and glance out the frosted, beveled panes of the high, narrow windows on each side of the front door. It was nine o'clock, black outside and brilliant, too, with a cold moon and the tinny night glitter of the water's edge showing its winter face to the sea, which reflected it back. And inside, the old stone walls of the villa, flowered sofas, firelight, crystal, dinner. Voices. Life.

She felt she had been warned. She was living inside a magic trick. Her happiness, like a rabbit, had come out of a silk hat and could disappear back into it just as quickly. If all this was illusion, then the best thing was to believe in it while it lasted. She went into the living room to call them for dinner.

It appeared they had settled for the moment the question of what or what not to do. They were agreed.

"If," Trigère explained to Djuna, "Ian does indeed line up the money while he's on this mysterious trip of his, we will remain, and we will instruct our agents to proceed with the matter of what is owed to us already. And there will have to be renegotiations. If, on the other hand, Ian arrives with an empty pocket—" He shrugged, not bothering to finish.

Maroga sighed. "To think he could have done this to us. He has always been such a gentleman. I have always wanted to do a film for him. Everything I ever heard was that everyone had lots of fun and he let you have anything you wanted."

Baker stirred his soup, waiting for it to cool. "He's a producer. To him this picture is only a vehicle for getting whatever it is he wants out of life this year."

"That's what it is to us, too, isn't it?" Joss' tone was all studied carelessness. He glanced at Djuna, sitting next to him.

Baker's face darkened. "What I'm saying is that he'll sacrifice anything, including us, to get this project off the ground."

"I thought we *were* the project. Do you think a shitty little story like *Lovers and Clowns* is worth a shilling without our names?" Joss said rudely and began to drink his soup. He looked at Djuna. "It's lovely, darling. Has it got watercress?"

She was not allowed to reply because Baker was suddenly saying with a very heavy stare at Joss, "Forgive me, McIvor, but maybe someone should point out to you that you don't know your ass about the movie business."

"Why should I forgive anyone for making a bloody remark like that?" Joss replied quietly enough, but his eyes watched Baker's. "I wouldn't go on like that if I were you."

Djuna put her spoon down. "Please. This is awful!" She looked from one to the other. "Stop it at once, both of you!"

"Sorry, darling," Joss said and patted her hand. He looked at her with his boyish smile. "It's a lovely dinner and Baker and I are monsters. Aren't we, Baker?" He lifted his glass and paused for a moment, weighing. Then he smiled and said, "To our difficult host from his difficult guest."

He drank. Maroga and Trigère and Djuna laughed with relief and drank, too. But Baker could not cope with the moment, and he did not reach for his glass. Instead, he continued to drink his soup. His ears felt as if they were reddening and he wanted very much to be in his dining room at the house in Los Angeles with the ballgame on and Djuna sitting across from him with earplugs and a book. That was peace and normality. These people were incomprehensible. Nobody here ever seemed to pay attention to a fucking word he said. They took the stupidest things seriously and made jokes out of matters that were really important.

Maroga was nudging his elbow. "You must drink with us, Baker."

The others were looking at him in surprise, still holding their glasses up. Waiting. Baker didn't want to meet Joss' eyes but he knew he had to. If he refused to drink with the man, then he had to look him in the face. So he did.

Joss, in honest surprise, embarrassment, and anger, measured for a moment the older man's dense, sullen expression and the unmistakable public insult that it was, and crushed the wine glass he was still holding into little bits.

Then he looked at his hand and said quite cheerfully, "Shit. Have a look at that!" He opened his fingers and stared at the shreds of glass mixed with his blood. He glanced at Trigère with a grin. "Too bad you couldn't have had this scene for the film, dear."

Baker lit a cigar. Maroga stared. Trigère got up and went around the table to look at Joss' hand. Djuna had also risen and was bending over it.

"It's nothing, I promise you," Joss said to her. "It only needs a wash, I should think." He got up, elbowing

Trigère playfully in the ribs. "Get back to your dinner, Doctor. I'm perfectly okay."

Djuna said, "I'll clean it up for you." He smiled down at her and they left the dining room.

"Everyone is so crazy!" Maroga said after a moment of silence. "Bernard, at least let me have a cigarette."

Gerard came through the swinging door and stared at the two empty places and the broken wine glass. He had come in to serve the second course but now he hesitated and looked at Baker.

"Oh, let's wait for them," Trigère said at once. And instructed Gerard. In French.

"Perhaps another bottle of that excellent wine would serve us while we wait." Maroga blew smoke at the ceiling.

Baker's face flushed a deeper red. Now they were telling him how to run his own dinner party. He looked at his watch carefully. How long did it take to wash off a few goddamn cuts? They should be back in three or four minutes, no more.

Trigère noted Baker's anxiety and felt only a little sorry for him. Baker was not a very likable man. His persona had a shallow, nonspiritual lining. Generally, the man grated on the senses. His problem was different from the predictable narcissism of actors. Most of them could abstract layers of feeling (it was a gift, of course; that's what made them different), but Baker had a blocked, inner density that precluded variations of light. He could project only the most mechanical subtleties. If he was very lucky, he might remain a successful film actor. But with his life he would continue to have difficulty.

Over the rim of his glass, Trigère continued to watch Baker watching the doorway. Poor devil. It was plain to Trigère that Joss was very much attracted to Djuna and she to him. They were not all that unlikely a combination. Certainly he had witnessed far more surprising couplings during the making of other films. They were both handsome people, with a sense of their own power, with original styles of their own. Of course, she was older, married, and they came from altogether different worlds. Not only that, but they would return to those worlds and those lives when the film was over. Still, there was the same causality to human eruptions as there was in physics, in nature. You struck a match against the right substance and you got flame. Powerful meetings between strangers were as simple as that. As mysterious as that.

He asked Baker where he got his cigars.

Upstairs, in the white tile bathroom, Joss was sitting on the edge of the bathtub, holding out his hand, while together he and Djuna searched for the tiny pieces and grains of glass.

"I told you, my love," he said. "It looked much worse than it is. Here, let's give it another wash and we're done."

She swabbed it with a dripping ball of wet cotton. "We don't have any bandages. Have you got a handkerchief? Then I can tape it."

He produced one and she wrapped it carefully around the lacerated hand, then taped the edges together.

"I'm a rotten nurse." She frowned. 'It looks all bulky and wrong." She thought she would faint at being so close to him.

"It's fine, darling. Really." He looked up at her. Then he took her chin and brought her face to his and kissed her squarely and very seriously on the mouth.

And that, finally, was that. Passionate information had been exchanged. The affair began its natural history.

What followed was the seduction of each other. Djuna was as blunt with desire as he. Gently he lowered her to the floor, and when he was about to enter her, they exchanged a long look, as if to mark the moment.

They finished with laughter and hugs. Smiling, he murmured against her hair, "You are an incredibly sexy lady. I've never made love in the loo before. Have you? Do you realize we didn't even stop to lock the door? Or turn on all the taps to hide the racket?" He drew his head back and regarded her gravely as they lay on the floor, their limbs still entangled. "Do I please you?"

She smiled a bit at that. "You please me," she replied. And added, "I promise you."

He looked to see if she were teasing him. "That's *my* line. You're aping me."

"Only because I like the way it sounds."

"We always said it when we were children. It was how we told the truth." He kissed the damp hollow of her throat and with one hand fingered the little gold chain.

"Why don't you ever put anything on this?" he asked.

"I don't know. I think about it, but I never do."

"It needs a locket." He grinned mischievously. "Aha! With my picture in it!"

"I'm beginning to worry about the door."

"Okay, everybody up!" he said in resigned fashion, and pulled her to her feet. "Everybody find their knickers."

Djuna looked around to find hers. "Knickers is a very unromantic word."

"On the contrary," he said, already buckling his belt and tucking in his shirt. "I find your knickers extremely romantic." He smiled at her and then looked at himself in the mirror. "Have you got a hairbrush for the famous mop?" He ran his hands through his hair.

"In the cabinet there." She turned on the water in the sink and began washing. He stood behind her, brushing his hair, and their glances met in the mirror, so they stopped what they were doing and kissed again. Then he began brushing her hair. After that she brushed his. And straightened his collar. They stood there another moment while time ran out. Then they opened the door and returned to the dining room.

When they were seated at the table again their naturalness was examined and judged to be authentic by the trio who had waited with a second bottle of wine and much unspoken conjecture. As for Djuna and Joss, what could have been more natural than how they felt about each other? It gave them the irreproachable air of innocents.

Chapter Fifteen

Item from Daily Variety

Lovers and Clowns principals Maroga, Joss McIvor and Baker Martin are reported ready to bolt their South of France location if Limey producer Ian Spencer doesn't deliver a new shooting date for the halted production. Martin's agent, Lily Dunne, on the horn from London, says that the Oscar (Supporting) winner will quit the pic by the end of the week if "matters are not resolved."

Item from Hollywood Reporter

English rocker Joss McIvor, on location for *Lovers and Clowns* (temporarily shut down), is sporting a heavily bandaged right hand, which didn't prevent him from pasting a French photographer and kicking his camera all over the tiny cobblestone streets of Vallauris where he was photographed emerging from a hotel with an "unidentified" companion.

Extract from Kat's Journal

. . . So everything has come to a halt, including me. Nothing is happening. Ian went to Paris and was supposed to be back this wek. No one has heard from him except Trigère, who shrugged and said, "He promises we definitely start on the first and that is why I am still here. I will wait this one last time."

Meanwhile, I'm blue and restless because I have more or less run out of things to do all day long, and everything is so expensive here, and the weather has been shitty and rainy—and also because of Joss.

I should have known better than to get all excited or to expect anything from him. After all, he is famous and I am not (yet), and I'm beginning to understand that it *does* make a difference.

Maybe I should be glad. It's practically impossible to have an intelligent discussion with him about any of the things I'm interested in because he is unbelievably prejudiced (and starts shouting) and because of his education—or I should say his noneducation. There are really embarrassing gaps in his basic store of information.

Then I find myself rationalizing, i.e., think of what he does with his music . . . think of his talent . . . think of how he makes love, and how really funny and different he is from anyone in my whole life!

But he takes me for granted, always calls me at the last minute, and we always have to do what *he* wants and never what *I* want. It makes me feel used. I am definitely caught in a very chauvinist relationship without, I am afraid, having enough character to get out of it. Yet.

I wish I could feel more for Jack. His girlfriend got laid off and went back to Paris. He and I are *completely* compatible and I know he digs me, but when I'm with him I keep thinking about Joss all the time.

Telegram from Ian Spencer in Paris to Theodora at home

LOVEY CRACK OPEN THE CHAMPAGNE. ALL IS SOLVED. ARRIVE HOME TOMORROW, PLEASE PACK MY WARM THINGS.

Item from International Ski Travel *magazine*

Mont Bleu, a brand-new ski resort in the French *Alpes Maritimes*, is at an elevation of 6,000 feet. It is overlooked by seventeen snowy peaks, covers 15,000 acres, has twenty-one ski lifts, forty downhill runs and the complex itself consists of eight stories (two of them underground), comprising four hotels, five apartment condominiums, seven restaurants, two nightclubs, one supermarket, three cinemas, four swimming pools, two bowling alleys, ping-pong and billiard rooms, thirteen shops, a bank, a post office, a health club, a church, a school, two hospitals and thirty-three elevators.

Extract from Kat's Journal

We are in a ski resort called Mont Bleu. It's like they glued Rockefeller Center together out of balsa wood and put it on top of Mount Baldy. It's the biggest, creepiest, most garish, confusing place I've been in.

But outside this tacky prison it's really beautiful. Lots of snow, giant peaks, sparkling air, sparkling sky. Joss told me you can ski into Italy from here—it's only a few miles.

We got here last night, everybody within hours of each other, and the confusion and bad tempers were really something, and, of course, we made quite a fantastic caravan winding up that scary, ribbon road. First Ian and Chin-Chan and Maroga and Trigère in the Rolls, then Baker and Djuna in a limousine with a chauffeur—Baker absolutely refused to make the drive otherwise (he's so full of Hollywood shit I can't believe it)—then Joss and me and Jimmy, who gets carsick and had to sit in the front seat which meant I boogied around in the back (and almost tossed *my* cookies) while he and Joss sang raunchy pub songs and talked about people and places they've been that I didn't know anything about. That is, they did that when Joss wasn't swearing at the car in front, the car behind, and trying to pass everyone and almost plunging us over the side a few times. But I liked the last part of the trip. Once we got up to the snowline it was really dramatic—steep canyons with green-water streams running over black rocks packed all around in fairy white snow.

Behind us came the production staff and the crew and the trucks with the camera and lighting equipment and all the sound stuff and wardrobe and props, and I found out today we don't have half of what we need, according to the art director. He is hysterical. He keeps saying, "I was hired to prepare a film in the color and mood of the

Côte d'Azur and all the fresh fragility of the flower fields of Provence, with a story and characters I understood. Now they tell me I am to have this infernal white stuff all over my picture. I ask you. What picture? There is no picture. The film we started down there has nothing to do with what we are all doing here."

The only happy person is Jack. He told me Hans hasn't shot a snow picture since the forties (and it was b & w) and is also terrified of height now that he is so old, so Jack will get a lot more responsibility and be able to do things his way. I have to take Jack on faith—I mean, I have never seen his work but I get good vibes from him.

What apparently happened, I mean the reason we're here, is that Ian cooked up some kind of deal with the owner of this place. It's only been open a month and doesn't have the prestige (or the customers) of a place like Chamonix or St. Moritz, and making a big movie here will help to promote it. Ian is a new man, now that he's got everything together, and is playing Genghis Khan again as if it didn't matter that, as the art director says, we don't have a movie.

When Ian told Trigère that we were coming up here and Trigère said he was stark raving mad, Ian apparently replied, "My dear boy, I am not the first mad producer you ever had. Adjust the script. Alter it any way you like. What difference does it make where we shoot this bloody story? We've got the stars, we've got you. We've got four weeks up here with these fellows footing the bill for absolutely everything."

I really feel sorry for Trigère. Four weeks is nothing, even if you have a picture to start with. And there's still the problem of postproduction down the road. Ian probably owes the studio plenty.

The interesting thing is that everybody came. No one refused or quit—even though the whole thing is absolutely ludicrous. And we came on about three hours' notice. I suppose it's because, crazy though it all is, we are already a unit. And the film, in its nonexistent way, already exists. I'm beginning to see that people don't walk away, as they would from an ordinary job. As long as the idea of the film is alive, everyone stays hooked into it.

I'm rooming with Chin-Chan. We have a two-bedroom apartment on the fifth floor and inside it is exactly like any skiing place I've ever been in—cabin furniture, cabin everything, in beiges and browns and oranges. It has a Pullman kitchen with a wooden dining booth that makes into extra beds and a whole wall of glass looking out on the slopes. We also have a terrace that has a heated floor. It's really kicky. You can go out there in your bare feet. Chin-Chan says everybody's apartment is exactly the same, except Randy's, where they've set up the production office, and that has three bedrooms and is on another floor.

I don't think Chin-Chan ever sleeps. She does everything for Ian. Everything. And she runs, she literally *runs* back and forth across his life like a dog racing frantically to fetch the ball or the newspaper or whatever for its master. She's worked for him for years and still calls him Mr. Spencer and says yes sir and no sir, and, of course, he loves it and treats her as if she were his personal servant. The truth is, Chin-Chan could run General Motors, but she's like the slaves in the South before the Civil War. She's never experienced freedom. She went straight from boarding school to Ian and is quite retarded about the world outside his orbit. She fools you with that petite Chinese face, the mincing little steps, the literal bowing to every one of Ian's commands—just a pretty little Oriental puppet on strings, you might think. The truth is, she's a bully. And a terrible bitch. Behind Ian's back.

I was hoping Joss would ask me to live with him, while we're here. But he didn't.

(Later)

He just knocked on my door and asked me to dinner. Ian and the others will be there. I wonder what they will think when they see me with him.

"This place is like a concentration camp," Djuna said, coming in the door of their apartment at last, after twenty-five minutes of wandering lost through dim faceless corridors that were slick with the wet of melted snow from skiers who had tramped on them all day. She was on her way back from the supermarket, where she had gone to buy coffee and fruit and other provisions. "I've been in five different elevators and found myself not only on the wrong floor but in the wrong building. Everything looks the same, nothing is marked, and there's no way to know where the hell you are."

Baker was in the living room, looking out the window wall at the fat, icy slopes. It was getting dark. Only a few skiers were coming down now. It would be the last run for everyone.

He turned. "Ian wants us to meet him in the nightclub, or a nightclub—I guess there are several—anyway, I wrote it down. About nine-thirty. Could we have dinner here? I'd like a nap before we go."

Djuna was unpacking the things from the supermarket. "I hadn't planned on that. But I did get some soup and I have eggs, if that's okay. Do you want a drink first?" She banged open a cupboard over the sink and looked in a drawer dubiously. "I'm not thrilled with the housekeeping arrangements. Why couldn't we stay in one of the hotels? Did I come all the way to the French Alps to cook and do the dishes?"

"It's part of the deal Ian made with the owner. This is the first season for the place. The hotels are doing pretty good but they had a hundred empty apartments. Did you get bourbon? That's what I want. On the rocks." He kicked at a black vinyl hassock and looked around the room. "This place is a piece of shit. Do you realize we don't even have a telephone?"

She handed him his drink. "Well, at least you're working again. As for this"—she also looked around—"the thing is, we're comparing it to the villa. Try to remember some of the locations you've had in the desert. It's really spectacularly beautiful here. When I went outside this morning it was like every terrific Sonja Henie movie I ever saw when I was a little girl . . . formally dressed waiters serving hot chocolate and croissants to people in deck chairs all wrapped in blankets, clinking their jewelry and speaking a dozen languages." She laughed. "It's trippy. We're seeing an entirely different slice of Europe than we had planned on."

She seemed so happy, Baker thought, feeling dull and troubled himself. She was as cheerful as a tourist, just along for the ride. What would it be like to be just a woman, just a wife, just along for the ride? He envied her.

"If you want to see the bullshit I'm facing," he said after a moment, "come watch us shoot tomorrow. We were out there all afternoon and probably got three feet of printable film. Trigère doesn't know what he's doing and neither does anyone else."

Despite Chin-Chan's meticulous instructions to Baker on how to find the nightclub, it took them fifteen minutes to find their way in and out of two wrong sections and three wrong elevator banks. They went down dim hallways stacked with skis and boots outside doors, past several circular areas with open fireplaces and phalanxes of flashing mechanical games, a compact row of cinemas, several shuttered shops, and a noisy pool hall.

When they found an ironwork stairway opposite a neon-lit milk bar, Baker said, "This is it. I mean these stairs. We go down two flights and turn right." They started down. "I feel like I'm in a nuthouse," he complained. "Does this racket go on all day?" he asked, referring to the recorded music assaulting their ears.

"It seems to be in all the public areas," Djuna said with a tight smile. She was on edge. The place was really fearsome. It was loud, ugly, incomprehensible. She remembered being lost at a carnival as a child.

As they reached the foot of the stairway, a different kind of music blared, heavy, brassy, real. They went down another five steps through a slim arch into a dark red-leather hole.

At the far edge of the tiny, varnished dance floor they saw Ian and Joss, Maroga and the American girl, Kat. The party with its two well-known faces had already attracted attention, and when Baker and Djuna walked toward the table they knew they were being looked at by everyone, including the wide-eyed members of the band, who were practically hysterical with awe and delight at the presence of Joss McIvor.

Ian stood up so that Djuna could slip in next to him. Baker sat at the other end, by Maroga. Kat was between the Italian actress and Joss.

The air was opaque with gloom and smoke. Baker lit a cigar. He was tired and he hated nightclubs. His nap had been unsuccessful. He had done nothing but stew and look at his watch and change the position of the pillows behind his head.

"A bit disorganized out there today," Ian said to him at once. "Bernard's upstairs working on the script. We'll be right as rain tomorrow."

"The experience today had nothing to do with acting." Baker puffed on his cigar. "Which is what I basically do. Is there some reason we're here tonight?" He looked around. "It can't be to enjoy ourselves."

Ian looked bland, unperturbed. "Actually I thought it would please Joseph. If we all appeared the first real night. In one of the public rooms."

Baker looked blank. "Who is Joseph?"

"Joseph is our fairy godfather," Maroga replied with an arch smile. "The creator and principal owner of Mont Bleu."

Baker looked at his cigar. "I'd like to meet him. Believe me."

"So would we all, darling," she laughed. "But he's at St. Moritz. On a skiing holiday. At least he has the taste not to patronize Mont Bleu. Don't look at me like that, Ian. You are not going to pretend that this place is chic."

"Don't be such a snob," Ian returned crossly. "Just because Mont Bleu is new and all your friends haven't been yet—"

"New!" Maroga tossed her head. "Vulgar is what you mean. All I've seen so far are shopgirls, hippies, and Germans."

"It's really a firetrap," Kat said. Everyone turned to

look at her. "The way the buildings are all connected and practically no instructions posted about how to get up, down, out. And there must be about five thousand people here."

"And all of them in this room." Maroga fanned herself with a cocktail napkin.

"She's right," Baker said, experiencing a sudden touch of claustrophobia. "The whole complex could go up like a book of matches. I didn't see any fire doors on the way down here."

Maroga produced a bored, condescending smile. "Leave it to the Americans. Always so busy, so sanitary, so efficiently prepared for disaster."

"I read something in the paper this morning, and it wasn't an American paper," Kat said with a flash of temper. "I read that forty people were trapped and died in a hotel fire because there were no exits." She paused and said directly to Maroga, "The hotel was in Rome."

Joss ruffled the top of Kat's hair lightly. "Don't be morbid, darling." He eyed Maroga, who had fixed a surprised cold stare at the girl. "And don't glare at her like that, Maroga. She's got a seat at this table same as you and she has every right to say what she pleases."

Djuna felt a violent spasm in her lower back. She only got those when she was afraid. The girl, the apprentice, Ian's bird—whoever she was—was she with *Joss?*

It wasn't what he had said, but how. That familiar, proprietary air . . . and the girl was sitting next to him, not next to Ian. Out of the corner of her eye, Djuna watched them.

Joss was listening to something Kat was saying with that attentive, hooded smile, the very same look—and then Joss must have sensed her signal because he turned slowly to regard her for a moment. He acknowledged her with his public mask. That was all.

Ian asked Djuna to dance. It was a slow number. "The only kind I can manage," he said jovially. But he was an excellent dancer. She tried to lose herself in the mindless, physical pleasure of the music and their movements.

After a moment he said to her with a mixed look, "I expect it—or we—all strike you as some kind of mad circus. Hauling our cables, as it were, to the top of the Alps and no act to speak of. What energy! What cost! What maniacal purpose! All over a film whose merits were marginal from the beginning." His eyes flashed with their cold, merry twinkle. "What clowns we are. Aren't we? Tell me what you think."

Djuna had mixed feelings about Ian. Generally, she didn't like the idea of him. It wasn't so much what he had done or not done since she and Baker had come to France, but more a matter of taste. She didn't care for the things he cared for, whether it was the pictures he made, the food he ordered, the people he kept around him, or what she sensed to be his indifference towards moments and feelings in which she found passion or beauty. She doubted that he believed in anything much, and when it came to emotion, his range had always struck her as narrow, ordinary, committed to quick gratification.

And yet, whenever she found herself with him she was reminded that he was not a character to be easily dismissed. He had lived a long time and had taken note of practically everything. If she took issue with him insofar as what he had chosen to retain, what he had chosen to let lie, she always found, when she was actually with him, that he was interesting and amusing, and that she enjoyed him.

She answered, glad of their conversation—it was something to do while she tried not to think about Joss and that girl—"I don't really know what I think." She smiled up at him. "Anyway I'm a non-pro. I'm only a relative."

He whirled her about in an expert turn. "That makes you family. You count."

"Tell me how I count, Ian. I could use the cheering up."

"Well, my dear, you're a part of *it*. Nothing is closer between people than being on a film. A film doesn't exist as a part of anything or anybody. It simply exists on its own. That's why we're all together. It's why no one gave notice when I, the mad producer, decided to switch everything from the Riviera to Mont Bleu."

"Do you think your troubles are over? Do you think you're going to make it?"

"I expect so. I've come this far. When the Americans backed out, when Vito tried his disappearing act, there was still me, there was still the film. It's more and it's less than my own survival as a producer and as a person. I don't know. I can't really separate any of it."

The band came to the end of the number and stopped altogether. It was their break. Recorded music instantly blared from all the speakers. Djuna and Ian returned to the table.

Yesterday, in romantically colored Antibes, when Djuna had been packing, the idea of Mont Bleu had spelled out new magic. Now it was all spoiled. It was more than the overwhelming size of the place, it was more than the young girl sitting so naturally next to Joss. She couldn't identify the name of the feeling, just that she felt misplaced and wanted to cry, wanted to get out, away, and down to the flower fields again.

Two days after the dinner at which Joss had cut his hand on the wine glass and they had made love in the bathroom, he had phoned her in midmorning.

"Baker is here at the hotel seeing Trigère, so I thought it would be safe to ring. I also thought it would be lovely to see you. Any chance?"

"Yes," she replied simply. "Yes."

"Would you like lunch? I'll come and fetch you. We'll go to Vallauris."

At the restaurant, they had steak and two bottles of wine and held hands openly for all the world to see and be glad. Then they went to the small hotel across the street, took a room, got out of their clothes at once and fell on the bed and made love. Then they made love again, and then they talked until the sun dropped away from the lace-covered window.

They could have stayed forever, but instead they dressed, pausing at the door of the room for one last kiss. When she hung on for the extra moment, he pulled away laughing and said, "You'll be flat on your back again if you don't stop that."

On the way back to her villa they teased each other a bit with the fresh iconoclasm of new lovers. They had a private language. Already. It had come to them as naturally as the original acknowledgement of their passion.

And at that point, each of them was quite genuine in respecting and believing in the separateness of the other. The space they occupied together was still open, as clear as light. There was no recognizable signal of dependency; it was, rather, an atmosphere of sheer power.

Djuna saw in Joss a heroic quality. Something remembered. Something old. Something new.

"You remind me of Tarzan," she said to him two days later. They had gone to the same restaurant, had exactly the same lunch, and now were in the same bed of the same hotel as before.

"What!" he asked, after a second or two, a bit wild, a bit absent. He was pleased—he was always pleased with nearly everything she said—but at that moment he was driving himself crazy at his own game, his body alive against hers. He had definitely passed the halfway mark where his brain could have assimilated even an intelligible remark.

"Oh!" she cried suddenly, and drew his face down to hers. "Stop doing that." But she closed her eyes quickly and arched her back, and he said slowly, between wonderful and horrible gasps for breath, "Why should I stop doing that, Djuna? Tell me, darling. Tell me!"

So it went. Later when they were sitting up against the pillows and drinking beer, he said, "What did you mean about Tarzan, anyway? I was too busy at that particular second."

"I can't explain it. It's just—" She waved her glass vaguely in the air, and then grinned at him. "I don't know. I see you as very strong and very hard and very brave. I like it. You can be my hero, if you like."

He looked at her almost shyly as he rearranged the sheets around her breasts. "You're really daft, you know."

But he had his own dream, too. What he saw in her was the physical reflection of a secret ideal, honest and beautiful, as bright with history and tenderness as a mother, and erotic beyond—and in a different way—any woman he had ever been with.

"How old are you, anyway?" he asked, slipping down into the bed next to her and propping himself on his elbow, staring up at her.

She made a face. "I prayed you wouldn't ask."

"Well, now I have, and now you have to tell me," he said with a satisfied air.

She reached for her cigarettes on the bedside table and he slapped her hand playfully. "None of that." So she put the pillow over her face and tried to hide. He got on top of her, pinning her down. "Tell me!" They rolled from side to side while she tried to squirm away, still holding fast to the pillow.

"Tell me," he said finally, wrenching the pillow away, "or I'll fuck you to death." He assumed an injured, innocent look. "Like you accused me of doing the other day." Then he addressed someone offstage. "Fancy her saying a thing like that to me."

"Well, you were. If I got up right now, I'd fall down. I'll probably never walk again."

They smiled at each other.

"You're forty," he announced brutally.

"Someone told you."

"Nobody told me. I knew."

She said, looking away, "There are times when I don't find your boyish candor all that attractive."

He kissed the top of her nose. "You're upset. I'm sorry. Don't you know how beautiful you are?"

"I'm not upset."

"You are," he said mournfully. "You're pissed off at me." And he kissed her again all over her face.

"All right!" she said with a laugh. "I'm pissed off at you. You could have pretended you thought I looked thirty-five."

"I honestly didn't know. It was a guess. I was teasing.

And anyway, do you think I give a shit how old you are? Here. Look what all that kissing has done. What you've done." He raised himself to a kneeling position over her. "Look at that, darling."

So she took him.

On the level of language they had kept it light. It seemed the only way. The phrase "I love you" had not been said. On this question each held out, as if by unspoken agreement, and the irony was that it only intensified the bond between them. It was one more thing they shared, and the words were all the more powerful for not yet having been said.

Sitting in the nightclub, Djuna understood that their coming to Mont Bleu had pushed the relationship into a new square. The pastel afternoons in the little hotel in Vallauris were already a remembered age of innocence. She mourned, and she also felt afraid.

The band was now filing in again after their break. They stopped by the table to shake hands, pay their homage to Joss. The leader, with some shyness, asked Joss if he would honor them by taking the stage himself. Joss listened politely and shook his head.

"I've worked all day, mate. Another night, perhaps. And thank you very much." He shook hands with the young man again and the band took up their instruments and began another set.

Djuna tore at her little paper napkin. Would Joss ask her to dance? Back to square one. Back to being fourteen years old. Nothing changed except one's style in handling it. Pain arrived prepackaged and apparently in a limited number of sizes and shapes. She had seen this one before. It was labeled Please Ask Me.

And then he was standing, taking her hand. Casually. "Come and dance with me, Djuna."

The dance floor was packed. Joss seemed to be turned on. By the music? By himself? By her? She couldn't tell. He was being cocky, like his act. He didn't look at her but seemed absorbed, connected to his own flow. She saw that

141

the other couples were leaving a little circle of space around Joss and her. She looked at their young faces, at all the long-haired girls and the young men, and then back at Joss. She felt her own inappropriateness. She was raw and exposed, too old to be jumping up and down on a dance floor to rock music.

"What's wrong?" Joss was shouting over the music, but he didn't look as if he cared. He was enjoying himself.

Mute and angry, she shook her head, refused to look at him, and continued to prance and rock her hips, feeling condemned by an offstage judge to dance until either the audience stopped laughing or she dropped dead.

Joss moved closer and said with a vexed expression, "If you're going to be like that you'll piss me off, I can tell you that straight away. You know we can't talk here, so what's the use of being a pain in the ass about everything?"

"I hate you," she said.

He came abruptly to a stop and said, in exasperation, "Shit." He quickly glanced toward their table to see if anyone was watching. Then he looked back at her stony expression and they stared each other down. Then he caught both her wrists and pulled her to him. And so the moment was healed with that simple, physical act, which has always been the most sensible form of human behavior. With their arms around each other, nothing was difficult, everything was absurdly simple. Holding each other, they held, they thought, everything.

He said against her cheek, "You're behaving like a little girl. You know that."

She answered with a wry flash of restored good humor. "Just because I'm old doesn't mean I'm grown up."

He laughed. "I'll say!" The music stopped and he asked, "Where were you all day? I was looking for you all day? I was looking for you every minute."

"I was unpacking, and you are a terrible liar."

He only had time to say quickly as they left the dance floor, "Stop it, darling. Come to where we are shooting tomorrow."

At the table Baker was yawning ostentatiously and stood

up before she could sit down. "Good night, all," he said firmly and took her arm. They left the night club.

They lost their way three times. Djuna nagged nervously, Baker exploded at her, and the echo of his voice ricocheted through the empty, unfathomable corridors. They finally found the right level, the right elevator, the right door and went straight to bed without saying much more than a weary, carefully civil good night.

In an identical apartment down the hall, Trigère stood in his living room staring at the black window glass. He could see nothing beyond it; only himself, backlighted by an orange glow from the mustard-colored ceramic lamps in the room.

A director had always to visualize the completed work and to create each sequence of images in accordance with how each of those moments in the dramatic pattern was going to be assembled—that is, if he hoped ultimately to make artistic sense and meaning for the audience. Imposing a time design on a film was, chronologically, one of the first tasks Trigère, like most other directors, set for himself. The impact of the finished work was directly connected to those first choices. Just as an action which takes up a lengthy space in a lifetime can be translated quite sensibly into a few minutes on film, a fleeting moment in individual or collective history can occupy many minutes, even an hour in a movie.

From the beginning, when they were still on the coast, before a camera had ever turned, Trigère had recognized that the script was thin, not powerful enough to act on him; therefore he must act on it. And in the flower fields he had thought he had begun to see his way. The environment, as always, created its own action, the size of the idea had taken its shape and the major flow of mood and style had begun.

One learned to deal with the violent aesthetic disruptiveness of always shooting out of sequence; that was the way production went, but the unexpected switch of locations was in the nature of an amputation. All those incomplete blocks of action they had photographed in the studio in Nice and along the Riviera would either have to go out with the dripping hospital garbage or be sewn back on. But how?

He turned from the window now and saw a weary but staunch Chin-Chan, lent to him by Ian, still sitting loyally at the typewriter, waiting for any further dictation he might give her. They had been up all night. She smiled daintily and recrossed her legs.

"Another coffee, Chin-Chan. Then I promise. We will stop."

"I think it sounds quite good. Really," she said encouragingly, and picked up the empty pot to go to the little kitchen with it.

He shook his head. "No." Then he smiled. "We are still asking the audience to contribute too much."

She giggled and put the kettle on to boil. "We could print little booklets and distribute them as the people go into the theater. It would describe the sequences the audiences have to imagine for themselves. Of course, if we could get back into a studio—"

"Chin-Chan, stop torturing me with obsolete fantasies. Ian says we can't count on that. I have to make the film here. All of it."

"And postproduction? I suppose we'll take it to Rome?"

"Not if Ian and Vito owe money there, too. The way things are going, we'll probably end up doing it in a hotel room in Honduras."

He turned back to the window. He had once or twice run into the problem of having to reshoot because the raw material simply did not contain what was necessary for the final assembly. It was expensive, frustrating, frequently embarrassing, and played hell with everyone's commitments. But never this.

He was going to have to forget all his pretty, seminal constructions on the coast. He was going to have to extract a film out of the three main characters themselves and what little was left in the shrunken bones of the script now that it had to play in the Alps. And he was going to do it tonight, or resign and go away in the morning.

They worked for another hour, but he felt he was only going around in shallow circles.

"Go to your apartment and get some sleep," he said finally to Chin-Chan. "I think that we have done all we can tonight."

When she had gone he picked up the pages she had typed while he had paced and smoked and haltingly dictated revisions in the major blocks of action, trying to find connections and authenticity, trying to find his way. He read them over. They were all separate and amorphous.

No. It wouldn't do. He would have to be more clever than that. He went out to the terrace. The railing wore a fresh, fat, silvery coat of snow. He traced his initials in it slowly, smiling a little. And then he knew.

He had been fighting the snow all along.

Any location dominated by overpowering natural elements, such as snow, sea storms, dust, could be chancy. You shot and then you went back the next day and absolutely everything was different. But a location could also generate its own excitement and its own theme. He realized that in everything he had written tonight he had been trying to impose his original conception and his sheer will upon this vast, white, powdery arena. He had been trying to film his picture in spite of the snow instead of allowing the picture to come out of it. He had been looking for a whole day at the slopes, at the peaks, at everything as if it were all on a static postcard where nothing moved or changed and the paint had dried on every detail. He had been trying to paste his characters and his story to that postcard. It was so stupid. So blind. One had to start with the earth where one stood.

How did one get so far away from what one knew?

He looked at the black night, the spectral peaks, and thought that perhaps, after all, anything was possible. He smiled, thinking of all the moments and the places in which—always at the last minute—he had opted for hard, fresh hope. And what had come forth had always been good, and sometimes beautiful. A line. A look. A new love. A new life.

He said to the night, I am a romantic. And, on the whole, I am glad.

He turned on the fire under the kettle again and went down the hallway to Chin-Chan's apartment, where he knocked softly on the door.

It opened at once. But it was Kat.

"Chin-Chan just took a sleeping pill," the American girl said doubtfully. "I think she's already out."

"Kat," Trigère asked, "can you type?"

Chapter Sixteen

They worked until the black night beyond the window glass dissolved to morning gray and the ghostly outlines of the sharp, icy peaks appeared through the early mist.

Trigère paced up and down, and around the card table where Kat sat obedient, amazed, blinking her eyes to keep them open. She had been ready to go to bed herself when Trigère had come knocking at the door for Chin-Chan. She had also been feeling confused and disappointed. Expecting to spend the night with Joss after they had returned from the nightclub, she had merely been given a kiss on the nose and a proprietary whack on the backside, and then he had whisked her into her own apartment and gone off.

She didn't understand him. She would never understand him. Perhaps, she sat thinking as Trigère paused in his dictation, she shouldn't even try.

She had had a lot to drink in the nightclub and what with all the cigarettes she had had here—and Trigère giving her endless cups of coffee—her adrenalin was racing. At the same time, she knew she was exhausted enough to drop. This imbalance made war with her body, her brain, while she sat, attentive, thrilled, wishing this priceless experience to be over, wishing this priceless experience not to be over.

This was her first time alone with the legendary director, whom she had come to revere even more than she had when he had been only a remote, glittery name on the screen. While they always said hello to each other on the set and had even exchanged casual conversation, she found she had butteries in her stomach now that she was actually on stage with him.

From time to time he would stop his pacing and throw himself down on the sofa, running his hands through his thick, graying hair, closing his eyes, sitting like that for minutes at a time. She would stare at him with surprise and awe at being allowed to see him so privately, there in the small hours of the morning, and she was moved in a fresh way by his aging physical grace, his long legs, the elegant, polished loafers, the tousled hair, the open white shirt, the fine strong hands that steadily lighted endless cigarettes. To her, his sudden vulnerability tonight seemed as tough—and as fine—as his strength.

He opened his eyes. "Another coffee?" he asked in his precise English.

"For you?" She started to jump up.

"No, for you." He smiled. "I have to keep you awake."

She shook her head. "No more for me."

"A glass of water? Orange juice? No? Then what about a glass of champagne."

She giggled. "You're kidding."

"Not in the slightest." He rose. "In the last resort, champagne will clear the brain. And we are almost done."

He went to the small refrigerator while she sat with her elbows on the table, her chin in her hands, watching him and planning how she would record this night in her journal. He returned with two glasses and the bottle of champagne, which he opened as quickly and easily as she would have opened a soft drink, poured the champagne, and they silently clinked their glasses together. Then he

147

sat down beside her and quietly, very surely, began to dictate again.

She was aware of his extreme exhaustion, and thought there was some kind of pain, too, behind his remote, slightly ironic expression. She would glance at him curiously during the pauses, trying to find her way inside that look. He would meet these glances for long periods of time, but he seemed to be only looking through her eyes, into the private reflection of his own thoughts.

He was very precise. Once he delivered a line, an action, an instruction, he never went back, never asked her to read over what he had said. But now his expression grew increasingly remote and the pauses grew longer.

During one of these pauses she asked, hardly daring to voice it, "You hate working on this film, don't you?"

He was silent for a moment, his eyes suddenly very sharp, sweeping over her face.

Then, instead of answering, he took her hand, turned it over, looked at it. He sat there, his shoulders hunched forward, his finger tracing her life line.

"Come to bed," he said at last, abruptly, looking her full in the face.

His expression told her very little. Only that he seemed to have gone as far as he could go. By himself. For now. His weary smile, it also seemed to her, was the last effort he would make on her behalf. She felt, along with the shock of his words—and the thrill—the noises of fear and warning inside herself.

She needed to gain time but she knew she wasn't going to get it. This wasn't a romance, or even a seduction. She had merely been asked to do one more thing for him. She felt the ground underneath her feet falling away. She was in a flying place she had never been before. An older place. A place she had not been prepared for. And in that moment, she resented it all violently, resented him for forcing something she would have wanted to dream a little about first.

He lifted her palm to his mouth and gently kissed it.

Then, with a wry smile, he took both of her hands firmly in his own and remained looking at her, oddly, curiously, sadly, as if he knew what she was thinking and was going to let her puzzle out her own answer.

But after a minute, when she did not speak, she thought she saw his eyes retracting again into that remote place she had seen all night. There was a flicker of resignation, old pain—what was it? Did it have anything to do with her at all?

In a flash, her whole life was behind her and she was jumping through the hole in the scenery again, into—she thought—the soul and body and life of Bernard Trigère.

When he was only thinking, behind his weary, intelligent eyes: I am tired and empty and I must put myself somewhere.

He must have perceived she had made her decision, because he kissed her mouth lovingly for a long time, and then drew his head back saying, quietly, "Yes?"

"Yes," she said.

In bed he did not kiss her mouth once. She floundered, clumsy and awkward, pressed into the sudden service of this possessed man.

She felt intimidated by her own lack of experience with older men, faintly put off—and excited—by the angular, different feel of his body, his movement, his need. Her sense of newness and fright toward the experience produced in her an unnaturalness that compounded her awkwardness. She wished wildly for it to continue forever.

She had thought he would make love to *her*, but she saw at once he expected the reverse from her. She found she could not. *Could not.* There was a low laugh in the darkness. He placed her on her back and entered her.

An hour later, the sun began to glow behind the heavy curtains and he was still riding her. He had not spoken one word. From time to time she had an orgasm. She was raw and sore, but this did not diminish the only desire she now had in the world—which was to have him stay inside of her.

At last, he rolled over beside her, one leg flung over her body. Eyes closed. A million miles away. She waited for him to open his eyes and see her. But he did not.

She fell asleep and when she awoke it was late morning. His side of the bed was empty. She waited for him to come from the bathroom, from somewhere, but there was no sound. She got out of bed and looked around the apartment.

He was gone. So were the pages she had typed for him.

When she got back to her own apartment, Chin-Chan greeted her crossly.

"I've spent half the morning correcting your typos," she said.

Chapter Seventeen

The sun sliced the snow everywhere with its morning rays of butter-yellow. The sky was brilliant blue, and the high-gloss telecabines were swinging along the cables out of the red tower, on their way up the slopes, over the heads of children, ski classes, and people just out for a breath of air.

Mont Bleu was up and had had its breakfast. Already there was activity to be seen at the top of La Tour, the highest run, where clusters of early-rising skiers were starting their first plunge down deep trails. Below, and in every direction, there were knots and lines of skiers hanging onto ropes and bars, all moving at a stately pace, orchestrating the scene, setting the rhythm of the day.

Billows of steam rose from the heated, aquamarine pool. Some children splashed at its shallow end, while their nannies stood at the ready, hands thrust in the pockets of their cloth coats for warmth, their faces tilted slightly to catch the promise of the early sun.

On the circular, varnished deck at the edge of the giant

complex, rows of pampered women in fur coats and sunglasses and men in tweed caps stretched their legs out under gay plaid blankets and read astrology charts and movie magazines. Waiters hurried by with trays of coffee and hot chocolate.

The only people left in the complex were the employees of the restaurants and shops and all the other services, a few passionate couples still busy at morning love amid rumpled sheets, the band sleeping the night off, and the usual complement of nonskiers—wives, servants, and children of the dedicated.

The film crew had been gathered a little way up the central slope since early morning, setting up for the day's shooting. The assistant director had at last managed to get the area blocked off from skiers and onlookers. Jack was tied to the rope tow and to a flat sled from which he would be making a tracking shot of a telecabine with Maroga in the window. He was rehearsing now, sweating with the exertion of coordinating the movement, as members of the crew manually operated the tow that would move him slowly up at the exact pace Trigère had instructed.

Hans was busy with the lighting crew and Trigère was answering questions from everyone who demanded his attention while he squinted at Jack and felt the fear in the pit of his stomach that perhaps he should have tried another way, not hand-held like that but—

"I thought," Conchita was upon him, "you said the white cap for Maroga. She is insisting on the black fur."

He nodded absently. "The white. Definitely the white."

"God Almighty!" the assistant director shouted suddenly. He was staring up the slopes. The script girl had just taken his arm and pointed to a figure in a bright red jacket at the top who had just started his run down the slope.

"Trigère!" the assistant director called now. "That cocky son-of-a-bitch is trying to ski!"

Trigère looked up to the top of the run. It was indeed Joss, unmistakable in the red oilskin jacket he had been given by Wardrobe.

"*Merde.*" Trigère turned to the assistant, his eyes flashing angrily. "Who let him go up there? Who's responsible for this? Do I have to do the baby-sitting as well as everything else?"

"Trigère," the assistant director answered with a moan. "Who can be responsible for a crazy shit like that? He was right here, I swear it. He must have slipped into one of the regular telecabines when no one was looking."

Ian approached, picking his way carefully through the snow. "What's up?" he called cheerfully. "Are we ready?"

Trigère nodded grimly at the slope. "Your superstar, who has never skied in his life, is coming down the hill there."

Ian peered up. "But why? What's that silly bastard doing? Are you sure it is he? That fellow is skiing *very* fast."

Trigère kept his eyes on the red jacket. "He is out of control. In a few seconds he will either get very frightened and try to stop or his luck will run out—in either case he will break only his leg if he is lucky or his neck if he is not." He turned away.

"Shit, Mr. Spencer," the assistant said in agony to Ian, "he asked for some skis and boots this morning so he could practice walking in them. Who would have thought he would do a lunatic thing like that? Doesn't he know you have to take lessons and start on small hills?"

Not for Joss had been the likes of lessons. Take lessons like some bloody schoolboy? At his age?

He hadn't liked being in a place where he didn't know how to do what was being done. Everyone, it seemed, skied except himself. The rich and the famous. Almost all of the crew. Djuna and Kat both. And all those bloody little toddlers whizzing about on the smaller slopes. Well, they hadn't spent their lives in a mining town or busting their grubby pipes singing for a living. Anyway, it couldn't be that difficult. It was obviously a question of will.

Now he was more frightened than he had ever been in

his life, but excited, too—beyond any remembered experience—and it was all going so fast that he existed only in the brute force of his will, his spirit, his breath, his legs. It was too late now to stop. There was nothing for it but to get balanced—that was it, get balanced, stay balanced, be balanced.

From below, Ian squinted at the bright halo of the hill, watching the wild, accelerating plunge of the red-jacketed figure. "Get a camera on him," he called to the assistant director. "Any camera."

"But, Mr. Spencer—"

"Do as I say!" Ian shouted in a rage. If Joss was going to kill himself he might as well be photographed doing it. He looked around. "Kat!" he called to the girl who was staring up the hill like everybody else. With that goddamn camera she always had, hanging idly from the shoulder strap. "Get a picture of that bloody fool!"

But she seemed not to hear him.

The only person on the scene who thought Joss might make it was Joss himself, which is probably why he did. Having been willing to offer up his own death as a fair trade for a necessary experience, nerve and muscle co-operated in his primitive transaction with destiny, thereby making it possible for him to land, finally, at the bottom of the run, on his head but alive.

They picked him up. He was exhilarated. He would not show his exhaustion from the physical strain or the terror; it was not his style. He would see out the rest of the day as if nothing had happened.

It was part of his bravura, Trigère thought as he watched everyone crowding around Joss. It was all so macho, Joss' particular brand of rash, raw guts. And somehow touching and nostalgic. All that outdated heroic romanticism, all those notions of seventeenth-century bravery and honor. It was so innocent. And so powerful. It was what one could still make films about. If machismo was bullshit, it also had its own kind of antique beauty.

And then Trigère turned back to his film, to his crew,

to his day. He stared thoughtfully at the set-up. Then he looked all around, at the peaks and the sky, and he said to himself, I am going to need a helicopter.

He looked down to see Kat standing before him. Green eyes in a sea of young freckles. He liked her face, and he smiled. She was really very lovely.

"Hello," she said, wondering if he knew how much it had cost her to approach him.

Ah, yes. Last night. It had been pure folly. His millionth folly. "You okay?" he asked, falling into the Americanism—always an aid to him for keeping a distance.

"Fine," she answered. Very sturdy. He felt admiration and relief. He was also—unaccountably?—a little ashamed. But Hans and Jack were ready for him.

"Yes?" He smiled at her kindly. " That's good." And turned to his crew.

Toward noon, Djuna picked her way across the snow and up a gentle slope to the patio restaurant that was being used for the day as headquarters for Wardrobe and Make-up, the catered lunch being set up now, and a dumping place for equipment and for anyone who had a minute to sit down.

She took some coffee from the aluminum urn at the main table and stood at the wooden rail, watching Trigère run through the same shot again and again. After a moment, Joss, whom she had believed to be in the rigged-up telecabine with Maroga and Baker, walked toward her. When he came up she silently handed him her cup and he drank all the coffee down. He sat on the rail next to her, tense and hunched forward, his eyes on the scene around them.

He glanced at her briefly before he turned away again. "Anyway, darling. Are you feeling brighter today?"

The sun was unpleasantly hot through her thick Irish sweater. She felt remote, barricaded behind her big black sunglasses, out of touch with the scene, Joss, herself. And that girl was here. She was at the edge of the set, sitting on a camera case, writing in a notebook.

Djuna exploded violently. "I hate this fucking place."

"Nobody likes it much." Joss' tone was critical, impatient.

He stared away again. She would get to the reason for her bad temper presently, but not without some striking out at him, at everything. She wasn't easy. Not that he'd thought she would be, but he realized he had been counting on special behavior from her; a woman, he had thought, would not react like a girl.

The scene was distressingly familiar. *Was* there a female on earth who was easy? And still interesting? He decided to take the bull by the horns.

"If you're pissed off about Kat, I'm sorry." He squinted up the hill to where he had begun his run. "But I need someone. That's the way I am. I'd rather that someone be you than anyone in the world. But you're married."

"Is she . . . are you . . . ?"

"She was assigned to an apartment with Chin-Chan. She sleeps at mine by invitation only."

Djuna said nothing to this, so after a moment he added, "Don't be angry. Can't we just go on caring for each other and being together when we can?"

She said bitterly, "Will you change the sheets when it's my turn?"

He slammed his fist into the railing. "I don't need this, Djuna. Truly I don't. *You* get into Baker's bed every night of *your* life."

After a moment she said, "Baker and I don't make love."

His head swung around. "I don't believe that."

"Why not?"

"I just don't." He was looking at her oddly.

"Baker is impotent. At least with me he is."

Joss' face darkened, and he had difficulty choosing his words. "Is that why you—" He stopped, tried another way. "I expect you've had others, then?"

"I am in love with you," she said, because it was time.

155

He was silent. At last he said carefully, as if delivering a rehearsed line, "I care for you very much but it is important for you to know that I am not in love with you."

"I wasn't asking for a trade." She took off her sunglasses and gave him her clear look.

He said, frowning, "If I were in love with you I would expect you to be—well, to be mine." He stared up the hill again. "All things considered, that possibility doesn't seem likely, does it?" After a moment he added, "You are more interesting to me than any woman I've ever known. But one of these days the film will be over. You'll go back to your life and I'll go back to mine. We have to be very clear and precise about that. Or you're going to be terribly hurt. You're like that. I could see it from the beginning."

"Isn't everyone? What about you?"

"Of course it will hurt me when we say goodbye," he said roughly. "But you've got to admit it wouldn't be exactly intelligent of us to plan a future. I'd only be lying if I made you any promises. The fact that you are fifteen years older than me isn't the least of our problems."

"Joss!" They were calling him.

He swung off the railing. Looking at her awkwardly. "I have to go. Are you very upset? Darling? You know I can't kiss you here. Give us a smile? Even a small one? Can you come to see me tonight? You know we're all right when we shut the fucking world out. And I've missed you terribly." He stood there like a boy. Dying to go. But waiting for some sign from her.

He was going to break her heart.

"Joss!" The assistant director was calling again. But it was plain Joss did not want to leave her. Not like that.

"Go." She manufactured a smile. "I'll try to come tonight."

"There's a love," he said, relieved, and ran off.

Extract from Kat's Journal

I am writing this sitting on a camera case in the snow, with a lot of hot French sun popping new freckles on my face. That's the warm part. My feet are wet and freezing.

The boots Chin-Chan loaned me are no damned good. Nearly everybody has the same problem. Nobody had the time (or the money) to get the right kind of gear before we came, particularly boots, gloves, and hats. And the prices in the shops are ridiculous. Of course, Maroga isn't suffering, not that she ever does. She brought all six hundred pounds of her clothes, which she apparently takes everywhere she goes. And yesterday, I saw Djuna in one of the boutiques trying on fur parkas and fur hats. She probably bought plenty, as she is very clothes-conscious and I think she thinks she is a movie star herself.

Joss is over there by the restaurant talking to her right now. It has become obvious even to me that he's got some sort of schoolboy crush on her. And how do I feel about that? I'm not even thinking about it this morning. I'm thinking about all the postcards I've been sending my family and friends about what a terrific time I'm having and how wonderful everything is.

The truth is I feel like throwing up all over France. All over the world, to be exact.

All I can say this morning is that I guess I don't understand men. I went to bed with Trigère because I thought the world of him and because I saw how much he needed me. Obviously these are fucked reasons for going to bed with anyone.

Jesus, am I learning.

Chapter Eighteen

At four o'clock on Friday of the following week, Chin-Chan tapped Trigère on the shoulder. "The dailies are back from Nice."

He nodded. "We'll see them before dinner." And was conscious of the high walls of his stomach.

"In the production office?" She put her mittened hands

over her delicate Oriental ears. It was cold; it was always cold there on the hill in the late afternoons.

"No. I want them projected. Set it up in my apartment. Ian, myself, you."

Her boots made a squeaking sound in the snow as she hurried away. Trigère turned his attention back to Jack and Hans, who were arguing about the lighting again. But his own light was inward, on himself. It would be his first look at any of the work they had done so far. There had been a delay at the lab and now everything had come on the same day.

He frowned and dug a small hole in the snow with his boot tip. It reminded him how, as a boy, he used to scoop out the earth in a perfect ring like that for his marble games. He had not seen a marble in years. Such beauties he had had. They had been objects of art and he hadn't known it then. Did children still play with marbles? Were the dailies going to be a disaster?

It wasn't only that in these difficult and unfamiliar conditions he had had to depend so much on Jack, with whom he had never worked before, but rushing at him now was the dead weight of his own responsibility. His blood felt gray with it. His choices. Had they been arrogant? Self-indulgent? Would there be enough to work with? Enough to go on?

He looked at his three stars, just off to the side, waiting, complaining of the cold, dressed at his direction in tones of ivory and white. Was it all sheer absurdity? Ever since he had imposed his stubborn color mood on the new version of the film, it had seemed as if everyone had taken a step back from him in disapproval, even suspicion. Jack had maintained a noncommittal but surly air and his commands to the crew were always terse and obscene. Even Maroga had violently protested her new stylized make-up, and the wardrobe girl always seemed to be hovering at the edge of his visual periphery, her arms loaded with scarves and hats in every color of the rainbow, should he change his mind. Or was he only hallucinating that she was always there? Judging him?

Trigère took a deep, angry breath. Damn it, had he lost all faith in himself? Had he not been confident all week?

After the night he and Kat had stayed up until dawn, he had slept only an hour. He had been up by eight o'clock that morning prowling the miles of Mont Bleu's corridors with Chin-Chan in his wake, taking notes, followed by the art director making quick sketches for approval every time they halted, using Chin-Chan's shoulder blades for an impromptu drawing board. When they had covered the interior they went outside into the glare of ice and color.

"Up there." Trigère pointed to where a spiny cluster of high firs came to a black V in the snow. "That's tomorrow. I want a camera on—something, I don't care—it has to be high. Check with Hans. No, check with Jack. Get one of the telecabines painted white. That's also for tomorrow. And have Wardrobe see me as soon as we're finished with this." He looked at the art director. "I need to talk to you more about this later, but I can tell you now that I will be wanting a gazebo."

"But for what scene? And what size? Really, old man—"

"Let me see some sketches. Something you might put in a Victorian garden. Then I'll tell you."

"A *white* gazebo, no doubt?" the man said with a touch of sarcasm.

"Be grateful you can draw, Carl. You'd never make it on your charm. Chin-Chan, we want six black-and-white dogs. And a sled." He looked at his watch and walked back into the complex, saying over his shoulder, "At lunchtime we meet again."

He left them there with their notebooks in their hands and murder in their hearts. They looked at each other.

"I knew I shouldn't have come up here," Carl began. "This place makes you crazy. This film makes you crazy. He was always so reasonable before. For a director."

Chin-Chan looked at her notes. "The production manager is going to shit. Well what are we standing here for? Let's be grateful he isn't Antonioni. He would have asked us to paint the snow."

"Not the snow darling. That's already white. It would be the sky. They want to be God. All of them. Let's go and have a drink."

"Are you crazy? It's nine o'clock in the morning."

"What does that have to do with anything? You're the straightest girl I ever met."

Trigère was clearly aware of the effect he had had on Chin-Chan and Carl that day and on everyone else since. It had been calculated. It had been the best method of dealing with the faltering production, the disorganized, cold, complaining company, the picture, and himself. It was important to know how to use one's power to stay completely clean and zeroed in. He had controlled the scattered human storm around him by holding fast and pushing everybody one step further than at any given moment they thought they were capable of.

Ian came up to him. "Did Chin-Chan tell you the dailies are here? A lot of people have asked me if they can see them. I know we don't generally do that, but under the circumstances—they've had a rough week. you know. You've behaved like an absolute cunt to everyone and there's nothing wrong with a little morale."

"We'll make that judgment after you and I have taken a look," Trigère answered curtly and turned away.

The assistant director saw him approach and thanked Jesus Mary Joseph that there was only a half-hour left of light. Every day out here in this fucking snow was longer than a winter.

That evening the entire company was invited to view the dailies. By nine o'clock they were all crowded into Ian's apartment, overflowing chairs and sofas, sitting on the floor. Chin-Chan served wine, Kat served cheese and biscuits, and Ian made a little speech.

"We thought we'd have a little party tonight. We'll be showing the dailies because—actually, Bernard is going to tell you about that—but I do want to say that I'm very grateful the way you've all put your shoulders to the wheel during this difficult time. I won't tick off the problems because you know them better than I. But I will tell you that Bernard and I feel blessed to have each and every one of you in our little company."

There was light, cynical applause.

Trigère did not rise to speak as Ian had, but remained sitting on the edge of Maroga's chair. Nevertheless, as soon as he began his remarks an attentive silence settled over the room.

"Any film is difficult in the sense that so much that will happen is unpredictable. On the production board it always seems organized, sensible. Doable. As you know, the reality is hinged to less sensible elements, such as flu and wisdom teeth, bankers, ego, and, not least of all, the weather.

"The one—how do you say—ace in the hole the film maker has, to deal with the thousands of unpredictabilities that emerge, everything from a simple error to a major hold-up—is adequate preparation."

Laughter.

"Quite so." Trigère smiled. "Preparation is hardly something in which we have abounded. Actually, *Lovers and Clowns* has so far proved extra-difficult in extra ways from any film I have ever done—and would wager you have ever done."

Applause.

Then, with a faintly ironic, quizzical glance at Ian, "Our esteemed producer and host, who actually has been on our side even when it didn't seem like it"—he paused and smiled at Ian—"informs me that the pay packets are in the production office, which as you know is Randy's apartment, and may be picked up in the morning. Or tonight, if he is still sober when we finish here and can find his doorkey."

Cheers and applause.

"Next . . ." Trigère paused. "I am told many of you had to come up here without the opportunity of getting together suitable clothing, and in connection with that, please see Chin-Chan before you leave and she'll give you

161

chits for some of the stores. Get what you need for warmth, comfort, et cetera, but anyone who abuses our tender-hearted—and belated—largesse will be in trouble. From now on, anyone seen in sequined Adidas, fur-lined Afghanistan parkas, or Balenciaga sunglasses will be shot at sunrise."

Cheers and catcalls.

"Now. We are going to show you what we have shot so far because it is the best way I have of telling you what I am doing here . . . and what you are doing here."

He nodded at Chin-Chan, who turned off the overhead lights while Kat got the lamps and the editor started the projector.

The screen flickered with soft silver snow. Radiant pinpoints of light gave way as the eye traveled through the frozen, cobwebbed dream to where everything was leaves, wet, glistening and icy, and then, a sudden rush forward into a face—Maroga's—a frame in chalky mists.

There were murmurs.

Next a glut of quick images: Joss in a spiny, brittle tree and the camera coming round at him. Then close-ups. Joss' profile as cold and sharp as the fine, jagged line of a winter branch. His double, falling twenty feet to the snow. Baker in black, from head to foot, standing over him with his shotgun.

Then all the late-afternoon shots, the long snowy traverses, sun, wind, the blowing of snow. And finally the antique white telecabine dissolving out of the mist, moving upward, endlessly upward, and again Maroga's face in the window, as pale and marbleized as the frozen scene itself.

The screen went blank. The show was over. A hubbub broke out immediately and Chin-Chan turned on the lights again. In the collective jubilation they all congratulated themselves privately for having done their own job well. What they had just witnessed, alone and together, was shining proof. It had worked. Everything had worked. Trigère was a genius. Jack was a hero. They were both forgiven for their shitty behavior.

Ian beamed and passed around paper-foil trays of little pizzas that Chin-Chan had bought in the supermarket.

It had been Trigère who suggested the party, after he and Ian had viewed the film. "I think we should give them something, even if it is only dailies and wine, to bring us all together. I have played Hitler until tonight, but now I know we have something and I want to concentrate on keeping the momentum going. I need them with me, Ian. I want them to care."

Ian looked around the room with a bright expression. It was more than a party. It was like a movie itself, bigger than real life could ever be. He could feel tears just behind his eyes. What a sentimental sot he was!

Oh, *Good God*. It looked as if Joss was passing out joints. He was! Ian started to move toward him and felt a hand on his arm.

It was Trigère saying lightly, "For an old scoundrel, you are incredibly antediluvian when it comes to other people's pleasure. Leave it. It's so harmless."

But Ian hated drugs and he hated stoned people. "I don't like it being done in my flat. It will stink it all up to bloody hell," he said coldly to Trigère. "If people want to relax, why can't they do it with spirits? Goddammit, look. There's Chin-Chan lighting up. Silly cunt. She'll be useless the rest of the night. Who's going to wash all these goddamn glasses? Oh dear dear *dear*."

"Darling Ian!" Maroga had come up to them. She was wearing black ski pants, a black turtleneck sweater, and no make-up except for the fringe of charcoal eyelashes and she looked very beautiful in her way, which was to look always very much like a movie star.

"What a good idea, this party of yours." She waved her wine glass at the room. "I can see that everyone will go to bed with a new partner tonight. Tomorrow there will be twenty romances launched, and if anything can keep a film together, *that* will."

She looked around the room and her eye fell on Kat, who was talking to Jack. The girl was dressed, as usual, in jeans and a Mexican shirt hung with gold chains, and she had on her little wire glasses. She was not really pretty, but she had something. It wouldn't photograph well, perhaps, but it would always draw men.

Maroga turned back to Ian. "Is it true that that girl really wants to be a director, God save her? If she is serious, why don't we let her do something besides hang around and take away all the men?"

Ian looked vexed. "She is *very* serious. I have the feeling that if I give her an inch she'll be running the cameras and even producing the picture herself. I can't think why I picked her up. It seemed like such a good idea at the time."

Maroga smiled at him indulgently. "You had money then. That's when everything seems like a lark."

At the other end of the apartment Joss was chasing Chin-Chan. In the narrow hallway between the bedrooms he grabbed her and ran his hands up and down the back of her silk shirt.

"Give us a kiss," he said, holding her to him, high on the evening, the wine, the joint, the stunning beauty of the dailies. He was trying to block the presence of Djuna. Baker was here and it was no good. He had exchanged a glance with her at the beginning of the evening, that was all, and he had wished, as he often did these days, that everything was simple. That she belonged to him.

He kissed Chin-Chan and she seemed to like that very much, so he went a little farther.

A door behind them opened suddenly. Djuna was coming out of the bathroom, her head bent slightly, looking for something in her purse. As she looked up, Chin-Chan had just opened her startled eyes.

Joss murmured, "Christ."

The trio stood frozen for an instant, and then Chin-Chan broke and fled back to the others.

After a moment Joss made a helpless gesture. But remained silent.

"Do you have to do it with everyone?" Djuna asked at last.

"It was just a bit of fun," he said quietly. "I'm sorry you saw, but I'm not going to apologize for anything more than that."

She saw that he meant exactly that, and in that sense she thought he was cleaner about himself than anyone she had ever known. Identifying who he was and what his rights were had never been one of his problems. He was simple and direct always, whereas she was layers and layers thicker. Older. And more corrupt.

It was crazy.

He was thinking the same thing. How to stop this affair? It wouldn't do. It was all getting very thick and he simply had to pull out. But when he looked at her face he wanted to drown in it, he always wanted to drown in it, in her, in her arms, her eyes, her soul. What was it? What was the violent pull between them? Surely the sexual attraction was most of it; that had been plain from the beginning. With each new experience of each other their passion had increased. When she had come to him two nights ago they had not spoken a word until after he had thrown her on the bed and torn her clothes off, so desperate had he been to get into her. He closed his eyes and played back the scene, the arch of her neck, her arms flung wide, the incredible craziness he had felt, and her eyes as hot as his as he rammed himself inside her again and again crying out God knows what. Raving mad things. He opened his eyes and saw her mouth. The mouth where he had put his cock, and he remembered her hair falling around his belly and his legs.

He might as well admit it, at least to himself. He was in love with her. That was plain enough. But he would not declare it because it would pass. It would have to pass. She had said she loved him, but after all, women said that a lot. And he had to keep himself together.

He watched her finger the gold chain around her neck. He would get her something for that. A diamond. Why hadn't he thought of it before?

But he wanted desperately to give her something now, not because he felt he had to make up for his asinine flirtation with Chin-Chan but to affirm in some ritual way the fact of his passion. Then he remembered the song he had composed on the journey from Nice.

"I wrote something for you," he said falsely. But it would serve.

"For me?"

He loved to watch all the quick changes her face made. Now it was the little girl, hopeful, not quite sure he meant it.

"Yes," he said. "On the way up here from Nice. I saw water rushing over the rocks, and since the rocks were packed in snow I wondered why the water hadn't frozen, too. Perhaps it was because it was flowing so fast. I started to think about you. I don't know anything about freezing points, and not much about complicated American ladies either, yet—what, are you crying, for Christ's sake?"

It had welled up again, her deep response to him, mysterious, archetypal, hinged to molecules, to tides, to stars—surely it must have to do with all of that. It couldn't have just begun the day they met. The root of their attraction was buried somewhere in an ancient article of faith. Wanting someone who wanted you—that had to have begun centuries before you ever met. It came down through everybody's blood, everybody's tears, everybody's experiences in different places, different times, alone and together.

"Of course I'm crying," she said. But she was laughing, too, because she was happy again. "I'm allergic to you. You make my eyes run." She wiped her eyes with a Kleenex. "Is my black stuff running?"

"Yes, darling. Here." He took over the Kleenex and carefully blotted where the mascara had smeared her eyelids. "You have to stop crying because I hate it." Then he sighed and touched her hair.

Separately, they returned to the main room.

Ian had imported the band from the nightclub and they were setting up their instruments by the big glass window. Djuna saw that Baker was in a corner window

166

seat with Maroga, so she stood for a while with the wardrobe girl and the art director.

"At first," Carl was saying, "when we got up here I didn't understand why Trigère needed me at all. I could have sent my assistant. Paint this, paint that, he says to me. Can you imagine? Now he wants me to be a carpenter as well. On Sunday the production manager and I have to build that dreadful gazebo. If we don't get more help I'll be dropping dead next. I'm all for esprit de corps, but Ian's such a miser it's really not fair."

The wardrobe girl drained her glass of wine. "Then go and work on another film if you're suffering so much. I can promise I won't miss you. I've been on pictures with you for fifteen years and all you do is complain." She walked off in search of another drink but the band had started to play and one of the electricians grabbed her to dance with him.

Carl watched the raven-haired woman for a moment. "Why is it," he complained to Djuna, "that women who work in films are so macho? Look at Conchita in those jeans. At her age. A bottom as big as a rock, and a face to match. They all have foul mouths and dark personal lives for which one is supposed to feel sympathetic. Retarded children, alcoholic husbands, mothers with emphysema. Ai! At night they spread their legs—for anyone who asks —as mechanically as they might wash out their underwear or put cream on their faces. They fuck like whores, with their sweaters on. On the set, in the production office, they are tough beyond belief, cunning, shrewd, paranoid. The only way to understand their basic mentality is to understand power and dirt."

"You're talking about another era, surely?" Djuna murmured in surprise and protest. "I don't know about Europe, but in the States it's not like that. You're making a very unkind generalization."

Carl shrugged. "Under the skin it's all the same. The major requirement of the female in the film business is to be an object with two legs and a hole between designed for fucking. If they can take shorthand and if they like to work like dogs they keep their jobs. That's the mentality. In time it turns them into aberrations. Like Conchita. Did you know she used to be one of Ian's girls?"

Djuna stared at the make-up woman's granite profile, the coarse arms with their bags of loose flesh. "But she's old!"

"So is Ian."

"Yes, but—he's so elegant. I mean, he's intact."

"He hasn't had to work as hard. Or be fucked so much. Or cry on Sundays."

Djuna winced. "Carl, you're the most depressing man I ever met. Stop it!"

"Now take little Miss Smart Ass over there," he resumed, indicating Kat. "She thinks she's different. She's going to be a director, she says. Not for her the secretarial and script jobs. She went to a fancy film school in America and she thinks she knows it all. She has a lot of surprises in store for her. Perhaps she has had a few already. Oh, look. It seems as if McIvor is actually going to honor us with a song."

There was an excited stir around Joss. The band leader had just handed him his guitar and Joss had accepted it. He was looking around for some place to sit, his expression tight and absorbed. He found the edge of a sofa but first drank down all the wine that was left in his glass. Someone took it away and the room became quiet as he began to tune up. Then he looked out at his audience.

"The piano is really my instrument," he said quietly. "But I'm going to have to make do with this thing. And the truth is that I really need my jolly back-up men plus several thousand quid worth of audio equipment, not to mention a lot of advance publicity, to make me sound any good. So don't tell anyone you heard me."

There was laughter and applause.

"On the drive up here, when none of you buggers would let me pass you on the road, I wrote a tune just for me and someone I love." For a moment his eyes flickered over Djuna. "If we ever get through this film alive and well,

168

I'm going to record it for my next album. So here is 'Ice on the Rocks.' "

He bent his head for a full minute. Djuna found herself staring at a stranger inhabiting Joss' face. He was as remote as a shadowy head of state behind the fluttering curtains of a flag-draped balcony. His eyes held an expression she was not acquainted with. A vast distance suddenly occupied the shallow physical space between him and the crowd. Then he began.

The song was different from the way they had come to think of him, most of them. The melody was plaintive and clean, with classical halts and turns in the way that music indicates memory and longing. The lyrics followed suit, frail and tenuous in their effect.

Save Djuna, Trigère listened and watched the most intently of anyone in the room. Here was a totally different Joss, different from the way he acted before the cameras and different from his off-hours self. What Trigère was seeing was Joss' special theatricality, a composite Trigère now remembered from television coverage of concerts, photographs in magazines and on record albums. The arrogance was refined, almost modest. And the grace! He was human glitter, all soul and performance. It was very winning and very powerful.

When Joss repeated, at the end, the icy little refrain, and then trailed away and stopped because that was how he wished to end it, Trigère noticed that everyone in the room had been touched. Joss himself, well-schooled in audiences and in moments, looked up, and for reasons of his own, broke the mood violently by introducing some fresh wild chords, flashing his playing-field grin, and in a clownish caricature of himself, broke into one of his best-known, exuberant compositions. The band tried to back him up and everyone hummed and yelled along. When it was over, Joss waved the guitar over his head for victory and handed it back to the leader. There was wild applause.

Ian, always the most starstruck of anyone, beamed at Trigère. "It's made the evening, old boy. Thank heavens I thought of having the band." He made his way to Joss and shook his hand.

Joss accepted his thanks and ran his hands through his shock of dark hair. "I need a drink," he said with his hooded smile. He was Joss again, young and impatient. "Where's my bloody glass? Someone has pinched it again."

Chin-Chan ran to fetch him a fresh one and poured him some wine.

Joss took a sip and looked over the rim of his glass, across the room at Djuna. He drank the wine, and the way she stood there looking at him, with her beautiful odd eyes and her clear smile, he felt as if he were drinking from her.

Trigère began to relax for the first time in weeks, which is why, when he looked across the room at Kat, he really saw her for the first time since she had spent the night in his apartment.

He had asked for something and she had offered it and he had taken it and then he had gone about his business. She had been very young—and he had been tired and greedy. He tried to remember, he tried to strain the experience back through his memory, but so much had come afterward, the new idea for the design of the film, twenty-hour days, the impossibilities of the terrain, the limited equipment, the pressure of time. Looking across the room at her now, he thought she was, after all, very charming with her little wire glasses, the silky red hair, the fine nervous hands. Suddenly he closed his eyes to block out what he had been blocking out all the time, which was simply the shame of having used her like that.

He reviewed her behavior to him over the last week and it had been perhaps a little subdued, but friendly. Of course, he had not paid that much attention. He would go and speak to her now.

She saw him coming. He saw her stiffen slightly. But she continued what she was doing, talking to Jack, drinking her drink.

"I'd like to have a word with this young lady," he said to Jack, feeling ridiculously pompous and wondering why he had chosen this moment, why he had not chosen another.

Jack melted away and Kat was looking up at him with a bright, prepared smile.

"The dailies were really terrific," she began to chatter nervously. "The tracking shots were a miracle. I—"

The sick, brave look on her face turned his guts over. "Do I owe you an apology?" he interrupted quietly. "I'm afraid that I . . . that I . . ." Then he realized it was all wrong, what he had said. What was the matter with him?

He decided to start over. "Would you—" But Maroga was suddenly standing there, taking his arm, saying, "Bernard, if we don't go downstairs this second they will close the restaurant on us. And I'm dying from hunger." She nodded coolly at Kat, who was already turning away.

Trigère watched her go. "And I am dying from weariness," he said to Maroga. "A quick dinner and then I must leave you. I'm going to get a good night's sleep for once."

But later, when he knocked on Kat's door, Chin-Chan answered.

"Kat almost never sleeps here," Chin-Chan said with an arch smile.

"I see," he remarked after a moment. And dropped it.

Chapter Nineteen

A week later Ian's bubble burst. Again. He could only handle, he estimated, another twelve days of production before his empty coffers and his shaky deal with Joseph came to light. He told no one.

Instead, he called Theodora in Juan-les-Pins and asked her to come up for a few days. "I miss you," he said and she replied, "Oh, dear, things must be dreadful."

"Not a bit of it, darling."

"Well, they are here. I've got nothing but tradesmen knocking on the door day and night."

"Then a week in the snow is just the thing," he replied, smooth as ever.

He hung up and wondered where Kat was. She was never around when he wanted her any more. He sighed and picked up the phone again, to make yet another long-distance phone call, the twentieth, perhaps, he had made that day. He had rung up people all over the world, looking for help, looking for money, and there was none for him anywhere. He left yet another message for Vito in Cannes. Vito had not returned any of his calls. Nor had anyone else. And the phone bill was going to be something. He looked up another address in his phone book and dialed again. Then he closed his eyes for a moment as he waited for the overseas operator to connect him with California.

Ian sincerely did not want to commit suicide. It seemed like such a beastly way to go out. Perhaps this call would bring fresh hope.

But the faceless secretary in that unknown office in Beverly Hills was saying, over the wire, "Mr. Parks is fishing in Cabo San Lucas and can only be reached in emergencies by radio-telephone."

Ian hung up and put his head in his hands. But the thoughts he was having were too awful to bear. Better do something quickly. So he straightened his tie (he had taken to wearing one every day to keep his spirits up), left the production office (the only one of the apartments which had a telephone), and took an elevator downstairs to the shops, where he charged a really smashing cashmere jacket for himself and a fur lap rug for Theodora.

Out on the slopes, the crew was almost ready to wrap for the day. Everyone was looking at his watch, waiting for the blessed moment when they could go in and adjourn to the bar, warm their feet and their throats, and get some space between today and tomorrow.

Joss, seated in the quaint gazebo, in full make-up, was also looking at his watch, but he knew tonight was an utter loss as far as seeing Djuna was concerned, unless he happened to run into her at one of the restaurants, and with seven of them to pick from, he didn't have much of a chance. With no phones in the apartments it was practically impossible for them to make—or keep—plans to meet.

Then Trigère was nodding to the assistant director. There was a hush. "Action!" rang out and Joss obediently did what he had been told to do. Take after take. They did it seven times. Trigère was, as usual, supportive, relentless.

Finally they were done. "It's a wrap!" the assistant director was calling. Joss saw Kat hurrying away and caught up with her.

"Let's have a drink," he said, throwing an arm around her shoulder.

"Later," she said. "I'm going to ski down."

"But it's practically dark." He frowned. "We're all going in the telecabines. Besides, where's your gear?"

She nodded toward the roundhouse. "Over there. I planned it this morning."

He was still looking at her disapprovingly. "It's late and there will be nobody around. It's not safe."

"*You* should talk. And besides, I never fall." She grinned at him cheekily.

"That's a good one. I've seen you ass backward many a time."

"Well, I meant a *bad* fall. Look, would you buzz off? I can take care of myself."

"True, darling." He kissed the tip of her nose. "But only so far. I'll meet you in the Snow Grill." He turned away and called over his shoulder, "Keep your knees together."

When Kat didn't appear after about half an hour, Joss walked to the window wall of the Snow Grill, hoping to catch sight of her, but the slopes were dark, almost black. He left the bar, took the elevator to the fifth floor, and knocked at her door but there was no answer. He went back to the bar.

Forty minutes after that, he was shouldering his way past the attendant outside the sauna and making his way into the gloom of the red-hot room where, after a few seconds, he was able to distinguish Ian, prone and naked on a slatted bench.

The older man looked up in surprise. "What are you doing in here with all your clothes on, you silly bugger?"

Joss grabbed him by his sweaty arms. "Come along," he said, dragging Ian from the room. "Those bastards in the main office are giving me a lot of trouble. Seems they don't give a shit that Kat hasn't come in from her run. They keep shrugging and telling me she's probably at the hairdresser or shopping." He was pushing Ian, who was only wrapped in a towel, out the door into the wet corridor. "Stupid bastards. You've got to talk to them for me."

When they found her, her face was white in the glare of the flashlights. She had been painfully trying to roll herself down the hill. When she distinguished Joss, who had skied to the spot with the ski patrol, she said weakly, "You're getting awfully good on the boards, McIvor." Then she fainted.

In the hospital, the surgeon took X-rays of her leg and ankle and announced there were no fractures.

"That's why it's going to hurt so much," he said pleasantly. "A break would have been cleaner. As it is, you've got a severe sprain. Stay off your feet for a few days."

Joss insisted on carrying her upstairs in his arms. In the elevator she said to him, "What's the matter?" and looked at him curiously.

"What do you mean what's the matter?" he said crossly. "Your ankle's the matter, that's what."

"No, I mean with you. Your face looked so white in the doctor's office. It still does."

"Well, you gave me a bad turn, didn't you?" The elevator door opened and he eased out sideways, carrying her carefully. "When I saw you, down like that in the snow, I felt very dicey."

"That's surprising. Coming from you."

"Why is it surprising?" He looked annoyed.

"You're a man of action," she teased. "Known for your heroic displays. Like when you almost killed yourself a few weeks ago and didn't turn a hair."

"Ah, but this is different. You're a *girl*."

"Oh Jesus!" And she collapsed against his shoulder laughing.

"Laugh if you like," he said, opening the door of her apartment and carrying her in. "I'm not denying you've got brains like us. But in some areas, my darling, ladies don't know how to take care of themselves. Now don't get all popeyed," he added with his mischievous grin. "I'd like to see you carrying *me* if I was hurt. How would Her Nibs manage *that*, I'd like to know."

He put her on the bed and began helping her out of her clothes. "Persist all you like in believing there shouldn't be any differences between men and women. Just don't ask me to say amen to it. Ah ha," he was slowly pulling her sweater off, "now here's a difference we can always count on." He bent suddenly and kissed the tip of her breasts through her camisole. He said after a moment, "Fancy them standing up like that."

Kat began to unbuckle his belt.

"Now look here," he said. "You've got that ankle—"

"*You* look here," she answered, drawing him out of his trousers.

It was better and different than it had ever been between them. He wondered why, and she wondered why, but when it was over he was content simply to float on it, while she lay looking at him thoughtfully.

He suddenly bounded out of bed. "I'd better get that heating apparatus on you."

"Joss?" she said after a moment.

"What, love?" He was fitting the hotpad around her ankle, frowning with concentration and pleasure, as he always did, she had noticed, when occupied by even the simplest of physical tasks.

The glow from the bedside lamp and the darkness of the room beyond lighted him in a way she thought she would like to remember always. The naked body, the

175

chestnut glints in his shock of dark hair, the aristocratic profile, the small scar on his left temple.

"What, love?" he repeated with a gentle look at her when she didn't speak.

She made, she thought, the first grown-up decision of her life.

"Nothing," she said. And blew him a kiss.

She had until now believed that complete honesty between a man and a woman was the essential ingredient in a relationship but she had begun to sense that it was like apples and oranges. The words didn't mean the same things as the feelings. *Didn't*. Period.

Sexual myth had been handed down by men since the beginning. Literature itself had been invented by males and it was they who had created all the words for love. They had fantasized and boasted and they had raped and they had lied to one another and to themselves. And the women had lied too; they had lied along the grain of the myth for their own gain, for their own survival, for their own pleasure and vanity. It was as if the myth was true simply because everyone believed it.

She wanted very much to tell Joss how she felt, and share with him, a man, the deep places of her soul. But she had just grown up.

That is to say, she had become cautious.

Kat's sprained ankle was an inconsequential mishap in the production history of *Lovers and Clowns* but it had its own effect on some of the players.

To Djuna, Joss' behavior over the next few days was incomprehensible. Traitorous. Cruel. He had abandoned her in order to wrap hotpads around that girl's ankle, to sit with her whenever he was off work, even to cook her meals.

"Why can't Chin-Chan do it?" Djuna hissed at him. She had skied to where they were shooting. "We see little enough of each other as it is."

"Because," he muttered through his teeth, "Chin-Chan

is a bitch, and couldn't care less about Kat." He glared at Djuna. "I just give her a bit of soup. Play backgammon with her." Didn't she understand loyalty to the fallen? It all seemed so simple to him. Kat was down. Therefore, she took priority.

"I'll bet," Djuna was saying, in a fury at him, in a fury at herself. For being irrational. For being betrayed.

"Look," he said sharply, "that's the way I am. Just because I love you doesn't mean I don't care for Kat—in a different way, yes. I mean, it's nothing like what I feel for you, you're—any way, if you don't understand it, I'm sorry, but I'm not changing." With that he walked off. Right into Conchita, who was waiting with a powder puff, ready to prepare him for the next take.

The magic words. I love you. Women give up their lives for that. For Djuna it meant hers had started. She stared after him. He had said it. He had thrown it out, just like that, in the middle of a sentence, as if, as if she was supposed to have known it already, as if she was supposed to have known it always.

She watched him take his place, listen to Trigère's instructions, and suddenly become an actor, displaying emotions and speaking words that were only lines on a piece of paper but that millions would see and hear and believe in. At the last second, just before they started, he glanced at her. It was only the briefest of moments, and it was a very proud and stubborn look.

She set her skis down the hill and went flying, her face wet with tears of thanks—and hope and fear.

Toward evening of the next day, Kat got out of bed and hopped into the living room. She tested the ankle gingerly, walked a few steps. It wasn't too painful. Perhaps tomorrow she would try getting her boots on so she could go outside.

She was about to sit down by the window to watch the last skiers making their runs when there was a knock on the door. She didn't feel like hopping all the way there, so she yelled "come in!" and sat down.

177

Trigère walked into the room. He was still in his anorak, and his boots were wet from the snow.

"Chin-Chan isn't here," she said at once.

He looked at her for a moment, then took off his anorak and threw it on the couch.

"May I stay a moment?" He didn't wait for an answer, but sat down in the chair opposite her.

They regarded each other for a moment, and she, nervous at his presence, at his silence, opened her mouth to speak, to say anything that came to mind.

"Don't," he said, very gently.

So she turned her head to the window and looked out at the slopes, wondering.

He lit a cigarette and they sat like that for a while as the darkness fell. She sensed that he started to speak several times, but he would always stop himself and take another drag off the cigarette.

Finally she said, and she knew she sounded resentful, but she was feeling a surge of rebellion at the way he always seemed to manipulate her, "Things not going well?"

He did not reply to this. Instead, after a moment, he asked, "How's your ankle?"

"Fine." What did he want? It couldn't be her. And if it was, goddamn it—suddenly she became so angry she could feel her face flushing—he could rot in hell. The circle of hurt and confusion he had started in her weeks ago was going round and round again.

She stole a look at him. He looked so defeated. So unlike Trigère. She felt betrayed all over again. She didn't want him to be defeated. She wanted him to be glorious. And she began to be afraid.

He sighed in the growing darkness and looked her over slowly.

She found herself saying, "You're messing up my image of you again." She paused for his answer and then looked up to see he was waiting, with his curious, sad look, for her to go on.

She rushed ahead with it, not caring how gross it sounded. "I'm not an automatic life-support system."

He got up and began restlessly pacing the room. Finally he said, "To take first things first, your image of me—and I assume that is what you have perceived me to be through my work—is not, really, my responsibility."

"Isn't it?" *Christ*, was she going to cry?

He walked to her chair and looked down at her. "No, my dear, it is not." Then he walked away again, saying, "As for your second blast," he paused, "is it so bad to be a —how did you say—a life-support system? Or to want one? Must we be ashamed if we need? If we give?" Then abruptly, "Why do I talk like this to you?" And he turned to the blackness outside the window glass, as if she were not there at all.

She waited for him to go on, while the pit of her stomach began to tell her a new story.

When he turned to look at her she saw the tired lines in his face and accepted, with gladness, how beautiful he was to her.

"May I get you anything?" he asked stiffly, glancing at the kitchen, then back at her.

"No thanks." She prayed Chin-Chan would not come back too soon. Tonight, one way or the other, she was going to get to know Bernard Trigère.

"Well, then," he was saying, "good night." He picked up his anorak, threw it over his shoulder, and left.

Chapter Twenty

The following evening Maroga was getting drunk in her faceless, rubber-foam beige-and-orange apartment.

She had been doing this every night for two weeks. Each morning, when she awoke to confront her hangover, her headache, her thirst, and her humiliation, she would angrily vow it was the last time. But each evening when she and Trigère left the Italian restaurant where they had their evening meal, he went directly to his apartment to work or to sleep and she, who had developed insomnia since her arrival at Mont Bleu, was forced to fill the hours —with something—until she could sleep.

At first she would pace her living room, a small glass of brandy in her hand, staring balefully through the window glass at the blackness where the slopes were and seeing only the reflection of the room behind her. The awful vinyl furniture that could never make you cozy. The neat, reproachful stack of new novels on the orange plastic coffee table; the novels she planned to read in the evenings and never did.

Sometimes she would go into the second bedroom, where her maid spent most of the evenings reading magazines and listening to popular songs on the portable record player Maroga had given her last Christmas. Maroga would stare at the girl sitting in such placid contentment with her modest commercial pleasures, and then back out again to resume pacing, holding conversations with herself, smoking a steady succession of cigarettes, filling the glass with brandy again and again. Just one more. So she could sleep.

Eventually she would begin staggering, bumping into furniture, and then she knew that if she went directly to her bed and lay down she might sleep. But sometimes her head whirled about inside so violently that she would have to go into the bathroom and throw up. Then the taste in her mouth would be vile and she would tremble and cry a little as she got back under the covers.

The night before, Trigère had been unable to have dinner with her. She had not gone downstairs at all, but remained in her apartment drinking, not caring about food until much later, when suddenly, ravenously hungry, she had staggered to the little refrigerator, found a thick slice of cold meat the maid had left, started to devour it . . . and choked. The inside of her head went hot and black as she accepted the fatal information that the piece of meat was stuck in her throat, that she could not breathe, that the maid was downstairs at one of the cinemas.

Should she try to suck in air, or dislodge the meat with her fingers or a spoon? Neither seemed possible—there wasn't time for anything; she was strangling. And she was overcome with outrage at the capriciousness of death. And how detestable, how ungrateful, how stupid she was to have brought about this unspeakable, silly suicide. It wasn't even tragic. It was vulgar and absurd.

She couldn't breathe in; very well, then, she would breathe out. She tried to cough. It was too late to try for help down the hallway. She would not make it to the door. For a time she knew she wasn't going to make it and then her brain saw a pin-point of light that conceivably (if she were good the rest of her life, God!) might allow her back into the world.

She held onto the edge of the stainless steel sink and concentrated on her tiny, bright vision. If she could keep from fainting she thought there might be room for a little air, just a little, until she reached the next stage, which was the fresh idea of surviving after all. It was going to depend on sheer will. She did not have the time or the wits to negotiate with God right now. Tears streamed down her face as she fought for air. And finally won enough to cough up the huge piece of meat.

And here she was, drinking again.

She knew she was beginning to look like hell. In the mornings she had to get up an hour earlier than usual to repair the ravages of the late night, the brandy, the fitful sleep. Extra doses of eyedrops, face-steaming, vitamins, aspirins. She wondered if she were becoming an alcoholic but she didn't think it was that. It was Mont Bleu. It was her life at Mont Bleu. It was her life, period. She had come to a dead end in this terrible place with its rabbit-warren apartments and blaring loudspeakers.

Robbie. He had turned his back on her and let her fall off the edge of the earth. And how she had loved him! His face floated before her in the window glass and she touched his mouth with her fingers, kissed his eyes.

After that she floated happy and sad with her memories. She poured more brandy, stood looking at the window glass and her reflection, talked to herself a bit, danced, and when the doorbell rang half an hour later, she staggered as she went into the hallway, opened the bathroom door and finally found the right one.

It was Theodora, her arms full of new novels, a box of chocolates, and a bunch of red and blue anemones.

"Darling! So glad you're still up. It took me hours from Antibes. The ice was *something*. Then Ian gave me dinner in a horrid little restaurant downstairs, but he says they're all like that. How are you? You look frightful. What on earth is the matter?" She deposited the things she had brought on one of the black vinyl hassocks and looked around. "But this is exactly like Ian's. Same colors and everything." She looked where the window was, where the snow was. "I'm so looking forward to skiing. Ian says the snow has been first rate."

Maroga staggered a bit and answered thickly. "How absurd, Theodora. To ski at your age."

Theodora frowned. "Oh, *dear*. A bit tight, are we? Well, I don't mind if I have a small one myself. Is that brandy? Lovely." She settled herself on the sofa and took out her cigarette case.

Maroga poured out a drink for her friend and, taking care to walk steadily, took it to the sofa. "Skiing is nothing but bravado and a wet bottom. A silly sport. Narcissistic. Neurotic."

"Neurotic? *Children* ski! How can it be neurotic? You see little *tots* on the slopes!"

"Merely another form of child exploitation," Maroga careened on. "They are forced to ski by their parents, who want to go on skiing vacations. And if they set the children to doing it as well, then they don't feel guilty."

"Oh, what nonsense! I can see you've been having a bad time of it. Even though Ian's been telling me such encouraging things about everybody."

Maroga looked at her. "This place is every nightmare I have ever had about hell, about death, about going down at the end of your life with no one to care. The *tramp tramp tramp* of boots along the wet corridors, a loud-speaker blaring at you every five steps, and every day that bright light on the snow until you could cry from it. A company of clowns. Yes, clowns—all of us!" She sat down heavily. "And the worst food in Europe."

"Darling, you've simply got a bad case of cabin fever. Why not escape for a day at the coast tomorrow? The sea air and the flowers, civilization, wonderful bread—it will make you right as rain again."

Maroga looked into her drink. "A good prescription for a reasonably depressed person. But I am beyond that. If I leave here I will never come back, Theodora. I will not come back anywhere."

"Tell me what's happened. I can't bear to see you like this." She lifted her glass. "And bottoms up, darling."

Maroga sat down on the window seat, stared at her lap. "I could tell you that I'm crazy. That would be one version. Another would be to tell you that my spiritual energies are depleted. That I have lost my nerve for living. Don't you see? Everything is a giant task. I wear thin, Theodora. I am used up."

"But Ian says you are splendid in the film."

"Ah, my work. Well, I keep myself intact for that. Haven't I always? The rest of the time I want to die. No. Not to die." And she smiled, remembering the night before. "I only want this terrible life to go away. This terrible me to go away."

"Location blues, darling." Theodora said firmly.

"No, it's much more than that. I'm tired of my act, don't you see? It has a hollow ring. Everything is repetition. Particularly the mistakes. I grow older, not wiser. Nobody notices. Nobody cares. But I thank you for listening. Thank you also for not giving me a lot of *merde* about being grateful for who I am. Who I *supposedly* am."

Theodora frowned. "Being rich and famous doesn't ease an ache in the heart or even make it go away faster, but you must admit it can make us comfy in our misery."

"Rich? Don't make me laugh. I am penniless."

"Well," Theodora shrugged, "so are we. It's a matter of how much we spend, not how much we have, that counts. I suppose."

Maroga laughed for the first time. "Yes, I suppose."

"There. You're smiling. You're not used up, Maroga. You're just lonely."

"I am not lonely!" Maroga shouted angrily. "How dare you say I am lonely! I crave solitude!" Then she put her head in her hands. "Oh, Theodora. I weep for Robbie."

Theodora sighed. "Darling, he is the most boring man in America."

"To you," Maroga muttered. "To you."

"I've always felt that if he hadn't thrown you over you would have done the same thing to him eventually."

"If that were true, if I have suffered and broken my heart over nothing, as you say, if I were capable of that kind of silliness, I should kill myself."

"Oh, rot. We're all silly. If we weren't, how would we all understand one another?" She paused. "Isn't Trigère keeping you company these days?"

"Yes, but he is so busy. He has his own craziness to deal with. He's got the film."

Theodora put her drink down. "Well, I think you'd better get yourself to bed. See you tomorrow. We'll have a lovely lunch." She stopped and frowned. "*Is* there a lovely place to lunch? Oh, never mind, we'll just have to make it lovely."

Maroga let her out and Theodora went back to Ian's apartment.

Ian was sitting up in bed, smoking a long cigar and reading *The Happy Hooker*.

"I thought you'd already read that," Theodora said to him crossly.

Ian examined his cigar. "When I was a little boy I always read books I loved over and over. Why should I be different now?"

Theodora pulled her sweater over her head.

"Christ," he said suddenly. "I wish you wouldn't do that."

She looked at him and realized he was staring at her head. The sweater had pulled her wig askew, so it was half on and half off.

"I don't know why you wear a wig anyway. You've got perfectly nice hair of your own."

Theodora removed the wig completely and stared thoughtfully in the mirror at her own hair. She pulled at a thin strand. "Frustration makes your hair fall out. It's a bloody wonder I'm not bald."

Ian changed the subject rapidly. "Did you find Maroga in?"

"In? What else can one be in this place but *in*? She was rather tight. And very miserable. Weeping over Robbie. Her life. You know. The usual."

Ian said calmly, "Actually, I think Maroga is finished."

"That's very likely what she thinks about you." Theodora sat down and began rubbing cream into her arms. "Why are we all such fools, Ian?"

"Darling, I'm simply not in the mood for philosophy now. Before you come to bed are you going to get us a lovely drink? Hot milk—with a dash of Scotch?"

"Do you suppose," she went on, "if we'd all used our heads we could have made everything come out differently? Better? I was very moved by Maroga's plight. I suppose it is the plight of all of us. Of the world."

Ian sighed and put his book down. "What is this fucking plight we are all in?"

Theodora closed up the cream jar. "We're fools, Ian. Everyone is a fool."

"I'm not a fool," he replied mildly. "Don't be an ass."

She opened her suitcase and took out a nightgown. She stared for a moment at the rumpled clothes spilling out of the suitcase. "Oh, the hell with it if everything gets wrinkled. I'm not in the mood to unpack tonight. Morning is for regrets."

She crossed to the bathroom. "The driver told me all

the gossip on the way up. Not that there was much. Sounds as if you've all been behaving yourselves beautifully. He says Chin-Chan has a crush on Joss. I wonder if she's given him any of her fancy Chinese massages. Dear Chin-Chan. An inscrutable Oriental she is not."

Ian reached behind him to plump up the pillows. "There's no one quite like you, Theodora." He glanced across the room at her. "On the whole, I think I've missed you. Did you miss me?"

She considered. "I never do the first few days. Even the first few weeks. It's heaven doing exactly what I like. Even if we don't spend all that much time together when you're home, still I always have to be ready. Have things ready. You know. But yes. I suppose I'm glad to see you."

"Well then!" His eyes twinkled. "Will I get my hot milk?"

Several apartments away, Baker and Djuna, their marriage several decades behind Ian's and Theodora's in chronological history but far older in defeat and confusion, were also in bed. Djuna was asleep. Baker was thrashing about in the growing hopelessness of his situation.

To Baker, the appearance of Joss in their lives had been the reason for everything that was so terribly wrong now. One might say that a more sensitive and intuitive man would have seen it as the result of the problem, not its cause. On the other hand, the phenomenology of cuckoldry is rarely characterized by sensitive or intuitive reaction on the part of the victim. Betrayal is one of the most painful of human experiences. The distortions that result from it are full-blown.

The reason Baker had not spoken out was that he was still dancing around the size of the issue, still describing it to himself as only a mildly alarming flirtation. He would not confront Djuna with the accusation that she and Joss were lovers, because he simply could not believe it. So he struggled all around it, felt terrible all of the time, and remained stuck in the fixed notion that if they had not come to France, if she had not been flattered by Joss,

Djuna would not have been "spoiled." She would not have "changed" and none of this would have happened. Not that their marriage had ever been all that successful (and he groaned to himself as mutilated images of their sex life flashed by) but it had been, until France, contained. It had been safe from outside dramas. Djuna didn't know about Lily Dunne—and besides, what he and his agent did was his affair.

Impatiently, Baker shifted his position and put a pillow over his eyes. His requirements had always been so simple. Perhaps too simple for Djuna. He had wanted to be an actor, a successful one. And if the breaks came, a star. He had wanted a nice home in Beverly Hills, a good-looking driveway, a game room, a pool, and money to gamble with. A wife who loved him and who was pretty and smart. Friends. Nice Christmases. Peace. Now and then, a novelty piece of ass.

He sighed and turned over again. It was getting like a broken record. What He Wanted. If Djuna asked for a divorce, would he be able to find someone soon to replace her? What faceless woman would share his life, sit at his table? Djuna had been the culmination, the first prize to all of his expectations. The package had been beautiful.

He had not handled it well. But neither had she. He felt she was violently flawed, marked in some way he did not understand. What was the dark secret of her ruthless, female search for—what? Perhaps women were all the same. Possessed, devious, far more complicated than men.

He listened to Djuna's breathing for a while. He began to stroke himself there, in the darkness, selecting images.

Trigère had spent the evening alone. He stood at the railing of the terrace in a thick sweater and a windbreaker, his gloved hands holding a last cup of coffee before bed.

He had completed all the necessary revisions and notes for Monday's shots. Tomorrow, Sunday, he would give himself a holiday. He would spend some time with Maroga, whom he had neglected lately. He had been too selfish and self-absorbed in Nice to see that she was at the end of her rope. He didn't like the signs. She was drinking, she was frightened, she was desperately lonely. He must spend more time with her. The main thing was to get through this film. And honor their old acquaintance.

He looked down the five stories to the ghostly pool where steam rose in thick mists, the underwater lamps shimmering, making the whole scene move in rhythm with the wavy lights. On the shadowy verandas the deck chairs were lined up symmetrically in tidy, expectant rows. The cables for the tows and the telecabines were invisible against the pristine scene, piled high now with fresh night snow.

How long had they been in this place? He had come to feel, here, uncomfortably dislodged from his past. Mont Bleu had encircled him in a way no location ever had. In a way that was beginning to disturb him. The only moments he felt connected to any idea of the future were when he was with Kat. Whenever he looked at her he felt a seminal replay of things remembered, a stirring of things to come.

But really, the girl was too young. Better leave it. She was not someone to bury oneself in, to float on. She would require attention.

He turned and went inside.

His last thought before he floated off to sleep—and in the morning he thought it might even have been a dream —was that he should take Kat under his wing. He had not had a disciple for a long time. She already had a substantial store of practical and technical knowledge. She seem-ed to have taste. And in her odd, American way, she was literate, imaginative, original. He owed someone a chance, to pay back the one he had been given long ago.

In the morning Chin-Chan knocked on his door to tell him that Theodora had asked him to lunch at half past one. He didn't want to go in the least. He had planned to read and sleep during the day and spend the evening with Maroga, but when one o'clock came he found himself hungry, wanting a drink, even a little restless. So he took a shower, dressed, and presented himself at the Spencers' door at the appointed time.

Everyone was outside on the terrace, where Theodora had arranged for a long, cloth-covered table set with drinks and little pots of pâté and baskets of bread. The sun was high, very hot and bright. But the north railing of the terrace was still packed with hard snow. The mountain air smelled crazily like summer. It was pretty to stand there with the ice-cream peaks in a perfect circle around them.

A record player, commandeered from Maroga's maid, played an old French ballad to the open sky and the sound was sweet and memory-laden.

"How festive," Trigère murmured to Theodora appreciatively. "How nice."

"Oh, well," Theodora replied. "It's all I really do, all I *get* to do, isn't it? To try to make other people's lives festive? I've ordered up a wonderful soup that we'll have in a bit, and marvelous things to make our own sandwiches with. Get yourself a drink and do go and talk to Maroga. I find her in a shocking state. We *must* do something about her. I'm counting on you, Bernard."

"She is on her own course. She'll get right or she won't. We can be supportive, that is all."

Theodora looked at him impatiently. "It's a real life we're talking about. Not one of your films. How can you be so detached about human suffering? About our dear friend?"

"On the contrary," he replied lightly. "I err in the opposite direction. Don't you know by now that directors not only have an obsessive compulsion to rearrange the furniture of every room they enter but that they also grow to feel they are required to play God to their friends?"

"She's still wild about Robbie, you know."

"She remains obsessed with the obsession, yes. She has nothing better to do. Nothing else to do."

"What has happened to everyone up here? You've all jumped into different skins. Maroga has taken to brandy as if it were mother's milk. Joss and Baker's wife are having some sort of an affair. Do you know about it? And can you imagine, last night Chin-Chan was trapped in one of the elevators and when they got her out she was stark naked!"

He smiled patiently. Theodora's prattle was putting him on edge. He also noticed she had not invited Kat. "I assure you, I cherish Maroga. But never forget she is an actress. That makes her very different from us. There is far more slippage to her reality."

"Nonsense. She is an intelligent woman. A woman first, an actress second."

"She has been a film star for over twenty years. You don't think that doesn't have its effect? Intelligence has nothing to do with it. People like her have a thousand mirrors held up to them all of the time. You've been around this business as long as I have. You really think an actress is like you or me?"

Theodora studied him. "Go and be sweet to her. I have things to do."

She went off, a cloud of bright hair on a willowy neck connected to a trailing, gauzy gown. She was positively pre-Raphaelite. His eyes followed her and he wondered for the first time who she really was.

Ian, standing nearby, noticed, and was suddenly beside Trigère, murmuring, "For an old girl you've got to admit she's got style."

Trigère looked at Ian in mild surprise.

"I'm feeling a bit mellow," Ian said, catching the other man's look and waving his glass in explanation. "I'm on my third drink. It's Sunday. And we're on schedule." His eyes twinkled suddenly. "That is, we would be if we had a schedule. Ever make a picture like this, Bernard? Don't answer that question. I know you are going to bring it all right in the end, no matter what."

"Are you going to get me my helicopter?"

"Oh dear dear *dear!* Must we go through that again? We can't afford it, Bernard. Really, what's got into you lately? *You* don't need gimmicks like that."

Bernard squinted at the massive peaks. "I need the shots,

Ian. I need to get big. I need to get high, to get close."

Ian looked into his drink. "Then pray for a miracle. Pray for Vito."

"Vito?" Bernard looked at Ian in surprise. "Has he surfaced again?"

"He rang me this morning. He's working on Henry Reed, this very minute, in Cannes."

"That American you had the lunch on the beach for?"

"The dreaded same." Ian turned to include Baker, who had come up to them. "I'm telling Bernard what I just told you. About our possible good news."

Baker munched on a handful of nuts. "Someone just told *me* about Chin-Chan. Where do you suppose she was going—or coming from—last night when she was found bare-assed in the elevator?"

Ian frowned. "My wife says everyone's gone bonkers since we got up here. She does exaggerate. But it *was* very odd. Chin-Chan has done five pictures with me and nothing like this has ever happened. I picked her up in Hong Kong when I was making *Blue Fox*. Got her straight from a very good finishing school. She's been absolutely everywhere with me."

"About this good news," Baker went on, "I assume Henry Reed knows that if he comes in he's got to kick up everyone's back pay."

Ian looked hurt. "My dear boy, hasn't everyone been paid every week on the dot since we arrived at Mont Bleu?"

"That's not the issue." Baker put another olive in his mouth. "No one was paid for the time in Nice."

"Let's not worry that one now," Ian said hastily. "Not on a bonnie Sunday like this. It's all going to come right. You'll see." He smiled and moved away, his tall figure erect and stately.

"He's full of it," Baker commented sourly.

Trigère shrugged. "He's a producer. Anyway, I think they suffer more than we do. Let's get another drink before lunch."

They moved toward the table.

Baker decided he would call Lily that evening and tell

her Ian's news. She was still in London. Maybe she would come over for a few days. He suddenly realized how much he missed her. She was comfort and strength, hard-nosed Hollywood sanity and fresh news from blessed home. In his mind he saw her kneeling before him, her sleek hair shining. New color came into his face. He looked about him with a keen rush of assurance.

Djuna was across the terrace, talking to Maroga, who was saying, "He's so good, your husband. I didn't see it at first, I was so preoccupied with myself . . . as usual. But he is marvelous to work with." And she meant it, because it was Sunday, because she wanted everything to be nice, because she wanted to float into the mindless afternoon forever.

Djuna was glancing at her husband. She had never thought, not really, that he was so exceptional an actor. There was a heaviness to him always, the same heaviness he carried around in his behavior, in his life. Up there on the screen, he was always, somehow, Baker, pretending for a lot of money that he was someone else. Even when he had won the Oscar and they had shown a clip of his winning performance she had looked at it and thought: He won for *that*?

Was it always thus? Did spouses of actors and actresses never feel the performance? Did they only, as she, see the dreaded dailiness, the mannerisms, the embarrassments?

She looked across at Joss, dressed in his usual navy sweater with the tip of a white shirt showing, his dark chestnut hair bright in the Alpine sunlight. There were sun-wrinkles around his eyes and on the bridge of his nose. Where had he got that hawkish, aristocratic nose? From some ancient, titled ancestor?

He had been watching her, and now they smiled across the terrace at each other.

Djuna loved Joss with all her heart and cherished in a profound way what had happened to her because of him. There she stopped. She could not take the idea one step farther. She was too afraid. It was more than the fact she was married to Baker. It had to do with Joss himself. He was young and famous. She was middle-aged. And—they were on location.

She would have been very much surprised had she known what was going on behind his handsome smile. The fact was that his preoccupation with What Am I Going to Do about Her had been growing daily.

He couldn't possibly marry her. It was out of the question. She was too old. He didn't want a wife anyway, not yet, and when he did marry he wanted children, didn't he? Or did he? Yes, he thought he did. He deserved a go at a son, after all. And Djuna was getting on for that.

But how to keep her for himself? She could divorce Baker and come to live with him. But shit, that wasn't going to work, not for more than five minutes, not the way he lived. How could she possibly fit in? It wasn't as if he came home every night carrying his briefcase, all ready for his supper. There wasn't any home, and supper was never until after midnight, and there were always people —young people—and things to be done. How could he ask her to give up her life to wait in hotels? Besides, what if he changed his mind, what if he got tired of her? Then he'd be stuck. They would both be stuck with their mistake. If only she were younger! Then she wouldn't have all that much to give up, and the whole idea wouldn't be so heavy for either of them.

He glanced at her again. He loved that wide, slightly tilted expression of her mouth, the fine wrinkles around her eyes, the suntanned face and hands that were no longer young. But he also feared them. They told a story that would never be his. Why had she married a clod like Baker? Why did she have to be so old? Why did everything have to be screwed up when two people loved each other?

When lunch was over, Trigère felt he could decently withdraw from the party, so he went looking for Jack. He found him in the first place he looked—the Snow Grill. The young cameraman was sitting with Kat in a rounded red booth by the window. He greeted Trigère with "Welcome to the outcasts' corner. We who were not invited to Theodora's party are drinking our lunch."

Trigère threw a large pad of paper on the table, called the waiter and sat down. "Let's plan our aerial shots, Jack. Let's pretend we're going to make them."

Jack took a sip of his beer. Then he grinned and reached in his back pocket. "I just happen to have here a terrific little map of the entire valley and all the peaks." He laid it on the table. "I also just happen to have the telephone number of Samuelson's in Paris. I knew we'd win this one."

Trigère looked at the young man thoughtfully. He had not made himself popular, this blunt, know-it-all soldier of fortune from America. He drove Hans crazy with his quick impatient air of superiority. But he was hardworking, meticulous, and a highly experienced cameraman for his age. Also, he had a natural flair for the alternative. Most importantly, he had understood instantly every idea Trigère had suggested to him.

"We haven't exactly won it, you know," he said to the young man.

"But you're pretty sure, aren't you?"

Trigère hesitated. "Sure enough to be here with you." He looked at Kat, who had remained completely silent. "Why not move so I can be between you," he said to her. "It will be easier for you to see what we're doing. I had a word with Ian upstairs about you. He has agreed to let you work with me. All those damn-fool errands you run for him may advance your knowledge of the business, but not of the craft. That is"—he paused—"that is, if you'd like to. It would be mostly following me around."

"Thank you," she said quietly. And knocked over her drink.

Extract from Kat's Journal

Just back from seeing this week's dailies. Really, Trigère is brilliant! Even Jack is willing to admit that now. In Nice Jack never had a good word to say about anyone. But when we got up here, and suddenly everyone had to pitch in and do anything and everything, Jack's documentary experience turned out to be very helpful to Trigère. Also, Hans (who is really too old for this—why doesn't he retire???) is superslow and indecisive. It was taking him hours longer to do anything, and he seemed afraid to even try, so of course Trigère got pretty impatient. Trigère has come to rely on Jack, not only because he is more reliable and confident than Hans but also because Jack has studied (which I didn't know) Trigère's visual style. He is ready to work to that every time, no matter what the problems are.

We *may* get a helicopter. Depending on what size it is, Jack says maybe I can go up with him. He says it won't do a damn thing for me but buffet me around a lot, but I want the experience.

Chin-Chan told me that Joss—for sure—is having an affair with Djuna. Chin-Chan likes making me miserable because she is jealous—not only of my relationship with Joss, but also because of Trigère taking a (professional) interest in me. Maybe Djuna and Joss *are* having an affair, but if they are, it is pretty non-existent because I have been with Joss almost every night. And I really can't imagine them together. What would they talk about????

Djuna really pisses me off and reminds me of my mother. She thinks she's the cat's ass because she's beautiful and spends her husband's money tastefully, when all she's ever done—like Mom—is make a big empty nothing of her life. Neither of them have ever done anything really on their own. They live like parasites on their husbands, and all their education ever seemed to do for them is to make them want more and more goodies. Without ever paying anything or anyone back.

In all honesty I must add that I know I haven't exactly got it all together myself. But I'm beginning to understand that because I'm a woman things happened to me generations before I was even born that I will continue to act out with my life, if I'm not watchful. It's easy to slip into just wanting to be taken care of. And along that line, my feelings about Joss haven't been too wonderfully healthy. But at least I'm working on myself.

I can't figure out Trigère. *Can't*. And now that I'm working for him, I'm terrified of him all over again. He's friendly but *very* impersonal. I am also friendly. But very impersonal.

Chapter Twenty-one

On Wednesday morning a long black limousine wearing a frosty halo of ice pulled up as close as it could to one of Mont Bleu's nine entrances. Lily Dunne, Henry Reed, a mink-wrapped blonde, and Vito descended into the vast, watery slush of the parking area. All around them, rainbow-clothed guests searched for their cars under mystery mounds of snow, called to dogs, scolded children, started the new day.

Henry and Vito and the blonde left their luggage with the chauffeur while they went in search of information, rooms, and the whereabouts of Ian and the company. Lily carried her smart canvas traveling bag with the alligator handles straight to the nearest elevator, and after riding up and down in several more, always to be deposited in the wrong place, finally found the door of Baker and Djuna's apartment.

"This place is a nightmare," she announced to Djuna, who appeared at the door sleepy and in a robe.

Djuna replied with a tight smile. "Do you want some coffee? I'll show you your bedroom. Baker wants you to stay with us but we'll understand, of course, if you feel you'd be more comfortable in one of the hotels."

"I'll never find it." Lily took off her black fur parka and walked to the bright expanse of window. "God! From here it's beautiful." She quickly scanned the crowded slopes. "Where are they shooting today?"

"We can't see from here." Djuna came to the window and pointed. "Round to the right, there. There's an especially steep run they've roped off. We'll go over if you like. It'll take me a minute to dress."

"Sure. And I'd love the coffee. No, go on. I see it's made and I'll pour it myself." Lily reached into her purse for one of her little cigars.

Djuna went into the bedroom.

"Have they shot any interiors?" Lily called after a moment. She had settled herself in the little dining nook by the kitchen and was stealthily looking through Baker's and Djuna's mail.

"Some," Djuna called. "More is scheduled, even though conditions are very difficult and Bernard would rather do it back at the studio. It's part of Ian's deal with the owner of the place. This picture is going to be the most expensive commercial ever made for a second-rate ski resort." Djuna appeared now, brushing her hair.

Lily inhaled deeply and blew smoke out her nostrils. "Well, Santa Claus and his busy helper have come to save the day. I drove up with Vito and Henry Reed."

Djuna stopped brushing. "That's terrific. Then Henry is in for sure? Oh, Lily, what wonderful news! You can't imagine the anxiety around here lately."

Lily smiled kindly. Of course she could imagine. Almost every evening Baker had called her from the public telephone at the end of the hallway. He had also said he missed her. Which was partly why she had come.

"I want to hear all about it," she said now. "Will these boots be okay?" She stared down at the loden suede beauties. "I had to buy a lot of new crap to come up here. What'll I ever do with the stuff in California?"

Out on the slope, Ian blinked and decided it was definitely not a mirage he was seeing. It was, indeed, his corruptible Italian partner trudging through the snow, his cheeks pink as a boy's, his tie flapping at one ear, his custom-made striped silk suit brilliant and somehow cheap in the pure alpine sun. Next to him, almost romping, came Henry Reed, sweating in a cashmere overcoat, and behind him strode the silver blonde.

"It's not the same girl," Maroga observed idly to Baker. Everyone had stopped to watch the trio descend on them. "He must have a whole brothel of them."

Baker squinted. "You mean it's not the one he had at the luncheon that day? How can you tell? She doesn't have her Davy Crockett hat on but she looks exactly the same to me. Anyway, who cares? This must mean something, those two showing up. This must be it, babe."

"Look, there comes your wife. There by the deck, and isn't that your agent with her?"

Baker went off at a run and Maroga turned to the wardrobe girl, who had been standing by them. "Can you believe it, Conchita? Are we to be saved after all?"

They were indeed to be saved. The news went around quickly when they broke for lunch. During the final morning shot, Vito and Henry had stood a little apart, with Ian. There had been much shaking of hands and Chin-Chan was summoned to take notes. Lunch was served in the outdoor restaurant, and instead of the usual gossip and chatter, everyone watched the corner table where Ian and Theodara sat with the new arrivals.

A novice skier came careening wildly down the gentle slope by the deck restaurant and plowed into the tables head-first. He was not hurt. Everyone laughed and Joss picked him up and loudly ordered him a martini. Even if he was only twelve. There was a general air of joviality and promise.

Kat took her camera from her bag and started filming. Everyone mugged and waved at the lens, even Trigère, and when he did, a cheer went up from the crew. And Kat's heart, unaccountably, leaped into her throat. The sun was hot and yellow, and the snow blazed with it all around them as the company celebrated their good fortune with spaghetti and beer.

Lily was taking a shower. Baker was in the living room, reading over his pages for the next day. Djuna was on the terrace, looking out at the dark, silent slopes. Baker appeared in the doorway to the terrace. "Don't we have any tonic? Lily likes it with her gin sometimes."

Djuna held the fur collar of her parka closer around her chin. "No. Sorry."

"Well, I wanted some too. You know I like gin and tonic."

"Yes, I know." She stared up at the sky. You could never see that many stars in Beverly Hills.

"Would it be too much to ask you to take care of a few little things around here? Like seeing that the refrigerator is stocked with what we need to give someone a goddamn drink?"

She threw her little knife. "Baker, are you and Lily lovers?"

He faced her with his cold actor's mask. "Come again?"

"Are you?"

"You're being ridiculous. And I can't stand here any longer. I'm freezing."

"Then put a jacket on. I need to talk to you."

"But I don't need to talk to you." He turned and went inside. He closed the glass door and she saw him sit down again with his script.

Baker stared at the words and felt his heart pounding. She had *always* ruined everything. She knew how to choose her moment, just as she had chosen it at the end of his mother's long illness, just as she had chosen it the night he had won the Oscar. On both occasions she had managed to cut him down, expose him in some terrible way. She had hated and resented his mother, and even though she continued to deny it, she was, at bottom, unimpressed by and uninterested in his career.

Damn! He threw the pages on the floor. What goddamn business was it of hers if Lily was his friend, his dearest friend? Lily was always on his side, she cared about him, she made him feel fine. He never had to pretend to be anything with Lily. He just had to be himself—and it was a goddamn relief from the constant obstacle course of Djuna's finicky, emotional requirements and her dissatisfaction with him and her life. What right did she have, anyway, to ask him about Lily after the way she was carrying on with McIvor? And why hadn't he ever confronted her with it? Why hadn't he asked her straight out—like she had done just now to him?

But he knew the reason he hadn't asked. It would have opened up something exactly like this.

There was no going back from here. Whatever happened, everything was forever changed between them, and in plain sight. He mourned for their sad, past life with its soft, rounded corners and places to hide.

Djuna came inside. "Well?" she asked, and her voice was hard. She took off her parka and lighted a cigarette. "You haven't answered my question."

"Djuna, for God's sake," Baker said angrily, in a low voice. "What do you want to start something like this for? She's in her bedroom now. She'll be coming out soon and she'll hear us. Why don't you go and get dressed? We're due downstairs in half an hour."

Djuna looked at him. "I don't like her staying in this apartment. I want her to go to a hotel. Tonight."

He rose heavily and went to the window. His own reflection obscured what was beyond it. "May I remind you," he said after a moment, "that Lily is not only our guest and my close friend of many years, but she is also my agent—half of my professional life. And what's more, she has been very helpful to Ian and Vito in handling Henry Reed and I don't want any more of your goddamn *crap!*"

Djuna stood up. "You know what, Baker? You and I, we save the best part of ourselves, somehow, for others."

He stared at her and said nothing.

After a moment she went on. "Frankly, I don't think you even like me."

He remained with his back to her. But he could see her in the black glass with all the swirls of cigarette smoke curling about her. "Do you like me?" he asked.

She took a breath. "Not much."

"Is that why you started fooling around with McIvor?"

"I was always lonely with you, Baker."

"Pathos is such an inexpensive emotion."

"That's a line from the picture."

"So what?" He turned away.

The heady musk of Lily's perfume preceded her arrival in the living room. Her blonde hair was pinned sleekly into a bun at the nape of her neck. She was wearing a black velvet pant-suit, and diamonds in her ears.

"I feel terrific." She grinned, waving her little cigar, flashing her diamonds. "A day in the snow, gallons of your hot water, new clothes from the undies out. And no telephone. When are we due at dinner?"

"How about a drink while Djuna gets ready?" Baker said, too brightly. "Then we'll go." He moved toward the little bar, Lily perched on a stool near him, and Djuna left the room.

It was cold in the bedroom and Djuna shivered. She opened the doors to the wooden armoire, cheap and mass-produced but smelling of pine and winter secrets. First, what to wear?

And how to identify and collect all the pieces and squares one was in a given moment to make an authentic self? Lily, Baker, Joss, this room, Mont Bleu, the picture, their home in Beverly Hills, her girlhood, the lingerie drawer she had just opened, her reflection right now in the mirror. Tonight, tomorrow, yesterday. She found the sheer, wispy stockings she was looking for and sat down on the bed to put them on.

It simply could not be done. All the sides of oneself could not be felt at once. A private thread ran through the moments and thus connected each to the other, but every single moment wore its own scenery. You gave it your full attention. Perhaps that was how you survived. The white or the beige skirt? She held one up. Then the other.

She thought, I can never decide whether eye shadow makes me look older or younger. There is a definite effect when I darken my lids like this, but is it my effect? Is it too theatrical? Too mature? Ever since Joss came into my life I want to look as natural as I can. I don't want to be phony with him. But of course I *am* phony with him a lot, I can't help it. I'm protecting myself so I won't be hurt.

Lately I've begun to see how lost Baker is. How disconnected. I honestly don't think he feels he betrayed me in the slightest by his relationship with Lily. That is what is so wasteful. That he understood me so little. And that for so long I understood him so little. Looking back, I see what amateurs we have been. Two scared people trying to please each other according to rules other people made up. I'm going to try to be more honest with Joss about who I am. And not be afraid.

In the living room, Baker and Lily sipped their drinks. Baker felt overwhelmed, manic. He tried to surface. "Then everything is signed and sealed?"

Lily smiled languidly. "And delivered. Henry and his people are in all the way. His greedy little eyes are all lit up at the pretty package he's going to tie up, including what he can realize by exploiting Joss. He's already talking about an album—"

"But that's bullshit. Joss doesn't sing in the picture. He's going to write the title song that will go over the credits. That's all."

Lily pointed her little cigar at him. "Believe me, Joss will sing in the picture or Henry will know the reason why."

"You mean perform?" Baker asked incredulously. "It doesn't go with the character!"

Lily shrugged.

"Jesus," Baker looked at her. "Trigère will shit."

"You like Trigère then?"

Baker considered. "Yes. As a director, yes. He's taught me a lot."

"So it hasn't all been wasted."

"Well, no. Only," he paused, "I think my marriage is over."

It was her chance. At last. "Are Djuna and McIvor having an affair?"

He looked at her with his heavy expression. "So you've

heard it, too. I don't know. I suppose so. You know what location is like."

"Do you still love her?"

"I wish you wouldn't ask me that, Lily."

She looked at him steadily. "I thought I had the right. Sorry."

He said abruptly, "It's just that I don't know where I'm at. Can you bear with me?"

"Of course I can," she replied softly. "And I think I'll move to one of the hotels tomorrow. You're welcome, of course, any minute, any hour."

"I need you, Lily," he said, suddenly desperate.

She saw his pain and his hope, and she was happy. Once she had him all to herself she would make very sure he never left her. She held the cards now, and didn't she know all the ways? After the divorce from Djuna, she and Baker would be married. At somebody's house. Somebody big. It would be very elegant and very well reported. She wondered if she was too old to wear white.

There was a festive air at Ian's table. A waiter was stationed at each end and the maître d'hotel hovered close by. There were bowls of fresh flowers and at each place there were three wine glasses and an extra array of silver.

Theodora and Ian waved cheerily to the American trio as they came into the restaurant from the dim, noisy corridor outside, where people were still hurrying by in ski clothes, hauling bags from the supermarket, flirting, going to a bar, to the movies, to the sauna.

Ian put Djuna next to him, patted her hand. "You look devastating. As always."

The door to the restaurant opened again, this time with a violent swing, and Joss came in. He was wearing a silk shirt and the velvet jacket in hunter green. He had just washed his hair and it was still wet.

"Dear Joss," Theodora murmured. "He always bursts in like a boy. Now, let's see. Where shall he sit. Ian?"

But Joss was going to decide that for himself. He walked directly to the empty chair next to Djuna, sat down with an innocent air, nodded his head at everyone, and rapidly drank a glass of water. Baker chewed on his cigar thoughtfully.

After a moment of unscheduled silence, Vito said tiredly, "This place is a piece of shit, Ian."

But Ian's eyes were glittering with triumph. Everything was going to be all right. Henry was in, the picture was as good as finished, and absolutely nothing could bother him tonight.

"Shut up, Vito," he said benevolently.

Vito eyed his drink with a weary smile and changed the subject. "How much work is left to do in the studio?"

"Here comes Bernard now. He can tell you in more detail."

Bernard and Maroga sat down together, at Baker's end. During the greetings and the fresh ordering of drinks, Joss reached nonchalantly into his pocket and dropped a small velvet jeweler's case into Djuna's lap. After a moment she slipped it into her purse. Then, pretending to be looking for a cigarette, she opened the box and, on a white satin lining inscribed Mapin & Webb, London, she saw a tiny, brilliant diamond in the shape of a heart. Her hand went to the little gold chain at her throat.

He had given her a present. He had sent to London for it—when? on what day? It must have only just arrived and he had not been able to wait until they were alone to give it to her. She wanted to cry. She looked at his wet hair, still matted over his forehead, and the intense, almost embarrassed way he met her quick, surprised glance, and she thought her heart would break. Why was that? Why on earth was that?

Henry Reed arrived. And his blonde.

"Christ, I forgot his dolly!" Ian murmured and quickly ordered the hovering waiter to set another place.

"It's been a good day. Very interesting." Henry settled himself and inspected the ladies. He glanced at Ian. "Trigère and I had a good talk and I'm confident everything is going to be swell."

"Yes," Trigère said, and added casually, for Ian's benefit, "I explained to Henry. About the helicopter. We are getting an Alouette sent here in a few days."

Vito eyed Trigère. "Helicopter shots? Hans is going to get into a helicopter? And go up? Waiter, another vermouth, if you please."

Henry looked puzzled. "I thought his name was Jack. The fellow you introduced me to."

"Yes, yes." Theodora took charge. "Hans is our director of photography, Henry. Jack is his operator."

Ian frowned at Theodora for interrupting and smiled at Vito. "We absolutely have to bring you up to date on everything. But first a toast!"

They all raised their glasses. "To Henry!" Ian cried. "So very glad to have you aboard." Ian looked as if he were about to cry tears of joy. And why not? He had been saved.

Everyone drank.

The blonde tugged at Joss' sleeve. "I have every record you ever made. I've seen you in concert three times. I'm really glad to meet you."

"Thank you very much." Joss inclined his head gravely. "It's lovely to hear that, I promise you."

It was Joss the celebrity, a Joss Djuna scarcely knew. And she thought, as she had once or twice before, that he wore his fame with a good deal of grace. On a few occasions in the nightclub when fans had approached their table, he had met their homage with the same serious, polite attention, the same princely inclination of the head. The boy who had given her the diamond was real enough, but so was this remote, internationally known figure sitting next to her.

His authenticity would lie in the sum of all his parts. Would she get to know them? She watched him out of the corner of her eye. After a time, his very presence next to her acted as reassurance. She found comfort in his sharp, familiar profile. She could almost feel the warmth of his body. And she began to believe again that all was possible.

Everyone had another drink before dinner, and then

there were a great many dishes served, all ordered by Ian that afternoon. Wine was poured, and for some, the party grew more gay.

Baker began to feel better. Food and drink. Lily sitting next to him. He could smell her perfume. Henry had treated him very respectfully, and Trigère praised his work in the picture to everyone. Tomorrow was another day. He exchanged glances with Djuna once or twice, and while her eyes came back at him like a private mirror of all their shared sadness, it was suddenly different from ever before. They had crossed the line. It hurt more looking back than ahead.

Henry, Ian, and Lily did most of the talking, with Theodora interrupting constantly. Maroga, who hated to have anyone order food for her, did not eat, but stared in a sulky rage at her dinner and drank more wine than anyone else, but she remained pleasant to Trigère, and they talked quietly to each other. Joss and Djuna remained silently obsessed with the presence of each other and the idea of the diamond. Vito, already weary of these people, and convinced for the third time this week that he had a heart condition, surreptitiously felt his pulse every few minutes.

The party broke up early. Tomorrow was a working day. The blonde asked for a doggie bag, and everyone smiled except Henry.

Chapter Twenty-two

The entire company was out on the slopes when the sleek green-and-white air bird dissolved out of infinity, out of the vast gauzy space to the south where the sky hung wide and silvery over the picture-pretty coast they had left so many weeks ago.

They cheered. Even Hans grinned as the helicopter

came in over the valley. The growing sound of its rotors as it hovered nearer was motivated music to their jubilant mood. Maroga turned a cartwheel in the snow and her wig fell off. She sat there, laughing and waving it at the chopper. Kat took pictures of that and of Jack and Trigère, standing together, squinting into the sky, their profiles lighted from the side by the metallic rays of the falling sun. Later, the picture would be published everywhere.

Lily said to Baker, "It's as if these people thought today was the dawn of aerial photography. It's as if nobody ever used a helicopter in a movie before."

Baker replied, uneasy with her scoffing tone, "We've been through a lot. The helicopter is our reward. After all, this hasn't been your basic, normal kind of production. We've seen a director pull a picture out of shit. I guess we're all happy for him. Maybe the zooms won't make the picture for the audience. But it will make it for us."

"Smile!" Kat called to Trigère and Jack. "I've got my arty shot. Now I want something for my scrapbook."

Jack stared grimly at the Alouette. "I'll smile when I know they've brought everything I'm going to need."

Trigère walked over to Kat and took the camera out of her hand.

"I think your scrapbook should carry a picture of *you* on this lucky day." He stepped back and adjusted the focus ring. "Your meter has been telling you a lie. I'm going to take it one step up. If I'm allowed. Up with the chin, please."

He continued to hesitate and fiddle with the settings. Her face, grainy and beautiful and larger than life in the lens, was a powerful connection, seductive and primal.

As if she had read his thoughts, she said impulsively, "Savages are afraid of having their picture taken. They believe that the photographer will snatch their soul."

"Quite so," he said with a dry smile, and clicked the shutter.

*

On the railing of his terrace, Henry Reed, who had slept late that morning, stood in bare feet with a Bloody Mary in his hand, his thinning hair in pin curls.

"Look, honey," he said to his blonde. "The chopper. It's here."

She was standing on her head with nothing on but sunglasses. "I have another minute to go. But I hear it, sweetie."

Henry looked down and across the snow where the *Lovers and Clowns* company could be seen in a state of great excitement, and he said with a pleased air, "Distressed property has always been a profitable sideline with me."

"Huh?"

He giggled and felt his pin curls to see if they were dry. "I was talking about all those lovers and clowns down there."

"Isn't that the name of the picture?"

"Yes, and before it's over I'll own more than the picture. I'll own Ian and Vito. They might even be profitable. Did you know Ian's older brother is a lord?"

"Older brothers usually are."

He looked at her, and she said from her inverted position, "Just because I'm a hooker doesn't mean I don't know my English history. It's called primogeniture."

"Don't bullshit me with your English history crap. You probably made it with a lord."

"Several."

"Did you know your boobs look funny hanging upside down like that?"

"Want some?"

"What I want is for my fucking pin curls to dry. So I can go out and join the fun. I *like* making movies!"

The chopper was hovering now, ready to land. Trigère handed the camera back to Kat.

She looked up at him. "Thanks. And congratulations."

He laughed down at her. "Did you think you would ever see an old director get so excited over a helicopter? What a lot you are learning about the realities behind the —what do you call it? The tinsel?"

She took a breath and said a bit awkwardly, "I appreciate it all. And you in particular. You've been very good to me."

"As someone was to me, once." He seemed to be studying her face. "As you will be to someone, someday. Film is something we pass on."

The helicopter landed on the marked-off snowy plateau that had been designated as its parking space. The festivities were over. The chopper was now part of the reality, a piece of the motion-picture machinery. Trigère and Jack stepped forward to greet the pilot..

Rehearsals for the first sequence of aerial shots began the next day. Trigère and Jack went off in the chopper with the pilot and a terrified Chin-Chan, who was to take notes. She had never flown in a helicopter before—she didn't even like airplanes—and the idea of flying a zigzag pattern in and out of the ghostly peaks had made her swallow two tranquilizers before climbing into the chopper and taking the seat behind the pilot. Jack was strapped into the camera mount, his legs hanging outside in the freezing air. It was unbelievably cold inside, as well.

The pilot was silent, hung over as he had been every morning for six months, since his girlfriend, a Dutch model, had disappeared from their apartment in Paris. Women were always leaving him now that he was forty and going bald. Last night he had picked up a skinny girl in the bar who said she was a student, but he could see she was well past thirty. On the whole, she had made him very sad. She had pretended her passion, and not very well at that. Besides, the hair on her pubis had bald spots, just like his head. Was that what life was all about, just going from person to person? And quality going downhill as one got older? Perhaps he would find someone here. There were always cute chicks around films, and that Chinese one behind him wasn't at all bad.

The Chinese one closed her eyes and thought she would be sick. Jack and Trigère shouted in the wind, planning their opening sequence of shots.

*

Back at Mont Bleu, most of the company was enjoying its holiday. Maroga and Theodora lunched together and then sat chatting away the afternoon on Theodora's terrace. Djuna and Joss took a swim in the pool. Kat wrote in her journal. Baker and Lily saw a bad print of *Gunga Din* at one of the cinemas. Vito bribed one of the women in the rental office to give him a desk and a telephone so he could do his business. In private.

Henry took a skiing lesson, while the blonde, who didn't want to have any part of it, and who would rather have been in the beauty salon or the bar, stood docilely by, producing studied, encouraging sounds from her dishonest throat each time Henry tried skiing down the gentle beginners' slope. He was doing *that* quite well; stopping was his problem, and several times he landed on all fours. The blonde remembered all the golf courses on which she had stood just as obediently as this, as well as the game rooms, tennis courts, and pit stops. An endless life of witnessing man's sport. You were expected to be there, a silent, decorative audience of one. It was as if they couldn't enjoy anything they did without the security of an appreciative appendage. How long was she supposed to stand here, anyway, freezing her butt, watching the old clown fall down?

She heard the helicopter and looked up. It had come out of the peaks and was headed for its landing place. She had met the pilot yesterday. He was Dutch, and he was cute. Oh, how she would love to ball a real man!

She was astonished to feel the tears in her eyes. This place was *weird*. It made you lonely and afraid.

White walls of steam rose from the pale, undulating surface of the outdoor swimming pool. Hidden in its grasslike mists were Joss and Djuna, treading the aquamarine water, splashing each other and now and then exchanging slick wet kisses, locking their arms and legs, going under. No one else was about.

They came to the surface again and Djuna giggled.

Joss shook the wet hair out of his eyes and reached

below the surface again for her breasts. "It's lovely to be together," he said said. "Bugger the rest of the world." He put his hand between her legs. "Hold still, darling, and I'll give you a surprise."

She laughed and swam away, floated on her back, and wished the fleecy clouds would halt their steady drift across the crystal-line sky, so that all time would come to a stop. "It's been a million years since we've been alone like this."

He swam near her. "No, darling. A billion."

She righted herself and began treading water again. They grinned at each other.

"I love you," he said. He dove under and disappeared. When he popped up again he said, "When did you start to love me? Tell me the moment."

She considered thoughtfully, delighted to play the magic game.

"I think right from the start," she said at last.

"At Ian's? The very first night?"

"I don't know. Maybe."

He swam around her in a circle. "We're an odd pair, aren't we?"

"Tell me how odd." She laughed and blew him a kiss.

He looked at her out of the corner of his eye, while floating on his back. "You're old and I'm young. You're neurotic. And American. I'm completely together, and gloriously English."

"Oh!" She lunged and splashed at him and he caught her and began to kiss her. They went under.

When they bobbed up he shouted, "Christ! We can't make love in this muck! Let's go where we can properly take care of the problem."

From five stories up, Maroga and Theodora leaned against the terrace railing and watched the lovers.

Maroga remarked enviously, "They are charming, how they play. Look, Theo, how beautiful they are."

"Baker would scarcely agree with you."

"Yes. But they are so happy. Why should it have to be

wrong? And who decides about things like that?"

"It's very easy," Theodora said with a frown. "If you're the one who is doing it, it's right. If you are the one who it's being done to, it's hell." Theodora left the railing and went back to the little table. She sat down and poured more tea. "Will you have some, darling?"

Maroga turned. "Thank you. Why do you suppose they ever married, Baker and Djuna? The more I come to know of them individually the more I find it incredible that those two ever spoke words of love to each other."

"No more incredible than they themselves find it now, I would imagine." Theodora tasted her tea and dropped another lump of sugar in it. "Don't ask the oracle any more questions. She's fresh out of answers. Now tell me, is there anything decent to be had in the shops downstairs? I haven't taken a moment to look yet."

Maroga sat down and picked up her cup of tea. "For instance, you and Ian," she went on thoughtfully, "I know you've been through many troubles, but as a pair, you have an unmistakable air of solidity, of Getting Through. One can see it. It's almost physical. I can always envision you growing old together, nodding by the fire."

Theodora looked at her friend curiously. "Can you?"

"Can't you?"

"I expect so. But probably for all the wrong reasons." She paused. "Oh, bother the reasons. They're too many to count and far too mystifying as well. When one gets past fifty, being honest with oneself isn't so crucial. By then one has usually settled for one thing or another, and the main thing is to use what one has. If marriage is both heaven and hell, then I have had mostly the hell. I settled for that ages ago. I must have known my limitations. That I needed a center. That center has always been Ian. I've never been strong enough to fly on my own. Even when it's hell, it's still my life, the only one I can manage. Now, Djuna down there in the pool with Peck's bad boy, she's trying to fly on her own."

Maroga stirred her tea. "They were fascinated by each other right from the start. We all saw it. Nothing on earth can stop things like that. But she had to have been ready. Is that what you are saying? She had to have already decided not to settle?"

"Some might say that she is exchanging one kind of unhappiness for another. Though I rather think it is what we choose not to put up with that keeps on defining us."

They were silent for a moment and then Maroga sighed. "I feel a little better today. I begin to believe again that there is, after all, an order to things. And to accept my part in my own process."

"Well! That's splendid. I do think you're coming round. You do know, don't you, that you *will* get over Robbie?"

Maroga replied slowly, "For a long time I have been afraid of that, afraid of getting over Robbie because with the dream gone, there would be nothing, don't you see? Without the pain and the hope I would have nothing, be nothing. I would have to start over without even a fantasy lover for company." She flashed her famous smile. "It has done me good to see Djuna and Joss down there in the pool. Our two wet lovers. That is joy and that is beauty. I was like that with Robbie. If I could not keep it, very well, then, I could not keep it. I must only remember how it was, how I was. Perhaps I had the experience all by myself. I would like to think that means I have kept the best part of it."

Theodora smiled. "Good for you. Trigère said you would come round by yourself. He knows you better than I do. I was all for organizing a help brigade."

"Trigère is spectral. He knows everything. I cannot imagine him ever having to lean on anyone. He is unto himself."

"What's he like as a lover?"

"Cold." Maroga frowned. "How terrible of me to say it that way . . . How can I explain it better? He is very practiced, very knowing; but afterward, I always feel as if I have participated in an act of absolutely no significance."

Theodora commented dryly, "Bed is a matter of taste."

"And sparks." Maroga smiled. "There have never been sparks between Trigère and me. Only love, affection, and respect." She paused. "It's a crazy world."

Ian appeared in the doorway, fresh from his nap. "Have your tongues been wagging all this time since lunch? Can a fellow get some tea?"

Kat finished writing in her journal and hid it under her mattress. With Chin-Chan, you never knew.

She decided to go down to the sauna. Her ankle was bothering her and the heat would be good for it. She left the apartment, rode the elevator to the main floor, went past the rows of shops with their international glitter-wares, entered the sauna dressing room, and got a towel from the attendant.

The dark, red room was empty at this hour. She climbed to the topmost slatted bench and lay down in the hot gloom, noting the time on the luminous clock. When her ten minutes were up she had become warm and woozy with the sense of her own perspiring flesh and decided to stay on a few minutes longer. She was about to get up when two figures entered, one a man, the other a woman with a towel wrapped in a turban around her head.

They sat down on a lower bench and the man said to the woman, "Kiss my cock, love. I don't think I can wait for upstairs."

There was a low laugh from the woman. "Someone might come in."

"Then let them see what happiness is," Joss said lazily, and pulled Djuna's head down to him.

Kat lay back on the slatted bench and turned her face to the wall. And had to listen to the sounds. Hers. His.

Chapter Twenty-three

The major aerial shots, the lyrical, filmic winding through the high, icy walls of the peaks, had been completed. The weather had been perfect. They got almost everything they needed on the first day. Only the final zoom-out remained.

"If we begin early enough," Trigère had told Ian on the evening before, "we might wrap that in one day as well. You understand we'll have to clear an enormous area for this. I don't want to see any skiers in the frame. The slopes, as the helicopter moves back, will have to be clean. The telecabines will have to be stopped. I don't want anything moving."

"Stop the telecabines, my dear Bernard? Have you any idea of the revenue Joseph derives in one bloody day from those things?"

"Spare me your commercial *merde*, okay? I'm not in the mood."

"Very well." Ian frowned. "Then it's definitely tomorrow?"

"Tomorrow it is."

Almost everyone turned up for the shot. Henry, Vito, Lily, and Theodora stayed inside, stepping out on their terraces every now and then to check the progress of the preparations. They would not go out until Trigère was ready to shoot.

All the others arrived quite early and stood around talking, drinking coffee, trying to stay warm. There were thirty-one of them. In addition to Ian, Chin-Chan, Trigère, Kat, Hans, Jack, Conchita, Carl, the production manager, and the three stars, there were the assistant director, the script girl, a second camera operator, an assistant cameraman, a gaffer, a best boy, two grips, the property master, Conchita's make-up assistant, the sound mixer, the boom man, the editor, the assistant editor, a carpenter, two stunt skiers, and the production manager's secretary.

And Djuna. She had gone skiing early, with the first light, and had now stopped at the place where the company was gathered. She stood by the coffee urn with Carl and Conchita, feeling raw and out of concert with the general chatter, the mood of anticipation. The last shot of the last day. The film. Over. Her life in France, her life with Joss. Over. Location was as illusory as a film itself.

Yesterday in the pool with Joss, and later, the magic clock had still been ticking. Here, in the chilly morning light, she heard its silence.

She stood there, hurting, smiling, drinking a cup of coffee while all of Mont Bleu hung out of its balconies to watch the movie people.

The slopes Trigère had designated were cleared. The telecabines hung still. Joss, Maroga, and Baker were in make-up, standing close together, waiting. Maroga was worrying that her wig would blow away when the helicopter began the shot, and then pulled up and away. In the final frame the three of them were to be seen as tiny human dots in the snow and gradually disappear altogether.

Joss had been watching Djuna out of the corner of his eye. He now took advantage of a further lull in the waiting to start across the twenty meters of snow that separated them. She noticed, and started toward him.

Yesterday afternoon had been very tender, very fierce between them and when they had had to part at six o'clock, nothing had been said. Nothing about today, nothing about goodbye. Nothing about forever. They were alike, he and Djuna, in that way. Their last moment alone was not to be spoiled. It was to be honored. It had been accomplished by unspoken agreement. It was one more thing to share. They had exchanged a kiss, very long, very sweet, and then, quickly, she had gone out the door.

The administrative, unbearable part would come now. He saw it in her careful, prepared face as she walked to meet him halfway. He knew it in the tightness of his chest, the dryness of his tongue. But he had made up his mind. It must end and it must end here. Let the pain come. Let the pain go.

They approached each other and stopped.

"Look," he said, frowning, looking about. "You'd better let me have your address in California."

She said nothing. So this is how it was to end. She would cry on the plane. But not here.

"Actually," he was saying, "I'd better have your phone number. I'm not much at writing letters."

"What would we say to each other?" she asked after a moment.

He took a quick breath. "This isn't easy for me either, you know."

She turned her face away. "We should have said good-bye last night."

The assistant director was calling him.

"I'll have to go," Joss said quietly. But he did not move. She had turned to face him again with that odd, tilted smile. A moment as large as all their days together went by.

The assistant director called for him again.

Joss scowled and looked away, up at the slopes. He appeared for some time to be studying them with fierce concentration. "The problem is, my love, that my boots appear to be glued to the snow. I don't know how to say goodbye to you, Djuna. I just bloody don't."

And she saw he was close to tears.

He continued, still looking away. "I never thought it would be so fucking difficult. Did you?"

The assistant director's angry voice on the megaphone boomed out over the pristine white valley. "Places!"

Joss turned to Djuna. "Will you be watching the shot?" he asked.

She smiled faintly. "Of course. I'll take all of you I can get," she said.

"As soon as it's over, meet me down there." He pointed to the bottom of the slope.

"Why?" she asked helplessly.

"Because we're not going to leave each other like this. That's why." He stared at her for another moment. "Promise me you will."

"I promise you," she said, and watched him run off.

From the terraces it looked as if the company was ready, so the others came down. Theodora noticed Djuna standing alone and crossed over to her. Lily, Vito, and Henry decided to watch from the Snow Grill bar.

The helicopter was parked in its usual place nearby and Jack and Trigère were walking toward it now. Trigère would not ride with Jack for this shot. When they had filmed the panoramic scenes, it had been necessary for him to direct Jack; they did not know from one moment to the next what they would see, what they would want. But today it wasn't necessary. The zoom-out shot had been meticulously planned, and first thing that morning they had done a run-through without the actors. It was very simple. Jack was to focus on the three stars lying dead (supposedly) in the snow and start the zoom-out as the helicopter pulled up.

When Trigère and Jack reached the helicopter, Henry Reed's blonde was sitting in the seat next to the pilot.

"What the fuck is this?" Jack growled. "Out, lady."

The pilot looked at Trigère. "She won't be in the way."

"Henry said it was okay," the blonde said with a giggle.

Trigère sighed impatiently. His mind was on other things. He said coldly to the pilot, "It's nothing to me one way or the other. Jack is the man you must deal with."

Jack looked at Trigère. "I told Kat she couldn't come. She'll be pissed off if I let this turkey ride with me."

The blonde decided to be magnanimous. And she would tell Henry about it later. "Well, why don't you go and get her? There's still room."

"Shit." Jack ran his hands through his hair. "Do I need this? Do I need asinine female aggravation on top of everything else?"

"You'll have to solve it yourself." Trigère was deeply irritated. Did everything about this picture have to be an absurdity? "I'm going back now. We'll signal you."

When he got back to the shooting area there was a further delay, so he walked over to where the coffee urn had been set up. As he was lifting the cup to his lips he noticed the telecabines were in operation. The little painted cars were swinging jauntily from the cable on their steep ascent toward the top.

He turned around angrily and began shouting at the assistant director, who ran up, holding his hands up in a sign of peace. "Don't worry. I fixed it so the still photographer could ride in one of them. They'll stop it in a moment. We decided that halfway up the hill was the best place for the man to get his publicity shots. I let some of the others go with him. They'll have the best view. Look, they're stopping it now."

"Where is Ian?" Trigère asked.

"I don't know. I think he went with the group in the telecabine."

"Who else is in the cabine?"

"I don't know exactly. Chin-Chan, I think, and—"

Trigère looked at his watch and then across the snow to the helicopter. Where was Kat? He looked around for her, and saw she was sitting on a case, writing in her journal. He went over to her. She closed the book and quickly stuffed it into her bag and jumped up.

"Do you need me?" she asked, and he would have liked to have said, Yes, I need you very much, I need you very foolishly, and when we wrap this final shot today, I would like to take you with me somewhere where it is sunny, where we could float in a warm ocean, just you and me and see if . . .

Instead he said, "I've been looking for you. Henry Reed's blonde has talked the pilot into letting her ride in the helicopter."

"That figures," Kat replied gamely. Only one more day, and she would be on her way to Nice, then on a plane to Los Angeles. In a month or two, when she got her head together, she would write Trigère a letter, telling him . . .

Aloud she said, "The blonde and the pilot were, shall we say, together for most of the night."

"There's only the three of them in the helicopter— Jack, the pilot, and the blonde—so there's room for you. That is, if you really want to freeze to death and see absolutely nothing but the back of Jack's head. I know you wanted to go up, and this is your last chance."

"Thanks," she said. "I know it's dumb, I just want to have the experience."

"Hurry," he said, smiling down at her. "They're ready to go."

She ran off. As she passed the place where Joss and the

other two were waiting, Joss whistled at her. At first she wasn't going to stop, but then she changed her mind. It was cowardly to run away from things you had to say, do, be, just because it wasn't going to feel good.

She had been blinded by fairy dust and seduced by the most engaging stud in Europe. She had almost been deflected from her original sense of purpose. With Joss, she had fallen into her own ancestral trap, the historical way of her gender, the two-faced mirror of the profession she had chosen. She had fallen in love with love and thought to make it a life. She had been romanced by a star, and forgotten who she was.

Joss walked over to her. "Where the devil did *you* disappear to last night? I thought we were having dinner together."

She squinted up at him in the sharp sunlight, and then looked down. Made a circle in the snow with the tip of her boot. Finally she said, "You never really asked me to be your girl, so I guess I wasn't. But I thought I was. Which is the same thing. Yesterday I found out about you and Djuna." She smiled then, because she knew it was important to show some style. "So I didn't think it would be a whole lot of fun to see you last night." She paused a moment. "Actually, it hurt. It hurt a lot." She continued to smile at him bravely.

"I'm sorry." He looked down at the snow for a moment. "I'm sorry that it hurts. I didn't plan it that way. I promise you. And I couldn't tell you about her, could I? I couldn't tell anyone. It was always a separate thing and—shit!" He prodded at the snow with his boot. "I've been straight about everything, haven't I? I never told you that I loved you."

"No, you never told me that you loved me." She had thought the experience in the sauna had been the worst moment. But the worst moment was now.

He was staring at her in dismay. "You're not going to cry, are you? Please don't." He took her hands in his. "I care for you, Kat. Truly I do. You've been lovely to me.

We've had sweet times together. Haven't we? I couldn't help it about Djuna, honestly I couldn't."

"I have to go," she said. If she ran as fast as she could she still might catch the helicopter.

When it happened, Lily, Vito, and Henry, the trio at the window bar of the Snow Grill, had the best view.

The green-and-white helicopter was hovering over the three actors playing dead in the snow. In a moment the pilot would begin to pull up.

"Looks good," Henry remarked to Lily. She nodded and lifted her glass of wine to her lips but kept her eyes on the scene outside the glass wall. On the stool next to her, Vito felt his pulse again. It was racing. He was going to get out of here today and go straight to Paris to see his doctor. He reached in his pocket to see if he had change for the telephone.

Lily eyed him. "What's the matter, Vito?"

He took his hand out of his pocket. "I don't feel so good." He reached again for his drink.

"Flu?" she asked, edging her barstool slightly away from him.

He shook his head. "I've been getting dizzy, and here," he pressed his chest, "I get pains."

Her laugh was without humor. "Nerves, Vito. Psychosomatic symptoms. Trophies of what we do, who we are."

"I should see a doctor. It's been going on for weeks."

"So has this blasted film. You should take tranquilizers." She had turned from him and was looking through the glass wall of the window again. The helicopter was slowly beginning to pull up for the zoom shot.

That was what he had told the girl: "It's all in your head. There's nothing wrong with you except that you're neurotic and feel sorry for yourself." When she continued to complain of her strange symptoms and asked to see a doctor, he had threatened to throw her out, send her back to Rome. Three days later she had died at Ian Spencer's dinner table. The death certificate had been impeccable;

it had told no lies. But, he, Vito, was implicated in the eyes of a vengeful God.

He felt the dizziness again, and the fear. He closed his eyes for a moment.

"Oh, Jesus!" Henry was suddenly shouting. The bartender whipped around to the window as Lily's glass crashed to the floor and people in the bar screamed and pushed forward.

The Alouette's tail rotor had backed into the telecabine cable. Three of the glossy little cabines were severed from the main cable and plunged down through space, hitting the slope and sinking deeply into the snow. The helicopter went into a violent spin.

They had had little warning, the three actors, lying there in the snow. Their eyes had been closed—they were playing dead, after all—and even when they heard the terrible unexpected noise and the shouts, professionals that they were, Baker and Maroga continued to act their parts.

Joss, who had never experienced the embarrassment of ruining an expensive shot because one had moved or opened one's eyes too soon, was on his feet at once, shouting at the other two. He pulled Maroga every which way in the snow as he frantically tried to calculate where the helicopter would fall.

She was looking up. Screaming. She jerked away from his grasp and ran in another direction. Stumbled. Joss started after her but looked up in time and ran backward to save himself, as the helicopter came down on Maroga, tipped over crazily, and caught fire.

A little way up the slope, the telecabines lay in the grim snow craters they had made. From one, bodies had spilled out in all directions.

"See if anyone is alive in that thing up there!" Trigère called to the assistant director. He ran toward the downed helicopter.

He came to a full stop by Joss, who was standing very still, staring at the flaming wreckage, his face streaked with smoke and sweat. Trigère looked at him, saw he was not hurt and continued toward the helicopter, but Joss pulled him back, saying quietly, "It might explode at any moment. They're all dead anyway. I've had a look. Maroga got it instantly. She's underneath. Jack—"

In anguish, Trigère was gripping Joss by the shoulders. "Kat—"

Joss looked at him, puzzled. "She's there. Right behind you." Trigère whirled around.

Kat was running toward them. No. She was running toward him, Trigère.

Joss, who had until now thought that the only fatalities were at the actual scene of the crash, suddenly registered the sight of the fallen, mangled telecabines on the slope, and the gathering crowd around one of them. "Christ," he muttered, "were there people in that thing?"

He began to run up the slope.

The beginning of Kat's and Trigère's story required only an instant, only one look between them as they met there in the snow by the burning helicopter. They embraced, kissed the tears from each other's faces, then turned to help where they were needed. They followed Joss up the slope.

The crowd had begun to step back from the bodies in a respectful, shocked circle as Joss elbowed his way through them.

He would always remember that even before he saw her, somehow, he already knew.

Djuna's sunstreaked hair spilled in a bright fan on the snow. She looked frozen. The other four bodies all looked frozen too. Joss knelt beside Djuna, and when a member of the ski patrol, who had just reached the scene, took his arm and tried to pull him away, Joss stood up and knocked the man out.

Then he picked Djuna up in his arms and kissed her dead face. The crowd made way for him. For a moment his glance went to the snow again, to Chin-Chan, who stared up at him sightlessly. To Theodora, with her matted cloud of ivory hair, lying face down like an old, broken doll. Next to her, Ian. Sprawled hideously. Wearing his college tie. And some distance beyond them, the photographer.

Joss turned and walked down the slope, carrying Djuna. He met Trigère and Kat coming toward him.

"Djuna is dead," he said to them tonelessly. Tears streamed down his face and mingled with the sweat. "Djuna is dead." And he stood there mute, wooden, holding his burden, his love.

"Let me help you," Trigère took his arm. "It's damn slippery here."

"You know what I keep thinking?" Joss said to him. "I keep thinking that if I had saved Maroga, if I hadn't just let her bloody die there at the last moment so I could save myself, Djuna would have lived. Djuna died to pay for my cowardice. Do you think that could be true, Trigère?"

"You tried to help Maroga. I saw you."

But Joss just stared at him blankly, unseeingly, uncomprehendingly.

"Come," the director said quietly. Kat took Joss' other arm and the three of them came down the slope together, with Djuna.

As they passed the helicopter, Joss paused. "Did *he* live?" he asked. "Did Baker live?"

"Yes." Trigère looked at the Alouette. Goodbye, sweet Maroga. "He got farther away than you but was caught by some flying pieces. They've taken him to the hospital. He's not seriously hurt."

They proceeded across the snow. Two men came toward them with a stretcher, but Trigère felt Joss go rigid, so he motioned the men away.

It had begun to snow. Like a film, Trigère thought. He himself would have used snow for this final movement. And music?

No. The scene orchestrated itself. The three of them— the four of them—coming slowly down the slope. The sound of their boots in the snow. The silence of the falling flakes.